INSANITY

2

(Mad in Wonderland)

FIGMENT

by Cameron Jace

www.CameronJace.com

Copyright

First Original Edition, December 2014
Copyright ©2014 Akmal Eldin Farouk Ali Shebl

Previously on Insanity:

Living in an asylum after killing her classmates in a bus accident, Alice Wonder is persuaded by another enigmatic patient, Professor Carter Pillar, to save people from the Wonderland Monsters. Professor Pillar, also known as Pillar the Killer, claims she is the Real Alice from Lewis Carroll's books. He tells her that other characters from the books are reincarnated as humans and living among us. And that a Wonderland War is coming.

Alice manages to solve the riddles by the Cheshire Cat killer who kidnaps girls and sews a grin on their faces. She saves a girl named Constance who turns out to be a descendant of one of the girls Lewis Carroll photographed two centuries ago.

In a mad adventure, Alice learns about the secrets of Oxford University, then she is introduced to the Duchess from the books, now posing as Margaret Kent, a dishonest Parliament woman who uses Wonderland Monsters as assassins to serve high-caliber politicians.

Alice and the Pillar then travel to the Vatican to meet the White Queen who is reincarnated as Fabiola, one of the most respectable nuns in the world, trying her best to help people. Fabiola leads Alice to the final clue to catch the Cheshire who is looking for his grin, which Lewis had stolen from him. The Cheshire's grin will grant him unimaginable powers in his quest to summon many Wonderland Monsters to use them in the mysterious Wonderland War.

Alice and the Pillar confront the Cheshire in a final battle in Ypres in Belgium, where a bizarre festival called Kattenstoet takes place. After the sky rains cats, Alice manages to save Constance with help of Jack Diamonds, the mysterious card-smelling boy who likes her unconditionally.

The Pillar shows Alice how to meet Lewis Carroll through a secret door in the Tom Tower in Oxford University. Lewis gives Alice a key and tells her to take care of it. Still, Alice is forced to give the Cheshire his grin back in exchange for saving Constance again. The grin grants the Cheshire the power to posses any one he wants.

In a final scene, Alice realizes that Jack Diamonds is actually her boyfriend Adam, one of the people she killed in a bus accident she can't remember. Then the Cheshire visits her in the Asylum and tells her that she is mad and that this adventure only happened in her head. It was all just a figment of her mad imagination.

Prologue

*Football Match, Stamford Bridge Stadium, Fulham, London,
Present Day*

The players at Stamford Bridge stadium had no idea of
the bloody horrors awaiting them.

The two opposing teams, Manchester United and
Chelsea FC, were fighting for the title in the final game of
the season. The winner's prize would be a huge silver grail
with ridiculously huge handles popping out like rabbit
ears from both sides. Although it was no *holy* grail, it was
to be handed, along with a few medals, by the Queen of
England herself.

Unfortunately, Her Majesty couldn't come. One of her
Welsh dogs had been suddenly sick. The poor dog, whose
name was Maddog, had gorged on a sizable portion of the
Queen's Brazilian nuts last night, eventually fated with a
terrible case of chronic constipation. The Queen demanded
she would not attend the game until Maddog pooped,
which apparently never happened.

Renowned Parliament member Margaret Kent was
sent on behalf of the Queen, excited to watch the game.

The watching spectators didn't care about the Queen,
her dog, or the pretentious Parliament woman. The
crowd's only concern was the long-awaited game. They
looked as enthusiastic as Wonderland rabbits, checking
their watches and knuckling their fingers, ready for an
afternoon of a brilliant football match—soccer game, if
you're American.

After a hard-working week, licking dust off their
bosses' shoes, and paying their taxes, all they wanted was
pure, mindless entertainment. They watched the players in
the field kick-start the match, frantically chasing after the
helpless ball as if their lives depended on it. Some would
wonder why they kicked the ball away if they liked it that
much, but that was a nonsensical argument for another

time.

"I can't see anything, Mummy." A chubby kid among the spectators pulled his mother's coat. The kid didn't really like football. He was here because his mother had promised him an *insane* surprise.

"Shhh," the mother said. The woman wore an absurd red fur coat and big black glasses. "Patience, my dear," she said. "Madness comes to those who wait."

The boy rubbed his eyes with his fatty hands, and then sighed. He rummaged through his snack box and contemplated whether he should eat one of those Snicker Snackers twin-bars, or maybe have a fizzy Tumtum drink. He settled for a rainbow-colored Lollipop Lane as he waited for the insane surprise.

Down in the field, a player kicked the ball so high it landed atop the banks of the opponent's fans. A man with a silver front tooth, wearing the club's shirt, hugged the ball as if it were his newborn baby. A few other fans went bonkers and began kicking him to give the ball back and resume the game.

In such cases, the chubby kid was told, another ball was provided to continue the game.

And so it happened.

One of Manchester's players was given a substitute ball, which they kicked and chased again. That was when the Wonderland madness began...

A few kicks in, the players felt something unordinary about the new ball. The game was halted as the referee approached to check it himself.

"The ball is a bit heavy," player number fourteen said.

"Yes, it is!" another agreed. "That's unusual."

"What's wrong with this bloody ball?" a sweating player asked impatiently.

The referee weighed the ball upon his hand. It certainly was significantly heavier than the standard ball.

Which was impossible.

All balls had to be previously inspected by FIFA, the

international federation of football. Each ball's design followed a set of standard manufacturing rules.

"I think there is something *inside* the ball." The referee brought it to his ear. "Listen."

The players passed the ball one to another, as they listened to something bumping inside it.

"It's pregnant," a player chuckled before another snatched the ball from him.

"Get me a knife!" the referee's curiosity ruled over any logic. "I have to slice it open. It could be a bomb!"

Back in the crowd, the chubby kid had his eyes glazed to the scene, licking his lollipop at a faster pace. A surge of excitement ran through his veins as the soundtrack of the movie *Jaws* growled inside his head: *Dum Dum, Dum Dum. Tarararaaaa!*

Something wicked was coming his way. And he loved it. "Is this the surprise, Mommy?" the boy asked.

Mommy, looking like a widow in a funeral with her dark glasses, said nothing.

"What's in the ball, Mommy!" the boy insisted.

She only squeezed her son's chubby hands for assurance, and continued watching the incident in the field.

Somehow, right after slicing the ball in two, players began to run away in all directions. The referee who had the ball cut open was the first to run. He ran like a mad chicken, panicked by the egg it had just laid. Then the players followed. They couldn't stand witnessing the horrible *thing* inside the ball. Most of the players ran aimlessly in the field, too panicked to look for an exit, going nowhere as if they were in the Caucus Race.

Shivers of panic waved like a storm through the stadium — more excitement for the lollipop-licking boy *and* his mysterious mother, though.

"What's in the ball?" the crowd moaned, sweet horror on the tips of their tongues, kaleidoscopic panic in their eyes.

"This is the surprise, right?" The boy was about to faint from excitement.

Mommy nodded. A thin, almost unnoticeable, hint of a smile curved on her lips.

There was one last standing player in the field. Player number fourteen. The player seemed paralyzed by fear. He bent down and picked up the thing that had been bouncing inside the ball. Holding it, he had to stare at it for a while. He craned his head back and forth, inspecting what he was really looking at. It didn't make sense to him why such a thing was stuffed inside a ball. Who would do such a horrible thing?

The cameraman, although scared, approached the player slowly, trying to broadcast this terrible incident that would cling to the memory of the world later. Player number fourteen held up the thing to the camera.

"It's a..." the player said.

Whatever it was, it was trickling fresh blood.

The chubby boy in the crowd couldn't hear what the player said. His mother handed him a binocular. The boy focused the binoculars at the player with the horrible thing in his hands.

Finally, he saw it. He saw what was in the ball.

A head.

A human head which had been stuffed inside the ball a few minutes ago.

"It's a kid's head!" the boy hailed.

Some of the crowd began to faint. The rest ran away like ducks, stepping on each other toward the exit door.

"Good boy." His mother patted him as she stood fixed in her place. It seemed as if people avoided them while they panicked and ran around them. "Now be an even goody-dooder and tell the crowd what's written on the head's forehead," she instructed her boy.

Shifting his angle, the boy saw the player, now shivering with his hands glued to the ball, showing it to the camera, eyes shaded with terror.

At this moment, the panic had reached an apocalyptic level, where the crowd stepped over each other out of fear and need to escape the stadium. Still, the player held the ball with trembling hands, showing the world on camera the written words on the head.

The boy smiled from ear to ear as he read it. To him, the scene was all beauty, and he was glad. After witnessing the dead girl with a grin in Oxford University last week, this was starting to become exciting. The boy's eyes glittered as they met his mother's nodding glasses. He hurled the binocular away, licked the lollipop one last time, and screamed from the top his fatty lungs, "You want to know what's written on the forehead of the dead kid's head?" he shouted while everyone was already escaping the place. "'Off with their heads!'"

Chapter 1

Alice's cell, Radcliffe Lunatic Asylum, Oxford

It's been six days since I last saw Professor Pillar. Six days since Fabiola, the White Queen, visited me in my cell and showed me that Jack Diamonds was actually Adam J. Dixon. Six days since the Cheshire Cat, possessing Ogier's soul, visited me in my cell and then pranced away, whistling a mad song about me.

Six impossible days of isolation, pretending none of last week's events ever happened.

When Waltraud asks me about Wonderland, I raise an eyebrow and tell her I don't know what she is talking about. When she mentions I wanted to save lives in the world outside, I reply, "How can I save lives when my own life needs saving?"

I don't need to wake up with amnesia to pretend I am insane. I don't need evidence to know that the Pillar, Cheshire, White Queen, the Duchess, and the whole Wonderland War are figments of a lonely girl's imagination. After the Cheshire's visit, the *sanest* thing to do is to admit insanity and give in to its consequences.

Even if I am not insane, and all of this did happen, I am better off believing it didn't. At least I am not giving Waltraud excuses to send me back to the torturous Mush Room anymore. Believe me, life without shock therapy is less painful.

I've marked each of the six days on the wall, among the dried blood of whoever suffered in this cell before me. Six perpendicular strokes, carved with my short nails as if I am the female version of Count of Monte Cristo, feeling clueless, betrayed, and imprisoned in a dungeon in a faraway island.

A shattered laugh escapes my lips when I stare at the tattoo on my arms:

I can't go back to yesterday because I was someone else then.

It leaves me wondering which *yesterday* the tattoo is talking about: me before my hallucinations of Pillar with a hookah in a VIP cell, or me before I killed my friends in a bus accident?

Occasionally, I run the tips of my fingers upon the tattoo. I do it gently and with care. I am afraid if I rub it too hard, a Wonderland Monster would answer my call.

I don't think you know what a Wonderland Monster can do to you. With all my pretending that none of last week's madness ever happened, one thing persists to feel so real to me; one thing never fails to scare me and give me nightmares.

The Cheshire Cat.

With no distinguishable face or identity, he frightens the very essence of me. I fear him so much that I need to pinch myself to make sure I am not possessed by him every once in a while. Had I not been scared of mirrors, I would have used them each morning to confirm the absence of his evil grin on my lips.

"You're insane, Alice," my Tiger Lily whispers behind me. She, who is supposed to be my one and only friend, has been mean to me lately. I wonder if they have done something to her when she was in Dr. Truckle's custody.

"*Eye. En. Es. Aay. En. Eee.*" She snickers like an old toothless lady behind my back. "The Cheshire isn't real." Her tone gives me goose bumps. "You made him up, Alice. He is just an excuse for you to avoid facing the world outside. That's why you see the Cheshire's face in almost everyone you meet. You're simply afraid of people, Alice. Any psychologist knows that."

I don't turn around to face her. Usually, when she talks to me, it means I am in my highest moments of insanity. I bend my knees against my chest and I bury my head between them, hugging myself with my own arms. I close my eyes and decide to clap my hands over my ears until she stops talking.

"Nothing is real." Tiger Lily refuses to shut up. "Even

Jack isn't real."

My hands stop halfway and my eyes spring open. A single sticky tear rolls down my cheek. I tremble as it glides down slowly. Then I catch it before it hits the ground. I stare at it wobbling in the palm of my hand. My tears are terrified of uh he unknown, the same way I am.

"I mean Adam," Lily teases. "If you killed Adam, then who is Jack but a figment of your imagination?"

Provoked, I turn back, only to find a harmless orange flower in pot near the crack in the wall. I am not even sure she was talking to me. Mentioning Jack triggered a bittersweet knot of pain inside of me. If there is anything I am certain of, it's that Jack Diamonds—true or imagination—is the only thing I wish is real.

Now that I was shown he was my boyfriend, I understand my previously unexplained strong feelings toward him. I don't want to resist my feelings because, in a world as mad as mine, they shine on me with rays of sanity. I don't even have these kinds of strong feelings toward my helpless mother or my two mocking sisters. Jack seems to be my only chance for family.

Lily is right, though. If Jack is Adam, the boyfriend I killed, he must be dead too.

A sudden pounding on my cell's door relieves me from the burden of thinking about Jack.

Chapter 2

It's Waltraud Wagner at my door, the head of wardens in the Radcliffe Lunatic Asylum. Torturing me in the Mush Room pleasures her above all else. "Did you change your mind yet?" she blurts in her horrible German accent, reeking of cigarette smoke and junk food.

"What do you mean?" I tighten my fist around my single tear, squeezing it away.

"You've been unusually obedient for the past six days, confessing your insanity and such." She slaps her prod against her fleshy palm. "It's not like you," she remarks.

"I'm insane, Waltraud. I'm fully aware of it."

"I hardly believe you. How would an insane person know they're insane?" She is testing me. Admitting my insanity doesn't appeal to her. It rids her of reasons to fry me in the Mush Room. "People are kept in asylums because they aren't aware of their insanity. Their ignorance to their insanity endangers society. That's why we lock them away."

"Are you saying insane people who are aware of their insanity don't deserve to be locked away in asylums?" It's a nonsensical argument already.

"Insane people who know they are insane are smart enough to fool society into thinking they aren't," Waltraud replies. I blink twice to the confusing sentence she just said. "Think of Hitler, for an example." She laughs like a heavyweight ogre. Sometimes I think she is a Nazi. I was told she killed her patients in the asylum she worked for in Austria. But when she makes fun of Hitler, I am not sure anymore. "Or, in your case, you're admitting insanity to avoid shock therapy."

A twisty smile curves on my lips. Waltraud isn't that dumb after all. "That's a serious accusation, Waltraud," I say.

"It *is* an accusation," she retorts. "But it's hard to prove.

Who'd believe me when I tell them you're an insane girl believing you're not insane, but pretending you are?"

"Such a *mindbend*." I almost chuckle. Waltraud's misery is always my pleasure. "Have you ever read *Catch-22* by Joseph Heller?" It's a book that tackles this kind of logic. I wonder if Heller was a Lewis Carroll fan.

"I don't have time to read books," Waltraud puffs. "Does it have pictures in it?"

"No, it doesn't," I say. Waltraud probably read *Alice in Wonderland* and is trying to provoke me. Anything to get me to do something foolish and deserve punishment in the Mush Room.

"What use is a book without pictures?" She snickers behind the door.

"It's a book that describes how something can't be proven until a previous thing is certainly proven. However, the previous thing can't easily be proven either, to put it mildly." I neglect her comment about a book without pictures.

"I don't understand a word you say." She truly doesn't.

"Think of a chicken and an egg. We have no way to know which came first."

"I don't understand that either," she puffs. "I hate chickens." I hear her scratch her head. "But I love eggs."

I wish I could drive her mad myself. Wouldn't it be fun to have her in my cell instead of me?

A scream interrupts our ridiculous conversation all of a sudden. I have been hearing this for a few days now. It's a patient girl pleading to be spared from the Mush Room. It's probably Ogier torturing her. The Mushroomers in the other cells pound on their bars, demanding the pain to end. The screams have tripled since I've stopped being sent to the Mush Room. Waltraud and Ogier have been compensating my absence with too many other patients.

"Why all the torturing?" I ask Waltraud. I'd like to scream in her face and punch her with oversized gloves filled with needles and pins. But the inner—relatively reasonable—voice stops me. If I want to forget about my madness, and if I want to keep avoiding the pain of shock therapy, I'd better keep to myself. When I walk next to a wall, I want people to only notice the wall.

I am not here to save lives. It's not true. Why should I care?

"It's not torture. It's interrogation," Waltraud explains. "A patient escaped the asylum recently while you were locked in here. We are authorized to use shock therapy to get confessions from the patients neighboring his cell."

I jump to my feet and pace to the door, sliding open the small square window to look at her. "Are you saying someone actually escaped the asylum?" I can't hide the excitement.

"You look so happy about it, Alice," Waltraud sneers. "Come on. Show me you're mad. Give me a reason to send you to the Mush Room. You want to exchange places with the poor girl inside?"

My face tightens instantly. I spend my days and nights in my creepy cell, safe from Waltraud's harm—and safer from my own terrible mind. I need to learn to control my urges.

Be reasonable, Alice. Last week was all in your head. You've never been to the Vatican, the Grote Markt in Belgium, or to Westminster Palace in London. If you want proof, it's easy. Think of why the Pillar never sent for you again. Why Fabiola never entered your cell again. Why your sisters and mothers never visited again. It's better not to care about the escapee as well. Even if you escaped, there is no one out there waiting for you outside.

"Play the 'sanity' game all you want," Waltraud says. "Sooner or later, your brain will be mine to fry." She laughs. An exaggerated laugh, the way they portray an evil person's in Disney cartoons. I am really starting to wonder why she isn't locked in a cell, unless she is like Hitler, knowing he's mad and persuading the world otherwise. "Now get ready," she demands.

"For what?" I grimace.

"It's time for your break," she tells me. "You're rewarded for your good behavior: a ten-minute walk in the sun."

Chapter 3

Walled garden, Radcliffe Lunatic Asylum, Oxford

The garden where I am taking my break is guarded with barbed wire and concrete walls, high on all sides. Very reminiscent of maximum-security prisons where they want you electrocuted if you try to escape. The walls are ten feet high; they almost block the skewed sunrays trying to shine through. I need to move to a certain spot and tiptoe to allow the sun on my skin. When I do, my pale skin feels nourished, loved, and spoiled. No wonder my Lily lives next to a crack in a wall. Now she silently dances to the beautiful daylight, as though she worships the sun.

Don't ask me why I bring her along, even when she is sometimes mean to me. I can't explain why I am so attached to her. Like Jack, I consider her family for some reason.

I close my eyes, spread my arms sideways, and inhale all the air I can. The more oxygen into my lungs, the saner I feel.

The earth underneath me is sand, gravel, and boulders. I kick my shoes away and walk barefoot. I wonder if I keep my eyes closed long enough, would my life change for the better when I flick them open again? Will the madness subside? I wish it were that easy.

Maybe that's why people only dream with eyes closed. To open one's eyes is such a dream killer.

I walk barefoot, and in the darkness of my shut eyelids, a vision shapes before me. A colorful vision that looks as if a rainbow has crashed onto it and spilled its paint everywhere, turning the place into a palette of different hues and shades. I see huge mushrooms, funny-looking trees, giant fruits, as well as oversized rabbits and cats. A dormouse. Flying pigeons. A hookah's spiraling smoke. Nonsensical music is playing somewhere nearby. The vision is so beautiful I don't want to open my eyes again.

My feet keep walking. It feels like I have stepped into the transparent bubble of my own vision, leaving the real world behind.

A thin orange hue occasionally seeps through my vision. I am thinking it's the sun over the barbed-wired walls, seeping through my eyelids and into my daydreaming vision.

My feet still keep walking. I can't stop them. Nothing can stop me from walking farther into my vision. I breathe in again. Air is such a precious thing. So underestimated. I feel the oxygen fill my brain. It's relaxing. It's soothing. This vision I am staring at with closed eyes must be real. The air is real, and the trees are real. There is no way I am hallucinating now.

Finally, I realize what I am staring at. It's the place I have been looking for. The place, maybe, everyone is looking for. I am staring with closed eyes at a memory of Wonderland.

My heartbeat shoots to the roof. I start to hurry barefoot in this amazing place, not even caring how I look like in the real world of the walled garden of the Radcliffe Asylum. Maybe I am standing there. Maybe I'm also running. Who cares?

My eyes inhale everything I see. Wonderland is huge. I mean huge. It baffles me that most of its vastness is blocked by the enormous fruits and trees. I run farther. I have no idea of my destination.

Could this be? Is Wonderland real? I can even smell it!

The farther I run, the more my vision dims. I don't know why, but I keep running. It looks like it's raining in the distance. It looks like the sun is fading in the distance. But the distance is where my footsteps take me. An inner feeling draws me toward it, away from Wonderland.

Why would my vision take me beyond Wonderland? I don't want to leave, but something urges me to go.

The last things I see in Wonderland are huge clocks

hung from thin threads in the sky as if they were laundry. The watches are as flexible as cloth. They haven't dried yet. Someone has just washed them, so no time can be told from looking at them. Someone has washed time away.

But then Wonderland disappears behind me.

Now, I am entering a normal life again, bound by time, chained by reason, and surmounted by human stupidity. It's not the present time, tough. A newspaper swirls in the air and sticks on my face. I pull it off. Through the noise of the crowd around me and the heavy rain, it's hard to unfold the yellowish paper. But I manage.

It's a periodical newspaper. It's called *Mischmasch*, owned and edited by Lewis Carroll. This is the fourteenth edition.

With a beating heart, I raise my head and discover that I am standing in the Tom Quadrangle in Oxford University, a century or two ago. Somehow I arrived here through Wonderland. I lower my head and check the date on the *Mischmasch*. The date is January the 14th, 1862.

Chapter 4

*Tom Quadrangle in Christ Church, Oxford University,
January 14th, 1862*

It's still raining heavily. A darker shade hovers over the Victorian atmosphere. The clouds are grey and cruel in the absence of the sun, blocked by the dirty smog and smoke all over this world. A world that reeks of pollution and stink. Poverty and homelessness overrule this not-so-picturesque vision of English Victorian times before me.

I snake through the crowd, all the way outside the university. I am outside at St Aldates. Deeper into Oxford, I see hordes of homeless people shading themselves with newspapers from the heavy rain. Coughs and vomits are heard and seen everywhere, as if there's been a disease. Young children with tattered clothes and bandaged hands, smitten with dirt, walk all around me. All they ask for is money. A penny. A shilling. Even a bronze half-shilling with the drawing of Queen Victoria upon it.

If they're not asking for money, they are begging for food, a loaf of bread, a single egg, or a potato, with open mouths. Some even beg for whiff of salt or a sip of clean water.

An old man with a stick shoos a few kids away. "Go back to London, you filthy rotten beggars!" he grunts before he trips to the floor himself. He is as weak as everyone else, upset that they're begging for his share of meals.

People don't seem to notice me.

Most people are conspicuously shorter than usual. Maybe they're not really shorter — their backs are bent over from poverty, a lack of nutrition and shelter.

I keep stepping over the muddy earth, realizing that what was Wonderland a few breaths ago has turned into a nightmare of older times.

Victorian times.

It looks like I am in a factually real point in history. Did I travel back in time?

I realize I can just open my eyes and escape this vision. But I don't. I want to I understand why am I having it.

Is this why January the 14th is so important? My hands crawl to the key at the end of the necklace Lewis gave me last time. One of the six keys to open Wonderland doors, he said.

I stop in my place and gaze ahead, only to see Lewis Carroll walking in a haze. He is wearing a priest's outfit, and a pile of papers is tucked under his armpit. A tattered umbrella is held loosely in his other hand before some kids steal it and run away, hitting the old man with it.

Lewis doesn't care. He tucks his hands into his pockets and pulls out a fistful of breadcrumbs. He offers them to the homeless children. The children circle him like ants around a huge insect they'd just trapped. The kids snatch the bread and then knock Lewis to the floor, the papers of his manuscript scattering in the air. They begin hitting him, asking him for money, but he is not fighting back, astonished by their aggressive acts. They steal his watch and his wallet, and rid him of his hat.

I run toward him. They have left him half naked. He seems to be the only one who sees me.

"Lewis," I yelp. "What's going on?"

"I couldn't save them, Alice," he cries in the rain. "I was too late. Couldn't save them."

"Save who? I don't understand," I say as a few kids suddenly are aware of my existence.

"I—I tried," he hiccups. "Th-those p-poor children." Lewis stutters.

I also realize my time in this vision is short. I'm exposed entirely to the children, and they are approaching. They'll rip me of my asylum's nightgown for sure and see if I have any bread or money.

"Run, Alice," Lewis demands, but holds to my hand for one last time. "Never tell anyone that I couldn't save them!"

I don't understand, but I have slid my hand away and am already running from the sinister Victorian kids.

Suddenly, my head hits something and my lips swell as if I have been punched in the face by a train.

My eyes flip open as my vision phases out, back into the uninteresting real world. As I regain my balance and momentum, I realize I've hit the garden's wall.

"This can't be," I whisper to myself. "I had to run from the kids, but I had to save Lewis. What was that about? Who are they, the people he could not help?"

I close my eyes deliberately again, wishing to re-enter the vision. It's not there anymore. I don't know how this works.

I stand, helpless and imprisoned in the choking arms of these walls of the asylum. Either I am mad beyond all madness, or I can travel through time. Either I was right about forgetting about that happened to me last week, or it's a terrible mistake.

What did Lewis mean? I couldn't save them, Alice.

Chapter 5

Director's office, Radcliffe Lunatic Asylum, Oxford

Instead of spending his money on his failing marriage, Dr. Tom Truckle, director of the Radcliffe Lunatic Asylum, spent it on surveillance cameras.

He even helped install them himself in the VIP Ward when the Pillar was away. Although Dr. Truckle's life was sliding down on an oily spiral of circumstances, his obsession with the Pillar pushed him to do maddening things. He needed more cameras—from every angle possible—to learn about the Pillar's secret.

How does Pillar the Killer escape his cell and return as if he's world's best magician?

Two days ago, Professor Carter Pillar escaped his cell again, leaving a trail of swirling hookah smoke behind. It hung in the air, shaping the word *Frabjous*.

Dr. Truckle had previously doubled the security guards on the VIP Ward. He also sent for England's finest magicians to ask them how such an escape was possible. They had no clue. Architects, too, had been consulted. Radcliffe Asylum was a two-centuries-old building, first built in Victorian times. Maybe the asylum hid secret tunnels underneath it. Secret tunnels only someone as devious and intellectually crazy as Professor Pillar knew about.

But no. Truckle's mind had been reaching too far—possibly an aftereffect of the many medication pills he swallowed like the kids gorge on M&M's.

The architects called the idea of tunnels implausible. In fact, they declared that escaping the asylum was physically *impassible*.

"Impossible, you mean," Dr. Truckle replied to the architects.

"No, we mean *impassible*," the twin architects had insisted. "Nothing is impossible." They had laughed, and

Dr Truckle hadn't understood why. "You've never read *Alice in Wonderland*?" one of the twin architects asked. Dr. Truckle shook his head. He hated *Alice in Wonderland*. "It's an inside joke," they told him. "You can only get it if you've read the book."

Dr. Truckle didn't want to *get it*. He wanted to know how the Pillar escaped.

Of course, the Pillar was expected to show up soon, claiming he was out buying a new hookah or something. Dr. Truckle knew otherwise: Pillar the Killer was almost *uncatchable*. He could escape and live in an uncharted island full of mushrooms for the rest of his life. But he didn't. He preferred to spend his days imprisoned in this stupid asylum. And his sole reason for that was Alice Wonder.

That, at least, Dr. Truckle was sure of.

But why Alice? What in the world did such a young and mad girl possess that was so valuable to the Pillar?

Dr. Truckle swallowed another pill — the fifth today — and closed his eyes to calm down. He stood next to his desk, his eyes monitoring the Pillar's cell through the surveillance screens fixed on the wall. The Pillar hadn't arrived yet.

One of the screens was broadcasting news on national TV. Dr. Truckle liked to watch the local news while he was waiting. Watching the madness plaguing the world helped him tolerate his relatively mad job in the asylum, particularly after the horrifying incident in Stamford Bridge stadium yesterday.

Since the incident, Dr. Truckle knew things wouldn't end just there. The incident of a stuffed head in a ball was a beginning of something madder. Soon enough more bodies would pile up all over Britain, if not the whole world.

And here it was, right in front of his eyes.

The news host on national TV was announcing the discovery of another chopped-off head, found with the phrase "Off with their heads" written in blood on its forehead.

"Ramon Yeskelitch, a Ukrainian immigrant," the news reporter—a nerdy middle-aged woman with red glasses and an uptight but fancy suit—reported, "who lives near Borough Market in London, a divorced and unemployed father of two, went to buy his weekly mouthwatering watermelon today. Mr. Yeskelitch and his family have a certain liking for watermelons."

Dr. Truckle leaned forward, excited by the morbidity lurking in the air.

"Arriving back home, Mr. Yeskelitch tucked the slightly oversized watermelon in the fridge for a couple of hours," the host continued. "Then, when it was dinnertime, he decided to serve the watermelon to his children, who were eager for their weekly dose, only to be shocked with what they saw stuffed inside when they cut it open." The woman shrugged for a moment, unable to comprehend the words she was supposed to read to the nation. "Bloody, blimey, bollocks!" Her tongue slipped as she adjusted her spectacles. She raised her head back to the camera with kaleidoscope eyes of surprise. "Mr. Yeskelitch and his children found a human *head* inside the watermelon." Then she stopped, her eyes a bit watery, like a girl in a Japanese Manga about to burst into tears. "Another human head like the one which was found stuffed inside the ball in Stamford Bridge," she continued, almost stuttering.

Dr. Truckle wondered if she hadn't been informed of the heaviness of the subject before going live on air. Or was she occupied manicuring her fingernails, cleaning her glasses, and showing off her expensive dress?

But Dr. Truckle wasn't really interested in the pretentious world of TV—although he secretly wished they'd interview him on *Good Morning Britain*. The doctor was wondering whether the news had anything to do with the Cheshire killer, thus the Pillar as well.

Was it possible that the Pillar was somehow linked to

the killings?

The doctor's eyes darted back to screens monitoring the Pillar's cell. The damn professor hadn't returned. Where was he?

Dr. Truckle snapped like a rubber band to the sudden ringing of his office's landline. Who used landlines these days? He had begun considering the landline operator as an antique long ago.

"Dr. Truckle speaking," he answered, adjusting his tie in the mirror.

"I'm Professor Pillar's chauffeur," a mousy voice replied. "I have a message from him."

Dr. Truckle looked around, making sure no one was with him in the room. "What kind of message?" He grabbed the receiver with both hands, trying to stick his ear closer and closer.

"Professor Pillar wants you to do something right now. He says time is not on our side. We need to move fast."

"I'm not doing anything before you tell me where he is right this moment." Dr. Truckle almost cracked the handset open with his intensity.

"You really want to know?"

"I do." He was almost panting like a dog longing for a bone.

"He's playing football with an oversized watermelon in Hyde Park," the chauffeur said. "Oh, wait."

"Wait for what?" Dr. Truckle panicked. "What's happening?"

"Oh, nothing," said the chauffeur. "The watermelon split open. There is someone's head inside."

Chapter 6

Walled garden, Radcliffe Lunatic Asylum, Oxford

Amidst my confusion and frustration, I sit on the walled garden's ground. I need a moment to catch my breath and decide what I am about to do. Lewis sent me a message through a daydreaming vision. I am not sure what to do with it. Nor do I have any idea whom he failed to help — or save.

Whether Lewis is my mind's doing or for real, I can't discard his apparent caring about the world. He loves people unconditionally. He wants to make things right. He wants to make the world better. Lewis, the stuttering artist, doesn't shy away from what he is, from his fears. I think this is why he impacted so many children in the world. Older folks usually wear their own masks when they deal with children, but Lewis opened up and let go. He accepted who he was and what the world around him was like, and decided he would only see the good in all the mess.

Unlike what I did the past six weeks. I know now it was a mistake pretending what was not.

If I am mad, make my day. I should have not avoided the Mush Room in order to pretend last week's events didn't happen. The Pillar's words ring in my ear again: *Insane people are only sane people who give in to the madness in the world.* I am not sure he said those exact words. I am remembering the meaning behind what he said — again, if he ever existed and wasn't a figment of my imagination.

As I sit, I hear the girl's muffled screams from the Mush Room inside the main building again. Her screams send shivers of anger down my spine this time.

Waltraud and Ogier must enjoy torturing her, laughing at her and buzzing her over and over again.

Don't even think about it, Alice, my inner voice warns me. *You're not meant to save other people's lives. You're just a mad girl trying to avoid shock therapy at best.*

I fist my hands and clench my teeth when the girl screams again. This could have easily been me. Each time she screams, I remember the unexplained visions of poor children asking for a loaf of bread. Did Lewis mean he couldn't save *them*? The regret in his eyes was unmistakable. Do I want to regret not saving the girl in the Mush Room now? Do I want to regret not saving myself?

I can't. I am no hero, but I just can't stand witnessing someone's unjustified punishment.

"Stop it!" I scream at Waltraud and Ogier from behind the wall. "Stop torturing her!" My voice seems louder than I can handle. A surge of electricity runs through my veins, and I can feel the pain of the Mush Room's instruments already. "Stop torturing her!" I repeat, pounding on the ground.

I still can stop. Maybe Waltraud hasn't heard me. But I am stubborn and I can't tolerate the screams. I throw boulders at the walls.

The screaming stops.

A few minutes later, the main door to the garden springs open. Waltraud stands in front of me, slapping her prod on her thick palms. A smirk, ten miles wide, illuminates her face.

"You were saying something, Alice?" she asks as Ogier approaches me. "I knew you couldn't play your game long enough."

The grin on Ogier's face deserves an Oscar for the Most Stupid Portrayal of Evil. He keeps grinning at me with such joy while Waltraud handcuffs me to send me down to the Mush Room — and it's not the Cheshire's evil grin.

I don't care anymore. I will stay my ground, and say what I feel is right, even if I am mad.

"So, you're mad after all," Waltraud grunts. "You still believe in Wonderland. You believe in it so much you're willing to exchange places with a girl you don't know in the torture room."

"Why don't you shut up and just finish this," I grunt back.

"Do you know I tricked you into this?" Waltraud lights up a cigarette. "I had to make the girl scream her best so you'd hear it. We weren't really treating her that bad. I knew you think you're born to save lives. Foolish you." She laughs and high-fives Ogier.

They pull me down and usher me along the corridor leading to the torture room. My lips begin to slightly shiver at the taste of the coming pain I know so well. The Mushroomers on both sides bang the bars of their cells again. "Alice. Alice. Alice!"

At the room's entrance, Waltraud's phone buzzes.

She checks the number and grimaces. "It's Dr. Truckle," she mumbles, and picks up.

Waltraud listens for a while, her lips twitching and her face dimming. She hangs up finally and stares disappointedly at me.

"You're very lucky, Alice," she says. "Dr. Truckle is sending you for further examination outside the asylum."

A faint smile lines my lips. This must be the Pillar. Something has come up. A new mission, maybe? I am baffled at how happy I am. Who was I fooling for the past six days? I am addicted to this. I am addicted to leaving the asylum, addicted to the madness in the outside world. I am addicted to saving lives.

Waltraud unties me, her lips pursed. "Go get dressed now. But remember, when you come back, your brain is mine. I'll mush it into mushed potatoes with ketchup made of your blood!"

Chapter 7

Entrance, Radcliffe Lunatic Asylum, Oxford

The Pillar's mousy chauffeur picks me up from the asylum's main gate. Instead of arriving in the black limousine, he's driving an ambulance. Two guards from the asylum escort me to the back door as if I am the most dangerous girl in the world.

I still don't get why an ambulance. Maybe to camouflage me being transported for inspection in another hospital.

The guards snicker as they push me into the empty back of the vehicle. I glimpse the words written on the back doors before they close on me: *The Carroll Cause for the Criminally Cuckoo.*

Now I am sure I going to see the Pillar soon.

Once the chauffeur takes off, he requests I sit next to him in the passenger's seat. This is the first time he talks to me. His voice is thin and annoyingly low. It's like he has tight throat or something. No wonder he doesn't talk much. I watch him comb his thin whiskers while he drives—sorry, but I refuse to call those *hairies* on his face a mustache.

"Where is the Pillar?" I demand.

"I am driving you to him." He hands me a mobile phone for communication. It's a new one with a fairly big screen. He pushes a button on it to show me a YouTube video.

I feel like a spy on a new mission, watching the latest report.

The YouTube video's purpose is for me to catch on. I learn all about the Stamford Bridge crime. The head stuffed into a football. No doubts this is the Cheshire's doing. The phrase "Off with heir heads" seems like one of his messages. Then I watch recorded local news about a man named Roman Yeskelitch who found another head in a watermelon he just bought.

I realize why I am out now. There is a new Wonderland crime happening out there, and I am needed. I can't deny my excitement. I am not going to lie.

Rolling down the window, I stretch out my hands like a child and sniff the day's cold air.

A few minutes later, the Chauffeur stops in front of a "Richmond Elementary School." At least the school bears a coherent name. I have no idea how no one comments on the name of the vehicle we're in, let alone why we're arriving in an ambulance.

"Why are we stopping here?" I ask.

The chauffeur points over my shoulder. When I look back, an old woman in thick glasses appears out of the school's main gate.

"You must be Alice." She approaches with welcoming sparks in her eyes. Her attitude screams "teacher," one of those kind-hearted and very talkative few in every middle-grade school.

I step down reluctantly. The woman pulls me in her arms, kisses me on the cheek, hugs me, and tells me how Professor Pillar never stops mentioning me.

She ushers me into the school, telling me Professor Pillar is so kind to agree to lecturing her kids. A lecture about the virtues of going after one's dreams. It turns out he told them I am the optimum example of achieving my dreams.

All I do is nod. The woman will eventually send me to the Pillar, wherever he is.

I want to tell her she has a dangerous serial killer in her school. I want to ask if she'd never heard about Pillar the Killer. But she doesn't stop talking, so I have no room to even comment.

Finally, she departs, leaving me at a corridor leading to a few classes. She tells me the school management preferred to give the Pillar all the privacy he needed in the classroom.

The word "classroom" bothers me. I ask how many children he has with him in there. The teacher nods with the happiest smile ever, and claps my hand between hers before she says her prayers and blessings, still enamored by the presence of one of the country's most renowned professors. All of this without telling me how many children. She tells me how kind it is that a man of the Pillar's caliber visits the children, and how happy they are about meeting with such an idol.

"Do you happen to know he's been convicted..." I can't help it.

"Of murder?" She laughs and waves a hand in the air. "Professor Pillar was so kind to explain the misunderstanding. Of course, there is the *other* 'Pillar the Killer' who is locked away in a sanitarium. This kind man in the classroom has nothing to do with it."

"How so?" I am curious enough to blow my cover.

"Ah, dear. I know you're testing me now. You know it was a case of identity theft. The madman used the honored professor's name. He told me all about it. Besides, how can a madman ever escape a sanitarium?" She laughs again.

I can't argue with her, actually. I myself am not supposed to be out of the asylum. I think the brilliance of my cover is that I am not expected to be walking the sane world. "And why would a madman visit a school and lecture kids if he'd escaped the asylum?" I am thinking out loud, trapped inside the logic he fed to the poor woman. It's scary how the change of a word or two can twist any truth into a lie.

I pat the woman and thank her, turning to walk the corridor. A few empty classes away, I find an occupied one. When I peek in through the glass in the door, I don't see children flying paper planes or practicing all kinds of chaos in the absence of real teachers. Instead, I see them all building things. Some kind of Lego structure, except they are putting together pieces of a few hookahs.

Chapter 8

Classroom # 14, Richmond Elementary School

The Pillar has his own hookah fixed on the teacher's desk. He sits on the chair behind it, taking drags as if he were still in his VIP cell in the asylum.

I glare at him from behind the glass door once he sees me. Allowing middle-grade kids to play with a hookah doesn't seem to nag his morality by any means.

"Boys and girls." He points his hookah and lets a spiral of smoke swirl around him. "Welcome your new friend." He points at me.

The attention of the young folks tenses me momentarily, but once they start calling my name, I have no choice but to open the door and take them in my arms.

"Alice!" a girl runs into me and hugs me. "The Pillar said you would come visit us."

"I wouldn't miss it," I say, and then gaze at the Pillar for explanation. He is not looking at me, occupied with chalking something on the blackboard. He draws a blind woman holding two scales, a hookah in each, and writes underneath: *...and madness for all!*

"Are you going to save lives today?" a boy asks me. I can't help but notice most of the kids are a bit overweight for their age, but hey, they need to eat to grow up.

"Are you going to catch the Watermelon Killer?" a girl asks. I feel dreadful that they know about the crimes, and shoot the Pillar a blaming look.

"That's TV's doing, not me," he says, and drags from his hookah.

"He is not called the Watermelon Killer," a boy objects. "He is the Football Killer."

"Why don't you all give me some privacy with the Pillar for a few minutes"—I pat a few children—"so I can catch that killer?"

"Kick his arse!" A tall and chubby boy fists a hand as if

he were Superman.

I guess that is TV's doing as well.

"Go back to your hookahs, kids," the Pillar says. "They're not smoking hookahs, just putting a few together," he tells me before I object. "It's basically like Lego."

I leave the kids and walk to him. The Pillar shows me out to a balcony. Once we get out, his funny face disappears. "The Cheshire is killing again," he says, not wasting any more time.

Chapter 9

"How do you know it's the Cheshire?" I ask.

"At least he is behind the killings. But this time it's different: grander, gorier, and bloodier. Whatever he has on his mind, we're way behind to stop him." He reaches for his phone to show me something.

"Stop!" I demand.

He looks confused.

"Seriously?" I sneer at him, tilting my head.

He blinks twice, wondering about my annoyance.

"You don't contact me for a week, leave me behind with so many unanswered questions, and then when we meet, you act as if I'm working for you or something?"

"Oh?" he says. "I suppose I should've written you a letter of fluffy words on pinkish watermarked paper that smells of summer roses."

"Of course not. It's just that unanswered questions keep piling up."

"I suppose I could answer a couple of questions." He checks his pocket watch. "If the Cheshire doesn't go chopping a few other heads and stuff them in watermelons while we do."

"Don't do this to me." I raise a finger. He is triggering my desire for justice and saving people.

"After Yeskelitch's watermelon, eleven more heads were found in watermelons across the country. In a span of two days."

"So fast?" I am perplexed.

"Also, the news hostess lied and kept vital information from the public," he says. "The head Yeskelitch found was one of his *own* kids."

"I didn't—"

"Yes, Alice. It's true." The Pillar purses his lips. "Each and every head is a *kid's* head."

The shocking revelation urges me to watch the kids

playing in class. Although I don't approve of them putting hookahs together, they seem so happy about their lives. They are looking forward for each coming day. How can someone take that from them?

"Thirteen heads so far, all kids between age seven and fourteen," the Pillar says. "It's a Jub Jub mess." He turns on the news on his mobile phone.

"This is insane..." My jaw is left hanging open, my eyes begging me to drop down my eyelids so I won't have nightmares from what I am looking at. Families are crying their hearts out, mothers vomiting upon seeing their children's chopped-off heads, and fathers cry hysterically and swear they'd chop the killer into a million pieces when they catch him. "This is insane," I repeat to myself, because I don't know what else to say.

"Well, no more watermelons sold in Britain," the Pillar muses. Now he has my attention, he starts playing sarcastic and cruel again. "People should stick to cantaloupe. Ah, not big enough to stuff a head inside."

"So, why is the Cheshire killing again?" I have to ignore his weird sarcasm. It's only meant to provoke me.

"I have no idea."

"You don't?" I frown. "I thought you knew how the Cheshire thinks."

"Usually I do, but this"—he points at the screen—"is some messy massacre. I don't understand its purpose."

"But the message on the kid's foreheads speaks for itself," I offer. "'Off with their heads.'"

"So does the idea of chopping off heads." The Pillar stares absently at the screen. I can tell he is genuinely confused. "It's definitely a Wonderland crime, committed by a Wonderland Monster like the Cheshire. I just don't understand why."

"The Cheshire said there will be a Wonderland War— whatever that is. Could that be a part of it? Just some carnage, messy massacre to ensure terror on humans?"

"Nah." The Pillar tongues his cheek from inside.

"Despite his unquenchable grudge against humanity, the Cheshire's main concern is to locate and free the Wonderland Monsters to help him in the Wonderland War." He eyes me briefly, letting me know I am not supposed to ask what the war is about, not now. "So, inducing chaotic madness upon the world isn't his thing. These murders are about something else. This is tailored work, a careful design of crimes. Whoever killed thirteen children all over Britain in two days had committed the crimes much earlier. We were only meant to know about them now. There is a message we're supposed to get."

"We?"

The Pillar nods. "Humans, although he detests them, are of no interest to him. They are merely puppets he uses. If he represents the black tiles on the chessboard of life, we represent the white ones. Well, at least you. I'm only helping you for now." He takes a moment to consider. "Last time, the Cheshire wanted his grin back, so he could retain his unstoppable power that would assist him in finding the Wonderland Monsters."

I am not following, not really. All I care about is stopping the crimes, so I am thinking. "Why don't we start with learning more about the victims' heads? It's clear that this is what the killer wants us to look at."

The Pillar shoots me an admiring look, as if I am his clever apprentice. "Good thinking." He points at the news showing the victims being transferred to the morgue for autopsy.

I take a moment to comprehend what he is trying to imply. "Wait." I take a step back. "You don't mean I am..."

"Going to the morgue?" His smile broadens.

"I thought I'd leave the asylum to see the world outside, go see Oxford University, the Vatican, and Belgium like last time."

"If you want to know about the dead mean's fate, the morgue is always a good start."

"Which morgue?" I sigh.

"The Westminster Public Mortuary, formally known as the Rue Morgue to the likes of Edgar Allan Poe."

"Poe?" I know he was a prolific writer who wrote a short story called "Murders in Rue Morgue," which took place in London centuries ago. Was he actually writing about *this* morgue?

I shake my thoughts away, and do my best not to succumb to the Pillar's distracting comments.

"There is a slight problem, though," the Pillar mentions.

"And that would be?"

"The Westminster Public Morgue has a most secretive section inside. They call the *Iain West Forensic Suite*," the Pillar elaborates. "A state-of-the-art mortuary that the government uses in such complicated cases. Security is almost impenetrable. You will need to find a way to fool the *living* to get in, and then fool the *dead* to get out." He admires his quote for a second then looks at his pocket watch. "My chauffeur will help you in." He utters his words in one sharp breath, as a non-negotiable matter of fact. He does it so on point that I feel dizzy. My lips are dry and zipped. I have never been to a morgue before. "What are you waiting for? *Too late, too late, for an important date.*" He clicks his fingers for urgency.

I nod and shrug at the same time. Going to a morgue still seems very unsettling to me.

"Oh," the Pillar says, "I almost forgot." He pulls out a small box and opens it. There is small mushroom inside. "You will need to eat this."

"What is that?" I stare suspiciously at the mushroom.

"A sedative. It will make you look dead for an hour or so." He pulls my hand and gently places this spongy thing on my palm.

"Why would I want to look dead?"

"Oh, Alice. How do you think you will get into a maximum-security mortuary? Just take a small bite." He nudges my hand toward my mouth.

I open the balcony and say goodbye to the children in class. They wave back enthusiastically, welcoming me with their Lego hookahs. I gaze back at the Pillar, wondering if I should trust him. It's hard to tell from the way he looks at me. It's hard to tell who he really is, or what he wants with me.

"Don't worry, you won't grow taller," he says, as he wants me to slip the mushroom into my mouth.

Suddenly, I am more than uncomfortable with the Pillar's suggestion. I still don't trust him.

The Pillar gets the message, but says nothing. He lights up his mini hookah and takes an unusually long and tense drag, puffing it out. "I understand," he says. "If you don't trust me, I understand. Sincerely."

"Really?" I squint. Something is wrong. "You will give up, just like that?"

"Who said I gave up?" he asks as I feel suddenly dizzy. My knees wobble under me and imaginary birds begin tweeting in my ears. I fall to my knees, realizing too late that I've been sedated by the smoke from his hookah.

The world fades to black. The Pillar fooled me. I don't think I am ready for the morgue trip yet.

Chapter 10

Somewhere in this mad world

I open my eyes to an endless darkness. A blinding kind of darkness I haven't experienced before. Many times have I slept in pitch black in my cell in the asylum. This present darkness is different. It seems as if it has a soul, a substance. It feels too close and invasive to my privacy. It's as if I am wrapped between its octopus arms. A claustrophobic kind of darkness.

No explanation comes to my semi-numb mind right now.

Where am I?

My body is numb, enough to chain me in temporary paralysis. Each of my limbs is heavy enough that I don't bother lifting any.

Somehow, I am sure this will subside.

A slow train of memories arrives. It's slow but noisy and heavy, like a locomotive breath.

The Pillar sedated me, and all the kicks and screams in the world are of no use—for now. I will have to face wherever I am.

Shouldn't I wake up in the morgue and inspect the heads of the deceased kids?

As the heaviness in my body subsides, I reach for anything I can get hold of in the dark. The tips of my fingers collide with some kind of a plastic. It's wavy. I can't see it. My mind finally registers a fact: I am stretched on my back.

A surge of panic alerts my weakened body. It's so threatening that my numbness subsides. I start to kick my hands and feet in the dark as unreasonable claustrophobia overrules me. The plastic darkness opposes me in every direction, as if I am imprisoned in an elastic balloon.

I keep kicking and scraping against the surface of this darkness. I need to get out of it before I choke or die from the lack of breathing, but I can't cut through without a sharp tool.

Panic captures me. Until my fingers come across a metallic thing attached to the plastic.

A zipper.

The thought that hits my brain almost puts me back in paralysis. I think I know where I am.

Thin rays of yellow light seep through the plastic bag I am trapped in as I pull the zipper down. I reach out with my hands like the dead out of their graves. Finally, I wriggle myself out of the black plastic bag. I feel like a dying cocoon evolving into a butterfly — it reminds momentarily of the deceptive Pillar.

I straighten up on the table I am on — it feels like a table more than a bed — and I realize for certain where I am.

I'm actually in the morgue. I was tucked in one of those plastic bags the deceased end up in. A body bag. This is what the Pillar meant by a maximum-security morgue that's hard to sneak into. The madman tucked me in a death bag and slipped in among the dead.

Paralyzed on the table, I can't even comprehend my surroundings yet. I do notice the chilling temperature of the room, though.

"Breathe, Alice. Breathe," I whisper as I hug myself, since I am all I have on this side of life. And I thought my cell was the worst place in the world.

The cold creeps up my spine, fluttering like a winter breeze through my blue shirt and jeans. The cold almost bites at the back of my neck. Goosebumps prickle like devil's grass on my skin.

When I am about to move my legs to get off the roller bed I am on, my bare feet give in to numbness. I have no idea where my shoes are. I fight the stiffness in my back and bend over to rub my feet. As I do, I glimpse a rectangular piece of cardboard attached to a string wrapped around my right toe. I think it's called a toe tag. It's how a coroner or mortician identifies a dead person in

the morgue. My heart almost stops. Why am I wearing this? I reach out to flip the toe tag so I can read it:

Name: Alice Pleasant Wonder.

Numbness invades my very soul.

Case: 141898

Then it mentions my hair, skin, and eye color. And finally it says:

Condition: Deceased in a bus accident.

The world around me freezes. It's like someone has a remote control for my beating heart and just clicked the off button. My mouth is dry, my skin is cold and numb, and I can't breathe. Why not? I am dead, after all.

And I thought I was mad.

I snatch the toe tag from its string and pull it close to my moist eyes. My mind advises me to blink and read it all over again. Nothing changes. I am still in the mortuary, reading my own obituary.

How can I be dead? The Pillar wouldn't go so far to scare me. Why would he do that, unless I was imagining all of this? How did I die?

The answer hits me like a freight train when I flip the card. Someone has written something in the back:

P.S. She was driving the bus.

My hands cup my mouth, suppressing a painful scream. It's only for a few seconds before I realize how much I need to free the scream inside me. When I finally do, in my loudest screeching voice, no sound comes out. I think I have lost my ability to speak. Why not? I am dead anyways.

Chapter 11

Iain West Forensic Suite, an extension to the Westminster Public Mortuary, London

Speechlessly, I slide out of the death bag, and carefully get off the steel table.

The morgue's floor is cold as ice. I am barefoot, and I still don't know why. Whoever toe-tagged me decided I don't need shoes anymore, that I should suffer against the cold floor.

I hop like a panicked kangaroo for a few seconds before I realize that I will eventually need some kind of shoes.

Rummaging through the plastic bag I came in, I find nothing. It feels awkward and unsettling searching through my own coffin-like bag of death.

Before my mind scrambles for solutions, my lungs screech from the cold. I cough so hard I am sure something will burst out of my lungs into the air. My back bends forward. My hand clamps to the steel table, preventing me from falling.

Why is my body in such pain? Is this what death feels like?

I cough again, my mouth agape it hurts so badly. The clothes I am wearing aren't helping against this freezing cold. It takes a hard effort to lift up my other hand, as if it's tied down to a weight.

My hand is faintly bluish. I shriek—then cough again.

I manage to straighten my back and then rub my hands together for warmth. I rub them on my body as well.

Then I hop like a kangaroo again. Amazing how much unexpected energy your body can exude when you're in danger.

Relax, Alice. None of this is happening. You're probably not dying. It's just part of the insanity you're enduring.

It occurs to me that if I am not dead yet, it's only a few

minutes before I freeze to death in here.

See? How could you freeze to death if you are dead already? Let it go. Confess your madness and it will all subside. Just do what you came here to do. Examine the dead kids' heads.

My inner thoughts freeze to the cold of the floor underneath me. I rub my body even harder and do more of my kangaroo dance.

I really need to find shoes now. I haven't looked hard. I need shoes — and a coat.

I try to rip apart a piece of the plastic bag so I can wrap it around my feet and body. But the bag isn't elastic enough. Of course not. It's durable enough to hold a dead person inside. Why would it cut easily?

I tilt my head. The cold room doesn't offer any visible solutions. It's a huge, rectangular room, reminding me of the corridor in the underground ward in the asylum. I take a long, cold breath to get some oxygen into my head. It hurts, but I need it to think clearer.

The floor is marble all around. The walls are buried behind the endless metallic drawers with corpses inside. There are only three bulbs in the entire place. One is hanging over my head, another a few meters away, and the third is a bit too far. I can't see it — I am too numb to walk that far.

The three bulbs are slightly shaking, as if huffed and puffed by an invisible wind.

Closing my eyes and clenching my teeth, I try not to think about the dead all around me. Thanks to the dim light, I can pretend they don't exist, like all the scary things in the night we dismiss.

The cold attacks my feet again, chilling through my spine. It's getting harder to force my eyelids open.

Seriously, *I am not dead. Am I? The tag is some kind of a morbid joke. Right?*

I miss the madness of my Tiger Lily. She would have spat some quirky words at me. She would have accused me of being mad and useless, but she would have also hinted to some solution.

I keep walking as fast as I can in the room to get warmth into my body. I am actually limping now. It reminds me of the Pillar's Caucus Race; walking fast inside the morgue, knowing it will get me nowhere.

Where the heck is the door?

I can't find it.

Please tell me I am not mad.

Mad or dead, which is which, and does it really make a difference?

Panting, I stare at the few tables next to me. They are lined with plastic bags of the corpses. Those I stopped by are different. The bags are all labeled with chalk on the surface: *Watermelon Murders.*

This is what I am here for. Cold or no cold, I have to examine the corpses.

Still tapping my feet to the cold ground, it finally occurs to me to check my jeans pocket for my mobile phone. I guess I was too panicked to look earlier—isolated living in the asylum does this too you; calling someone for help isn't the usual reaction for a person with a Certificate of Insanity.

I find the mobile and pull it out. I am surprised there is a signal inside the morgue. Thank God. With numb fingers, I dial the only number on my contacts.

Beep. Beep.

No one picks up.

I hate those *beeps.*

My face reddens when the call ends. Some programmed woman's voice tells me that no one is picking up, that I should try later.

"He has to pick up!" I scream at her

"Well, sweetie. Let's try again," the woman chirps.

I almost throw away the phone, shocked by the woman's response. Isn't this supposed to be prerecorded?

But then I succumb to the madness, which means basically ignoring it and not giving it much thought. I push the button again, almost hurting my forefinger.

The Pillar has to pick up, or is he a figment of my imagination, too?

Finally, someone picks up and says, "Carroll's Cause for the Criminally Cuckoo. How can I help you today?"

Chapter 12

It takes me a moment to realize this is the Pillar's cool, nonchalant, and all-mocking voice.

Once I am about to fire all anger at him, he interrupts me, munching on food. It's not that *nom nom nom* sound. It's *brauch brauch brauch,* deliberately provoking me. "Hello," he says. "Who's this?"

"It's me, Alice!" I growl, and try to furrow my brow against the cold. I can't say my face went red, as it is still numb. I start tapping my feet against the cold floor again.

"Alice," he munches. "From Wonderland," he welcomes me, slowly sipping a drink from a straw. "Did you inspect the corpses yet?"

"Not yet." I am too chilled, too little blood flowing in my veins, a bit too numb to fire back or scream. "It's too cold." I rub my sides.

"Dead people usually are." He pops open a bag of snacks.

"I'm not joking. I am cold and will freeze in here." I begin to walk around again, looking for some kind of shoes again. "I know the toe tag is your doing; a sick prank from a sick mind."

"Toe tag?" More sucking and slurping. *Krrr krawww.*

"The one that says I died in a bus accident." I keep looking for something for warmth. A mortician must have left a coat behind or something.

The Pillar stops munching. "No, I don't know anything about that. I admit I sedated you in the school, but that was for the greater good. All in Britain's name."

"Then who did that to me?" Still looking for shoes, I don't have the nerve to argue about him sedating me now.

"My chauffeur sneaked you into the morgue as a corpse. It was the only way we could surpass the security system. He must have added a toe tag, but he never told me he'd write you died in a bus accident."

"I don't believe you," I say. "And I'm tired of your games." I rummage through a few weird-looking instruments on a table, metallic, scissor-like cutters. I can't even begin to think what they do with them. "Get me out of here before I freeze to death."

"You can't get out before approximately thirty minutes." The Pillar starts munching again. "A mortician will pick up your corpse after she receives a fake call from my chauffeur informing her your corpse has been misplaced, so we can get you out again. That's the plan."

"I will freeze to death in here. I need shoes and a coat."

"Why is that a problem?"

"The problem is I can't find any." I try my best to express my anger. The tightness of my face doesn't help much.

"If I were you, I'd roll out a corpse from the infinite drawers and fetch me a dead woman's shoe." He stops munching again, as if waiting for my reaction to his suggestion.

I don't hesitate. I walk back to the drawers, pull one out. The steel drawer is much heavier than I'd expected.

The corpse's smell isn't that bad. Unlike the corpses on the table, the ones in the drawers have been examined and cleaned. It's the corpse's sight that imposes a dreadful atmosphere upon me.

Dead or mad, what would it be? I realize I'd prefer being mad.

"Alice?" I hear him on the phone's speaker, but ignore him. I have to do this. It's just borrowing a dead man's shoe. We need to look out for each other, don't we, the living and the dead?

But then I am hit with an imaginary hammer on my head when I realize the corpses in the drawers don't have their clothes on. I let out another angry growl.

"No shoes?" the Pillar mocks me.

Too weak to even talk, I close my eyes, trying to argue with reason. Why is he doing this to me?

"To spare your breath, you'll not find clothes in the drawers," he says. "Corpses in the drawers had their autopsies already. You need to try the bags on the metallic roller beds. Those are the fresh ones. Yummy!" He bites into what I think is a greasy hamburger.

I walk silently to one of the death bags, not those marked with *Watermelon Murders*, as I don't want to mess with evidence.

I pull the zipper open only to realize the one I chose is a man's corpse. What can I say? I am picky. I want a woman's shoe, and I want it my size.

I zip the bag and try the one next to it. A woman.

Now, these are the smelly, rotten corpses I expected. Dead, stinky, and bloodstained. I am too exhausted to even care.

The woman's shoes turn out to be too small for me. I go back and pick up the man's shoes. My size. Being picky isn't helping when you're trapped in a morgue.

I put on the shoes, enjoying the warmth in my feet—a dead man's warmth. *Oh, the mad world outside.* I realize I want to go back to the asylum again, a tear about to squeeze out of my eyes in this terrible cold.

"Reebok or Nike?" the Pillar teases.

I don't answer him. Instead, I rip off the dead man's duster jacket and put it on. If I am blunt enough to put on a shoe, I better put on all that will save my life.

"I am ready." I tighten the dead man's bloody duster around me, my feet not jumpy anymore. "I came here to accomplish something." I take a deep breath, fooling my mind into thinking I am wearing Cinderella's slippers and a beautiful wedding dress. "Should I open the dead kids' bags and look for clues now?"

"I thought you'd never ask." The Pillar sighs. "I'd do it as fast I can, if I were you. Like I said, a mortician will soon arrive to collect you, so you'd be sent to another morgue. She'd need to find you intact inside the bag you came in."

"Yeah. You said that before." I've already pulled the

zipper of the bag of one of the victims. "Thirty minutes."

"That was thirty minutes when you arrived at the morgue, Alice." He sips and then burps. "You only have twenty minutes left, or your cover will be exposed. Time is slipping away."

Chapter 13

Twenty minutes to go...

I am doing my best not to think about the dead man's shoes wrapped around my feet. Still, I cringe at the thought. Strangely, the only way to get rid of it is to occupy my mind with a twelve-year-old boy's corpse.

I put the Pillar on speaker as he keeps reminding me of the eighteen minutes I have left before the mortician arrives. Then I lay the phone on the edge of the metallic table and begin my work. I feel like Nancy Drew already.

Unzipping the first plastic bag, my hand shivers and trembles when I see the kid's corpse.

Somehow, I am not really sure of the corpse's gender. The face is so mutilated, my stomach churns. The sentence "Off with their heads" is scribbled in sticky blood on the forehead. This feels like one of those unnecessarily gory scenes in one of those slasher horror movies.

I intend to reach for the kid's face but realize my hands are still relatively numb. Not from the cold this time, but from the horror before my eyes.

I can't even swallow, feeling a lump in my throat. What is it about the real world that makes people commit such crimes? It's a kid, for God's sake! He was supposed to have a whole future ahead of him. Why am I staring at his chopped-off head in a morgue right now? Why?

"Too much gore?" The Pillar's munching echoes slightly in the boxed room. "Which reminds me, I need barbecue sauce for my snack."

Instead of screaming at him, I buckle down on my knees and vomit on the floor. I don't even have a chance to resist the urge.

"You're not vomiting, Alice. Or?" The munching stops. "Can't you see I am eating here? That's so Jub Jub."

The cold and fear seal my lips. I can't speak. All I do is wipe my mouth with the edge of the dead man's bloodstained duster. Last time, when I saved Constance, I hadn't come so close to a corpse. Let alone a young boy or girl.

"I need a minute," I tell the Pillar. His annoying attitude doesn't disturb me now. Seeing the corpse stirred the same emotions I felt toward Constance. Someone has to stop the Cheshire. At least stop the killings from spreading. Someone has to stop this *sane* world's madness.

"You don't have a minute." The Pillar's voice is dead serious. "All you have is sixteen minutes left before the mortician arrives to pick up your corpse."

"I just couldn't believe what I saw." I am on my feet again. Words worm their way out through my lips and cause me pain. I wipe my mouth again, and force myself to stare at the chopped-off head. "I'm ready now, unzipping all five bags." I still do my best to suppress my inner screams. "Two boys, two girls, one I am not sure about, since I can't tell from the head."

"That's fine," the Pillar says. "If we see it's necessary to know its gender, you can check the rest of the body later."

"I only unzipped the bags a few inches to examine the heads," I explain. "The rest of the bodies should be down there if I unzip it totally open."

"No need for that now," the Pillar says. "You came to check the heads. They are the body of the crime, after all. The bodies have been collected from the kids' houses after the discoveries of the heads."

"So the killer chopped off heads in the houses and took the heads with him? That's horrible."

"We're not sure, Alice. He could have chopped the heads and then sent the body back to the house. Anyhow, read the toe tags, please. Let's see if a name clicks."

I read the names, but none of them rings a bell. I read them aloud to the Pillar. They don't mean anything to him either.

"Strange. I thought the names would have a clue. Fifteen minutes." I don't know why he feels he needs to remind me. I'm aware of the scarcity of time. "Try to look for anything the five heads have in common."

"Nothing but the 'Off with their heads' message," I say as I look harder for any details I might have missed.

"That's it?" The Pillar is disappointed. I can tell he has no clue of what's going on.

"No, wait!" I reach for one of the metal instruments on the table and use it to part a corpse's mouth. "There something in boy's mouth," I say. "It's wrapped in a small plastic Ziploc."

"What is it?" I've never heard the Pillar so curious.

"A muffin."

Chapter 14

I bend forward to check the muffin inside the mouth. "How come the police didn't find this?" I ask.

"The police are lazy, logical creatures. They think the world they live in is actually a *sane* one, so they tend to think of all the useless CSI-like evidence of a crime; fingerprints and other silly things," the Pillar says. "My bet is that some officer saw the muffin but didn't see its significance, especially if the boy is fat."

I can't tell if he's fat, as I am only inspecting his head. I don't have the guts to pull the zipper down to inspect the body yet. Who knows what the killer did to it. I might check this a few minutes later, so I don't vomit again.

"Besides, this is the coroner's job. It looks like he hasn't inspected the body yet," the Pillar adds.

"Why delay inspecting the body of the most important crime in Britain right now?" I am angry at the lazy system that postpones the autopsies of five innocent children. A system that postpones the possibility of justice.

"Well, that's a good point," he says. "Maybe the coroner has been told to delay the matter."

"Told by whom?"

"Parliament? There is always someone benefiting from he death of someone else, Alice?" He is hinting at something that I might not be ready for yet. I witnessed the Duchess Margaret Kent's corruption last time. I know I am still naïve to how the world outside operates.

"I can't get it out." I cut off my thoughts, trying to pull the muffin out. "Why Ziploc the muffin?"

"An intact muffin is a useful clue," he explains. "Whatever we're supposed to learn from it would have been lost through the victim's saliva otherwise. The Cheshire is saving the muffin for us."

"Got it." I manage to pull it out. "Should I open it?"

"If only people wouldn't waste time asking questions.

Thirteen minutes."

I open the bag, using the metallic instrument to pull the muffin out. It smells sweet. Very sweet and fresh. My mouth runs for it. Such tempting baking.

"Don't tell me you feel the urge to take a bite." the Pillar guesses.

"Momentarily, I was." I blink, to shake myself awake from the muffin's magic. "How is that possible?"

"How is what possible?"

"How can my mouth run for a muffin in such a horrendous situation? I feel like I'm a bad person." It's true. I feel an uncontrollable urge to eat the muffin. NOW!

"You think you will grow taller if you eat it?" he teases.

"Now, you're silly."

"Shorter?" He munches softly. "Does it say 'eat me'?"

"Stop the nonsense."

"Maybe you need it to get shorter to escape the morgue."

"I don't need to eat it anymore, Pillar. I'm over it," I stress. His comments get on my nerves. "But really, how is that possible? How can a muffin do this to me, even temporarily?"

"That's how the food industry lulls kids — and adults — with their products all the time." He sips some fizzy drink again. Will he ever stop eating today? Where is his hookah? "I'm the best example at the moment. Whatever they put in this food I am gorging, I can't stop eating it. Tell me this food isn't addictive with all its crap, sugar, and saturated fat. Anyways, tell me about the muffin in the boy's mouth. Look closer."

"It's just a muffin."

"There must be something about it. Or the Cheshire wouldn't tuck it in."

I work with the muffin from all angles. A surge of electricity stings my spine. The muffin has the Cheshire's grin drawn on one side.

I tell the Pillar about it. "Is that some narcissistic thing, the Cheshire having his face on the muffin like the Cheshire Cheese before?"

"The Cheshire Cheese has a cat's grin until this day on its package, believe or not. So does the muffin you're holding, by the way."

"You know this brand of muffins?"

"They call it a Meow Muffin. Someone put it on market a week ago, after the Cheshire's killing. You were in the asylum, so you probably didn't know about it."

"Are you serious?"

"Contrary to popular belief, I always am." The Pillar finally puffs his hookah.

"Why would a manufacturer draw a killer's grin on food mostly appreciated by children?"

"To make money. Lots of money."

"Are you saying the Meow Muffin sells?"

"Irresistibly. It's an instant bestseller in Britain. Of course, the Americans are discussing *Americanizing* the product now."

"I can't grasp how you can sell a muffin inspired by a ruthless killer."

"The same way you can almost sell anything with Darth Vader, Michael Myers, and Dracula on it," the Pillar says. "Villains make great business. Kids love it! Bad is the new cool. Parents pay double the price to buy their kids a Meow Muffin these days—four pounds each, and never sold in a pack, by the way—so the kids buzz off and stop annoying them. So tell me, do all the kids have Meow Muffins in their mouths?"

"They do." I wasn't waiting for him to ask. It already crossed my mind, and I checked.

"Hmm..." The Pillar ceases all munching and drinking. "Other than the fact that you only have seven minutes left, I think we have our first real clue. The question is—"

I cut in, thinking aloud: "Why a muffin?"

Chapter 15

Iain West Forensic Suite, an extension to the Westminster Public Mortuary, London. Seven minutes to go...

"So he stuffs Meow Muffins in the children's throats." I am thinking aloud. "What kind of clue is that?"

"Honestly, as much I'm satisfied we found it, I have no clue about the *clue*." The Pillar sounds honest. I think I have spotted a pattern, which I can't explain. It's more of an intuition when he has no idea about what's going on. Particularly when it's about the Cheshire. I wonder how those two dealt with each back in Wonderland.

"So that's it?" I haven't gone through all of this to end up empty-handed.

"I'm afraid so, Alice." The Pillar sighs. "The Cheshire's clue makes no sense. It only points at his involvement in the crimes."

"Think harder, Pillar," I demand. "I'm supposed to do the hard stuff, like entering the morgue as a corpse. You're supposed to have explanations. You're the one with memories of the Cheshire and Wonderland. This muffin has to mean something."

"Did you ever read about muffins in Lewis Carroll's books? I haven't for sure," the Pillar says. "The first killing in the stadium had one purpose only: to attract our attention to the case. Now this muffin should lead somewhere, but it escapes me."

"Then we have to think together."

"Six minutes, Alice," the Pillar warns me. "If I were you, I'd be zip myself back. We could think about it together when you're back."

"I'm not leaving without a lead to catching the Cheshire," I insist. Sometimes, I feel I want to be the Real Alice. Sometimes I don't. This is one of the times that I want to be Alice so badly it scares me. I will bring the Cheshire to justice.

"Then you might never leave this morgue."

"Let's just think again. The Cheshire chops their heads off and then stuffs them in watermelons. Doesn't that ring a bell?"

"Don't be fooled," the Pillar says. "The watermelons mean nothing. It's just a scare factor to imply nonsensical chaos. The British police are supposed to look in the watermelons matter. The muffin is for us. The Cheshire is clever. Five minutes and counting."

"Can't be five minutes yet."

"Okay, I lied." He chews on the words. "Five and a half minutes. I want you out. There is no point of blowing your cover. The world isn't ready to know about the Wonderland Wars or who you are yet. Trust me."

"The Cheshire planted the muffin so we'd get the message." I am surprised I am so adamant about solving this, but I like it. I am surprised by my lack of consideration about what happens to me.

Because you have no life, Alice. I hate the nagging voice in my head. *You're insane, probably a murderer, and no one cares about you, not even your mother and sisters. Why would it matter what happens to you? Convict or mad girl, it's all the same. That's why you're the perfect Alice for this insane job. A lonely Alice.*

But I do have someone I care for, I confess in silence. Remembering him curves a weak smile on my face. It's a smile nonetheless.

"Four minutes," the Pillar counts. "Do you have any suggestions to where you want me to bury you if you die in there?"

"Anywhere but a cat cemetery." I take a few steps back and stare at the five kids. There must be more than a muffin for a clue. "Why those kids in particular?" I ask.

"What do you mean?"

"Last time, the Cheshire chose the girls for specific reasons: they were all descendants of women who had been photographed by Lewis Carroll. Why these kids this time?"

The Pillar is silent. I hope he is thinking it over. "Okay. I will give it until one minute in." He sighs. It's the first time I force him to succumb to my wishes. "Let's see. The names you read on the toe tags do not have anything in common. All we know for sure is the kids' ages, which isn't much of a lead we can follow. Boys and girls, so there is no gender issue here. I checked a few names while you were talking; all kids are either poor or middle class. None are from rich families. But then, most crimes are committed against the poorer people in the world — "

"Could it be the Cheshire didn't stuff the muffins inside?" I interrupt, clicking thumb and middle finger. "Could it be that the kids bought the muffins themselves first?"

"I don't know of kids who like to bite on *Ziplocked* muffins. Doesn't sound so tasty."

"You're not following, Pillar. The Cheshire later *Ziplocked* the muffins they bought." I'm not stating facts; I am thinking out loud. "What I am saying is the kids might have been chosen because they bought a Meow Muffin — or wanted one so badly."

"Could be," the Pillar says. "So?"

I try to figure it out, staring at the kids again. Why would he kill kids who buy these muffins?

"Two minutes."

"Wait!" I raise a numb finger in the air. "Forget about what I just said. I was wrong."

"Admitting failure is a rare virtue."

"But I'm right about something else," I say in a louder voice. "The kids!"

"What about them?"

"They are..." I squint to make sure. Could it be that the clue has been so easy to figure from the beginning? Damn you, Cheshire.

"*What?*"

I hurl toward the death bags and unzip the kids fully

from top to bottom to see their whole bodies. Why was I so scared to look at their bodies before?

"What is it, Alice?" The Pillar is both worried and excited.

"The clue isn't in the heads!" I shriek.

"How so?"

"The same way the watermelons are designed to elude the police so we could find the muffin, the kids' heads are also a misleading trick to elude the police," I explain. "The real clue is in the bodies." All of the disconnected bodies are intact, with not one drop of blood visible. "The bodies are dressed neatly." I tell him what I see. "I don't suppose the kids wore those at the time of the crimes. The kids have been dressed up later. I mean the kids' *bodies* have been dressed up later."

"So, the heads were more of an 'x that marks the spot.' Makes sense, since the police located the bodies in their houses, a few hours after locating the heads." The Pillar is excited. "So what is the clue? Almost one minute, Alice. You better get going."

"The kids' pockets are filled with endless candy, bars, and tarts."

The Pillar is silent.

"Snicker Snackers chocolate bars, Tumtum cans, and Queen of Hearts Tarts," I say, reading the labels. "Are these known snacks sold in Britain now?" I don't remember any of those two years ago, but then again, I don't remember anything two years ago.

"They are. Everything Wonderland is trending in the food industries since the Cheshire's killing last week. Less than one minute, Alice. Hurry. Tell me about the clue."

"At first, I thought the suits were too large for the kids, and then now I find the pockets stuffed with candy."

"How large is too large?"

"Considerably large. XXL, I think," I say. "I mean, a fourteen-year-old boy or girl shouldn't be that—"

"Are the kids overweight, Alice?" the Pillar asks

bluntly.

"Almost as the overweight kids I saw in Richmond Elementary School. What's up with that?"

"Are *all* the deceased kids fat, Alice? Are they all overweight?"

"Yes." I nod. It's unmistakable. It finally becomes evident when I roll all the kids on their backs and see huge *XXLs* marked on the backs. This is definitely the killer's doing. "What kind of crime is this?"

"So, the clue is that all kids the Cheshire kills are fat?" The Pillar seems amused.

"It definitely is."

"Great. Take off your duster and shoes, Alice," the Pillar says. "And jump in the bag. The mortician should arrive—"

The signal fades.

"Pillar," I pant as I take off my shoes and duster and throw them behind a desk. "Can you hear me?" I get into the bag and start zipping myself from inside, which is really complicated, but I manage to zip up to my forehead as I lie on my back.

Inside the bag, I tuck the phone in my pocket and silence it, afraid it will ring while the mortician is present.

I begin breathing as slowly as I can.

Calm down, Alice. In only a few minutes you'll be safe.

I close my eyes as I hear footsteps nearing from the outside. A metallic door opens.

I take a deep breath and try to think of something relaxing so I won't panic. I can only think of one person who makes me feel that way. The one person I think gives meaning to my life, and the one I really care for, even it makes no sense, and even if he is mad enough to call himself Jack Diamonds.

Chapter 16

The footsteps of the mortician are that of a slightly heavy woman. The marble floor squeaks underneath her cheap sport shoes. Or so I believe. It's hard to tell for sure.

Heavy steps. Very slow. Trudging.

I try to slow my breathing, as there isn't enough air inside the bag. This should be over soon. I need her just to roll my table out of the room. She's probably looking for my ID or something to identify my *corpse.*

The mortician stops a few tables away and waits.

Then she walks again. I hear her tap what I assume is a paper chart. Her breathing is heavy, like a shivering gas pipe about to explode.

I try to occupy my mind again with anything that will calm me down. In the beginning it is Jack. *Oh, Jack, with all your absurdness, your silliness, and your cute dimples.* But then Jack's image fades to the sound of music outside my bag.

The mortician woman probably uses an iPod with small speakers. A song I know well: "Don't Fear the Reaper" by Blue Öyster Cult.

Interesting.

This might take some time. I don't think she is in a hurry. All I can do is wait for her to pick me up.

A flick of the mortician's cigarette lighter drags things into an even slower pace. I don't blame her. Time is probably worthless for a woman who spends her days *living* among the dead.

She inhales her cigarette shortly and then exhales, coughing. Smoke seeps through the bag and into my nostrils. I manage not to sneeze. *Dead people usually don't,* I imagine the Pillar saying.

But I know the woman is near.

I hear her pick up the paper chart again, and tread slowly toward me. She starts whistling with the song: *"Don't fear the reaper...la la la la la la."*

I want to wiggle my feet to the rhythm, but I hold back.

I wonder if she listens to the same song each day. While the Pillar's favorite subject is madness, this woman is surrounded by death. Maybe she grew too numb to it. That would explain her easiness and relaxed demeanor. I wouldn't be surprised if she orders pizza. *Two slices, chopped-off heads topping, and some mayonnaise, please. I'll tip generously if you slide me a Meow Muffin from under the table.*

"Alice Wonder," the woman mutters, flipping the chart. "Where art thou?" She taps her heavy feet, and then sucks on the cigarette.

I am imagining her in a white coat, a bit too tight for her size. Big-boned, almost square; red curls of thick hair with a pencil lost inside the bush. Fat cheeks, bubbly and wavy, too.

The waiting is killing me. I am about to zip up and scream at her: *Here I am. Just take me out!*

"So, here you are." She stands real close, reeking of cigarettes, the cheap stuff, and some other smell I can't identify. "Someone made a mistake shoving you here." She kills the boredom by uttering everything she does aloud. I know because I used to do the same in my cell. "Your sorry *arse* belongs somewhere else, young lady."

This blind game isn't fun anymore. I realize I will probably never know how the mortician looks like after she delivers my corpse to the chauffeur's car. Then she stops again and coughs. This time, she coughs really hard, as if puking. I hear the cigarette swoosh into something. What's going on out there?

A heavy thud causes a ripple through my metallic table. The rollers skew sideways. The woman chokes.

The tune of Don't Fear the Reaper continues in the background, but the woman stopped whistling, if not breathing.

"Help!" she barely pronounces, while her fat hand slaps like a heavy fish on the side of my bag.

What am I supposed to do? Help her, right?

And blow my cover?

What is happening to her?

Surprisingly, the woman stops choking.

"Bloody cigarettes," she mumbles. I hear her stand up. Her voice is a bit rustier, the music in the background making the whole incident sound like a joke.

There is a long moment of silence, only interrupted by her heavy breathing. She should also stop smoking. And eating—what's that smell again? Yeah, she somehow reeks of baking.

She decides to change the song on the iPod. Am I ever going to get out of here?

I am not familiar with the new tune. An American sixties song. A merry song, actually. Funny and quirky.

"'I am a Nut' by Leroy Pullins," the mortician documents. Then the lighter flicks again. "I love this song!"

What? She is smoking again?

This time she takes a long drag, as if her near-death experience rewarded her with an additional lung.

She moves toward me again, tapping her paper chart. Her feet aren't as heavy. I wonder how.

She takes another drag and whistles along with the song. The singer is a *nut* himself. All he says is "I'm a nut," a few fast words, then "I'm a nut" again. Then he stops to a stroke of a chord of his guitar and says, "*Beedle-dee-bah, beedle-dee-bah, beedle-dee-ree-pa-dom.*"

I have to check this song out, if I ever get out.

I hear the woman stop and swirl in her place like she's Elvis Presley on mushrooms. I am about to laugh. What happened to this mortician woman? Am I back in the Radcliffe Asylum already?

She approaches my bag and taps a hand on it. "Here you are, Alice Wonder," she says. I picture her with a big smile on her face, pushing against those chubby cheeks. "Time to take you were you belong."

Finally! I sigh. This took forever.

The smell of baking on her breath makes me hungry. I should have had a big meal back in the asylum. What's with all the mentioning of food today?

I don't care. I just want to get out of here.

Instead of being rolled outside, the woman's hand reaches for the bag's zipper. Maybe she wants to check out my face. I wonder if I will look dead enough to her.

Hold that breath, Alice.

The zipper slowly reveals my face to her, and the reeking of baking strengthens in my nostrils. There is a long silence, followed by the end of the nut song. The silence doubles up uncomfortably. I do my best not to open my eyes. But I don't know if I can hold my breath any longer.

"Very paradoxical, I must say," the woman says with a satirical tinge to her voice. "If you hold your breath long enough, you're dead. If you give up and start breathing, you're mad. Isn't that so, Alice from Wonderland?"

My eyes snap open.

I inhale all the air it can. I am in utter shock. A silent shiver pinches through all of my limbs, and madness almost blinds my vision.

What did she just say?

Although the mortician looks exactly like I imagined her, the smell of baking on her mouth says otherwise.

It's the smell of a Meow Muffin.

Chapter 17

I am paralyzed with horror. All my wishes to rid the world of the Cheshire evaporate in his presence. His grin, plastered on the poor mortician's face, is unmistakable. Damned are those who lay eyes upon that grin too many times, for it's unforgettable and will guarantee a lifetime of nightmares.

"What do you want from me?" I scatter the syllables on my tongue. I wish there was a way to camouflage my fear—maybe some hookah smoke like the Pillar's that I'd hide my real fears behind.

There is none.

"Love you, too." The Cheshire flashes a chubby grin and then takes a long drag from his cigarette. His view from down here makes me feel like an ant. His posture is like a towering building of nightmares.

Instinctually, I slide myself out of the bag and jump off the other side of the table.

The Cheshire doesn't move. He watches as I wound my left knee and almost twist my ankle. I run toward the faraway bulb, the one I hadn't come near before. It turns out it leads to a metallic double door leading outside. I limp a few times, fall, and pick myself up again. Part of my escape is me hopping on all fours like a rabbit.

The Cheshire still stands still. I know because of the muffin smell. He is behind me, dragging on the mortician's cigarette, enjoying the show.

I am such a coward, running away like that. I reach for the door's heavy handles. I don't think I am ready for the Cheshire yet.

"If you don't know where you're going, any road'll take you there," the Cheshire mocks behind me.

I stop in my tracks. I don't know why. A flash of a Lewis Carroll in Victorian England flashes before my eyes. It's like an electric shock. Painful but effective. It wakes me up and unwraps me from my spider webs of fear.

I give up on the handle and turn around to face the Cheshire. This is what I should do. I shouldn't run. I am here to catch him, not escape from him.

I don't know what Carroll's dream was about, but I know I don't want to end up regretful like him. I don't want to say, *I couldn't save them,* a week from now.

"Oh." The Cheshire licks his paws. Cat's habits. He stands between two rows of corpses on his sides. It's totally funny, in a very sinister way, to see the mortician gleaming with evil intentions. "So, you might be the Real Alice after all."

I stand with my back to the door, grimace, and shake my head, wondering why he says that.

"A Real Alice wouldn't run away from me," he elaborates. "The door is locked, however. But you didn't know that, did you?" He jingles a keychain in his hands. "Someone could still open it from outside, but no one knows you're here, Alice."

"How do you know that?" Frankly, I am shocked the door is locked. I don't know if he is lying to me. Maybe he is tricking me to see if I'll go back and try to open it. I stand my ground, fists clenched.

"Nobody cares for you, Alice." He grins. "You know that."

I can't argue with that. Only Jack seems to care. Where is he when I need him?

"You've always been like that," he continues. "Even in the books, you were a lonely, possibly mad, girl wandering Wonderland—which was probably all in her head." He laughs and smirks and grins and confuses the hell out of me when he says that. "You never made a real friend in that book, remember?"

"My sister was waiting for me when I woke up," I mumble, my head slightly lowered. The Cheshire hit a sensitive tumor in my soul. I am not only mad. I am lonely. I get it. *It's time to get over it!*

"Your sisters hate you, Alice. They hate you so much none of them bothered telling you the details of how you killed your friends. And your mother is too weak to protect you." He is enjoying this. "And your friends?" He kills the cigarette under his heavy foot and rubs his chin. "Oh, you killed them."

"You're lonely too!" I take a step forward. It actually unsettles him. He didn't expect that. "You've always been lonely, Cheshire. Humans killed your parents. You swore revenge on the world. Such a lonely lunatic who has no one to love him." The mortician woman's face knots. I press harder: "Even in Wonderland, no one cared for you. You and your silly grin, neglected in the Duchess' kitchen, then hiding on trees in the forest, appearing and disappearing, and commenting on the world only to take away attention from your miserable existence."

"Interesting." He steps forward, squinting at my face. "Tell me more. Is that really you, Alice?"

I shrug then lift my head up. "Why is it so important if I am the Real Alice?"

"Oh, it's important. You have no idea." He still glares, taking another careful step forward. "What puzzles me is that you don't remember any of it. I wonder why. What is it that the Pillar knows about you that I don't? Who are you, Alice?"

The Cheshire steps forward, the collective sum of the hate in the world glimmering in her eyes.

Chapter 18

"I don't care about either of you." I take another step forward, not knowing how this will end. Will I fist-fight a cat eventually?

"What do you care about, then?" His tone is investigative.

"To stop you from killing children and stuffing their heads in watermelons all over Britain."

He laughs. "Neatly executed crime; very artistic, you must admit."

I feel disgusted. I don't know how I look when disgusted but my face is in pain.

"Do you know how hard it is to stuff a head in a watermelon?" He is creepily sincere. Human lives don't mean anything to him. "No one appreciates art anymore." He rolls his eyes. "Is it because I am a cat?" The mortician's fingers turn into hairy claws, like Wolverine. "Do I have to change my name to Da Vinci or Picasso for you to appreciate my work?"

"You don't want anyone to appreciate you. The more you're hated, the more you love it," I say. "But since you asked, how about you just die? The world loves dead artists."

"Then I shall never be loved." The mortician slightly raises her meaty arm and waves her hands sideways. "Because I can't die." He smiles thinly at my attempt to humiliate him. "And the killing of fat kids won't stop. The *real* killings didn't even begin yet." She points at the dead corpses. "Humans are nothing but pawns in this Wonderland War."

"Why kill kids who are overweight?"

"Are you afraid to say 'fat' kids?" She smirks. "Is that politically incorrect? Is the blunt truth always politically incorrect?"

"Wow. You do have a grudge against 'fat' kids." I don't

like the sound of it on my tongue, but I need to speak his insane language so I can read between the lines.

"You will understand what I mean if you figure it out, Nancy Drew." She breathes into her paws. "You and your hookah-smoking Inspector Gadget." This seems to amuse him to death.

"If this is an old grudge between you and the Pillar—"

"It's not that," she cuts in.

"If it's about the grudge you hold against humanity, please remember that this happened so long ago." I don't even know what I am doing, conversing with the enemy.

"Nothing is long ago." She still scans my face, as if she wants to spot evidence of me being the Real Alice. I catch her/him staring at my neck as well. "Don't you watch the news? Humans are walky-talky apes, still stained with barbaric behaviors after so many centuries of evolution. They might dress better, talk mellower, and invent cool gadgets. They will say that they prefer love over war, but it's all nonsense. Humans are still monsters. Always will be." He stops and takes a breath, not finding what he was looking for in me. "But then, all my grudges aren't what the Wonderland War is about."

"What is it about, then?" If the Pillar refuses to tell, do I expect the Cheshire to?

"If you were *the* Alice, you would've known," he says. "Right now, I need to put you to continued tests, until you prove you're her."

"By killing children?" I can't digest his logic.

"Whatever it takes," he says. "Besides, you can still minimize the killings by solving the riddles." He cocks his head with another grin. "Think of it as a Catch-22. Either you don't solve the riddles and I keep allowing the murders, or you solve the riddle, I know you're the Alice, and we start the Wonderland Wars." He rubs his claws together.

"What kind of sick lunatic are you?"

"The *unkind* type," the mortician sneers. "Let's not

waste time, Alice." She starts smoothening her fingernails with one of the metallic instruments on the tables. "You were smart enough to get the muffin message, and smarter to realize all the victims are fat kids." He cocks his head at me as I glimpse a mallet resting against the wall behind the tables. Why is there a mallet in a morgue? "I see that you and your Pillar haven't benefited wisely from the clues I left you." Although spoken in a woman's voice, it has this sinister undertone to it. Something I can't explain. Something only nightmares can produce. "So here is my final clue." He raises a hand in the air, his thumb and middle finger close enough it looks like he is about to snap them. "Are you ready for my major clue, Alice?"

"I am." I'd say yes to anything until I get close to that mallet. I need to have some weapon prepared.

The Cheshire snaps his fingers, and a few corpses on his left and right come to life. They abruptly sit straight up and grin at me. Four on his left. Four on his right.

I freeze in place.

I barely learned how to deal with lunatics — other than myself, some might argue. But I am not prepared to deal with the living dead. This is beyond absurd. Why are there eight corpses coming to life?

"You didn't know I can possess nine lives at the same time?" She laughs, picking up two fork-like instruments from the table. What is she going to do, cut them open? "I can even possess them when they are dead. How *kewl* is that?" The Cheshire seems to be catching up on the lingo. "Let's dance, Alice. Let's dance."

I really wish I was mad now. This can't be happening.

Chapter 19

The two instruments in the Cheshire's hands are used in the most unusual way. I never expected it.

He waves them at the corpses, like a conductor guiding his musicians in an orchestra. On cue, the eight living-dead corpses on the table prepare to chant a melody of sorts.

I grimace, confused, perplexed, and overwhelmed as I watch the first headless corpse pick up its head. It adjusts it slightly off above the neck, and begins singing:

"Do you know the Muffin Man?"

It says it as if it's an obedient girl in school—she is actually one of the five kids. Then she tilts her loose head toward her friend on the table next to her. The other corpse fiddles with his chopped-off head, unable to place it correctly. So he decides to hold it out in both hands, and let it do the singing:

"The Muffin Man, the Muffin Man?"

The corpse shakes its own head to the left and right when it says "Muffin Man," like a happy kid in a school choir. The head in the hand swivels toward the next corpse, indicating its turn. The third corpse has its head placed upside down on its neck, still good enough for singing with upside-down lips:

"Do you know the Muffin Man?'

It repeats the phrase, arching an eyebrow at the fourth corpse—downward, of course. The fourth corpse doesn't belong to the Watermelon crimes. Some old lady with an intact head, almost seventy, dressed as a cook with big a white hat. Her face is burned—she must have died in an oven, my guess. The lady finishes the rhymes with a raspy but faint voice.

"Who lives on Drury Lane?"

This time the old lady looks at me with no teeth.

I am not going to remove my head and sing a song!

The Cheshire gazes at me. So do the other four corpses on his right. "One more time." The Cheshire waves his forks. "With feeling!"

In unison they sing it all once more:
"Do you know the Muffin Man?
The Muffin Man, the Muffin Man?
Do you know the Muffin Man?
Who lives on Drury Lane?"

Following the Cheshire's conducting, they end the verse with a double clap from their dead, blood-stricken hands.

And then they repeat it. Louder.

I hold my head with both hands and consider screaming. Rarely does screaming solve any problems, I know.

If there is a clue, again, I don't get it. If the Cheshire's intention is to drive me insane, he has done an exceptional job. If none of this is really happening and I am just imagining it, I'd prefer shock therapy in the Mush Room over singing corpses in a morgue. I feel like Alice in the book, falling down an endless rabbit hole where the falling will never stop.

As they keep singing, the desire to hit the Cheshire grows inside me. I step forward and pick up the mallet, my hands trembling. I want to hit the Cheshire so the madness stops. It's not like me, but I've lost it. The pressure is too much. And their voices too noisy. It's all become too much.

I raise the mallet in the air and plod closer to him. He doesn't move. His grin widens.

"Are you going to hit a fat, poor mortician woman, Alice?" he asks calmly, backed up with the maddening rhyme. "You don't know if she has children, takes care of a mother or a husband, Alice. You can't do that to her."

"I can!" I flip the mallet back to gain momentum. "The madness has to stop!"

I wave hard and then...

And then...

I stop, midair.

How am I supposed to hurt an innocent woman working in a morgue? She is annoying, smokes too much, and doesn't take care of her health, I know. But I can't kill her. She hasn't done anything bad to anyone. And I am no killer.

Even though I killed my friends on the bus.

Still, I am not a killer. This isn't how I see myself. If I hit this woman, the Cheshire will probably beat me and possess one of the many dead people in here. Not that I know how he does it, but I can't do it. He has me cornered in a way I can't react to properly.

"That's why you aren't *the* Alice." His eyes scan me thoroughly. "The Real Alice would hit and never blink. Because she knows that evil has to be chopped off by the roots and burned so it never grows again. That was the whole point of Alice's madness. She was strong. Powerful. Never afraid." He says the words with much admiration as resentment. "She was M-A-D. That was her trick. But you're not her." His voice saddens. He wants me to be her. God only knows why he needs her that much. Tears begin trickling down my cheeks. I don't know why. Am disappointed I am not her? Am I disappointed I can't kill him and save the world? I just don't know.

"The Pillar will tell you it doesn't matter who you are," he elaborates. "That it doesn't matter if you're mad or not. I'd say it matters a lot. How can you take sides when you don't know who you are? You know what the world's most common sin is, Alice?" He reaches for the mallet to snatch it from me. "It's indifference. Indecisiveness. Hesitation when it's time for swift justice."

He is about to pull the mallet away from my trembling hands when something inside me surfaces. Something I haven't met or thought of before. A strong urge to correct things, to stand for something, and to help as many people as I can. A strong urge to see behind the Cheshire's mask.

I can pretend it's not me as I bring down the mallet on

the mortician's woman's legs, enough to hurt her but not kill her. I can pretend I am not that kind of girl.

But it's me. Truly me. Maybe not the Alice the Cheshire is looking for. But the Alice I want to be from now on.

Chapter 20

A tear trickles down my cheek as the mortician woman falls to her knees. I do the unimaginable and catch my tear in the palm of my hand before it hits the ground again. If I want to win this, I can't cry. If I could squeeze that tear back in, I would. This tear is me balancing the insanity I am thrown into.

I help the woman in her fall so she doesn't hit her head against something. She stares at me with a horrified expression, unaware of what happened to her. The absence of a grin on her face tells me the Cheshire left her body.

Why not? He wants me to suffer the guilt of hitting an innocent woman.

The mortician keeps sobbing uncontrollably, more in need of an explanation than to mend her wounds.

The corpses have stopped singing and zipped themselves back into their death bags. I can't see the Cheshire anywhere.

"Who are you?" The woman starts to shake me hysterically. Her leg is swollen and bleeding.

"Please calm down," I tell her. "I need you to trust me. There is an evil presence in here."

The woman's eyes are wide open. She scans me from head to toe and then stops at the string wrapped around my toe. Slowly, she raises a reluctant finger, pointing at the empty death bag. "You're dead..." she stutters.

Before I can explain further, she faints.

I help her to the floor and pat her. I can't complain. She did me a huge favor and saved me a lot of time.

Turning around with the mallet in my hands, I look for the Cheshire. I don't know how his soul-possessing works, but he must be in the room because the door is still shut.

What kind of game is he playing with me now?

I walk slowly toward the door, the corpses supposedly resting in peace at my sides. Holding the mallet as if it's a sword does give me confidence somehow. It's amazing what fear does to you when you decide to finally face it. My bare feet, and my body, are still exposed to the chilling cold of the morgue.

Closer to the door, I hear my footsteps echoing. It's unexplainable, but I keep walking.

If the Cheshire has the ability to be invisible, then I really don't have a way to fight back.

Why am I hearing echoes of my footsteps?

I keep limping to the door with a mallet in my hand. Horror movies aren't even close to the condition I am in.

Closer to the door, I realize that what I am hearing aren't the echoes of my footsteps. They are someone else's. And they are approaching from the other side of the door.

How did the Cheshire leave the room without opening the door? And why is he mirroring my footsteps? He must be trying to scare me, that's all.

I grip the door handle, my mallet ready in my other hand. A deep breath helps me to lower my blood pressure, just enough to think straight. All I have to do is pull the door open and then hit hard. That's it. I hope I am really thinking straight. I have no combat training, after all—or if I did, I don't remember it.

I grip the door tighter, and then pull.

I didn't expect that. But like the Cheshire said, the door is locked.

The keychain in the mortician's hand!

I turn around to go fetch the keys from the woman's hands, only to see her standing on her feet again. There is a slight problem with her posture now. She has her head chopped off and holds it in one hand. The other hand holding the keys.

"Looking for these?" She grins.

The Cheshire is back. Who was approaching the door from the other side?

The horrible scene chains me for a moment. But I am about to run full throttle against the Cheshire and hit him.

Let's get done with this.

The door behind me suddenly flings open.

I close my eyes, as I suppose another Cheshire-possessed human is behind me. How am I supposed to kill him? Am I supposed to kill the nine of them?

"Alice!" a voice calls from behind me. "Here you are!"

A hefty smile forms on my face. The voice behind the smile is so dear to me. It's Jack Diamonds.

Chapter 21

The mortician's face knots in anger when she hears Jack Diamonds' voice. Jack prefers not to enter the room. It's hard to understand why. He just opened the door from the other side. The Cheshire can't actually see Jack from this angle. I haven't seen Jack yet either; I've only heard his voice.

Please God, don't make it just a voice in my head. But come on, the door is open. It can't be a voice in my head.

It drives the woman mad that someone is saving me.

"Come on, Alice," Jack urges me. I can only see his hand, reaching out from behind the door. "It's so cold where you are. I don't think I can get in."

"But I have to kill him first, Jack," I say.

"Kill who? Is there is someone with you in the room?" He wiggles his hand. "They are all dead."

"Who are you talking to, Alice?" the Cheshire blurts in anger. "There is no one there behind the door."

"Don't play games with me, Cheshire." I raise my mallet, ready to strike, as he is approaching again. "Who else do you think opened the door from outside?"

"I don't know." He shakes his shoulders and puts his head on. Sometimes, I really don't understand his intentions. Is he trying to give me a message so I continue my investigation, or is he trying to hurt me? The more time I spend with him, the more nothing makes sense. "But I know there is no one out there." Now he grins again. "And I know you can't kill me. You might have wounded and injured a poor woman, but you can't kill me."

"Alice!" Jack finally pulls me outside. He does it fast and with a bang. Never have I thought he was that strong. He pulls the door behind me and locks it with a digital code on a pad next to the wall. The code is 1862. The date in my vision when I met Lewis was 1862. What are all these puzzles, and what are they supposed to mean?

"Are you okay?" His hands search my face, looking for a bruise. He makes sure I am all right. Never have I seen someone so concerned about me. "Thank God you're okay, Alice. I was so worried." His cuteness doesn't match his seriousness, but it's understandable. When I lay my eyes on Jack, all I think about is fun.

"I am so glad to see you, Jack." I wrap my hands around him as he touches my face with his gentle hands. His touch is warm. I need it, even inside a morgue. *Who the hell are you, Jack? Why do you always come to save me?*

With my emotions flaring, I hug him tightly. I embrace his body and feel I'd like to hide inside it. Maybe he could shelter me from the mad world; maybe he could shelter me from my mind.

"Wow," he jokes as he pats me on the back. "It's too soon for that. I like a girl to take it slow, who takes me out for dinner first and tells me funny stories."

I hit him lightly on the chest while I am in his arms. His silly jokes make me think this world isn't worth any anger. I wish I could be like him.

"I was thinking about you, Jack." I stare at the closed door, waiting for the Cheshire to open it from inside at any moment. "You make me feel..."

"Funny?" His hands run through my hair. I can feel his breath on my ears.

I nod.

"You're a funny girl, too," he says. "You just have bad taste in clothes. Always stained with blood."

"Come on, you confessed you liked me in the Vatican. I heard you in the booth," I tease.

"Guilty as charged." He raises a hand to his chest.

"We have to go, Jack." I stare at the door. "He has a key."

"Who has a key?"

"The Cheshire."

"Who?"

"You remember the nasty old woman chasing me in Belgium?"

"Wow. She must hate you so much." He rolls his eyes, not even questioning what is happening.

I nod, not having the strength to explain.

Suddenly, sirens blare outside the asylum as we speak. I gaze at Jack for an explanation.

"It's the police," he says. "We need to get you out of here."

Chapter 22

"I guess someone reported suspicious activity in the morgue," Jack says. "We need to hide from the police. They will not understand."

"What will they not understand, exactly? I have no idea what's really happening."

"Nor do I, Alice," he says. "But it doesn't matter. What matters is we're together. Come on." He pulls my hand and walks me to a side door leading to another doctor's room. I look behind me one last time, wondering why the Cheshire didn't come out. Maybe it's the code Jack entered. Does it prevent the door from getting opened manually with a key?

"Jack, where did you get that code you just entered for the door?" I turn to him.

"There is senior nurse who I saw use it on all other doors, so I gave it a try," he replies. "Let's rid you of this thing in your hand." He tries to pull the mallet away as he closes the door behind us. It's a doctor's private room. "You look like a maniac."

It shocks me that my grip is still tight on the mallet. I can't give it away. My hands are stiffened with fear.

"It's all right, Alice." He gazes straight into my eyes. "It's me, Jack. I won't hurt you." He loosens my hand, finger by finger.

The sirens are getting closer outside.

"Wear this." He hands me a nurse's uniform from the wardrobe. A pair of nerdy glasses and shoes he'd brought from a storage room nearby complete the ensemble. "You will pretend you're the nurse, and I will hide in one of these." He points at one of the death bags on the tables. There are three of them. "You play the nurse and I play dead." He smiles. "Don't forget the nametag." He hands it over. "All you have to do is pull me out and tell the police there were intruders in the morgue. It's common. Thieves love to steal corpses and sell them."

"You think it will work?"

"It's the only chance we have," he says. "Neither of us know what to tell the police when they arrive. Now I have to turn around, so you dress up."

We both turn to opposite sides as the sound of police cars surrounds the morgue. I peek over my shoulder and see if he is checking me out while I am getting dressed.

He is.

But he turns around and clears his throat once I see him. I blush and turn back, facing the wall. I feel awkward being the weak one with Jack, now that my heart is unconditionally open to him. I wonder how intimate we were when he was Adam, my boyfriend. I know we were in love because my heart tells me so, but how intimate?

"Jack," I say, unbuttoning.

"Yes?"

I am contemplating asking him if he knows anything about our past lives, but don't want to turn him away if he thinks I am crazy. "How do you always find me?" I ask instead.

"I don't know, really," he says. "It's strange. I'll be sitting somewhere, and then feel this need to see you. This intuition that you are in danger. And suddenly I find myself near you."

I don't know what to think of that. I pull on the nurse's dress and glasses.

"And you?" he asks. His voice is muffled now, having zipped himself inside the bag.

"Excuse me?" I put on the glasses.

"Aren't you going to tell me where you live so I can pick you up for our postponed date?"

I turn around and smile at his persistence. My face changes when I realize I can't tell him I live in an asylum. He might be a weird guy. But I am nutcase. At least my life fits a nutcase. The song "I am a Nut" replays in my head.

"If we survive this, I might tell you," I say as I roll the

bed out to the entrance.

Outside, the main doors spring open, and an endless horde of men with guns enter. I am surprised when they greet me with concern. They ask me if I am all right.

I play shocked for a while and recite the story Jack told me. I point at the Cheshire's room. Funny how they buy it. There aren't any signs of breaking in. But they believe me. They are good to me. Maybe it's my looks, wearing a nurse's outfit.

Is that what the world asks of me? To blend in? A nurse's outfit or a doctor's would do the job? Is that mandatory to fit into any society, to become a recognizable stereotype?

I feel like I've had too much Pillar in my head lately.

Still rolling the bed toward the main door, I am expecting to meet the Pillar's chauffeur on the way.

"Wait!" Someone summons me right before I leave through the main door.

I turn around, and it's another nurse. A buff policeman stands proudly next to her. I hope my cover isn't blown.

"Yes?" I adjust my glasses and wiggle my nose.

"Who's that you are taking out?" the nurse asks.

"A patient who'd been wrongly admitted about an hour ago." I twist the truth. "An ambulance is waiting for him outside to transfer him to another morgue."

"Him?" Her face knots as she reads the charts.

"Oh, silly me." I play nerd of all nerds. "I mean her. It's a deceased girl."

"What's her name again?"

I shrug. "Wonder," I say. "Alice Wonder."

"Hmm..." She nods as the curious officer peeks into her charts.

"She died in a bus accident."

"Oh. That's right." The nurse points at the name on the chart. "Poor girl. She killed her friends, driving a bus herself."

"Really?" I try not to grimace.

"Aren't you from around here?" The police officer chuckles, hands proudly tucked in his belt. "The incident was all over the news a few months ago," Mr. Know-it-all says.

"Ah, I've only worked here for a month." I smile like a weird girl. What am I doing about the fact that it's impossible the corpse is still unharmed when it's a few months old? Why would I be moving it at this point? "I am from a small town near Oxford."

"That's why," the nurse says. "Haven't seen you here before. You're good to go." She waves a hand without looking at me.

"Thank you," I say. "But wasn't this girl admitted to an asylum?"

"Nonsense." The policeman laughs with the nurse. "It's such a rumor. She is dead like the rest. How could she survive the accident when the rest died?"

"Then how did you know she killed them?"

"A note, honey," the nurse says. "She left a note with her sisters before she did it. You talk too much. Now get going. They say we have an injured mortician inside."

I nod and roll Jack outside.

A few strides into the red-and-blue-glaring street, the chauffeur, dressed as a medical driver, approaches me. It takes him a moment to realize I am the one rolling the bed, not the one inside it.

"I believe things didn't go as planned," he says in his mousy voice. Seriously, he has to shave the whiskers off. I shake my head as he ushers me toward the ambulance.

"We thought so when it took you too long to leave the morgue." He opens the back doors for me. "The toe tag prank was the Cheshire's, by the way," he says, and stops me from rolling the bed inside. "Don't ask me how he knew you'd be at the morgue. I guess he expected it."

"A friend is hiding inside," I whisper.

"A friend?" The chauffeur's mousy ears pop out like two pointed parachutes. "Who?"

"His name is Jack."

Suspiciously, the chauffeur zips the bag open, and then stares with confusion at me.

I don't understand the conflict at first. But then I look into the bag. There is no Jack inside. Just the corpse of some guy I don't know.

Chapter 23

The Pillar's ambulance, driving through London

The Pillar is sitting on the opposite side in the back of the ambulance, curiously inspecting the corpse I mistook for Jack earlier—however that happened, I don't know. I can't even think about it. I just thought I had a grip on the thin line between what's real and what's not. I was wrong again.

The nameless corpse is stretched on the ledge between us. The cold metal of the ambulance is set against my back. The chauffeur is driving us to the outskirts of London, so we take the Pillar's limousine back to Oxford and then to the asylum. He is struggling with activating the ambulance's siren, slowing us down. Foolishly, he sticks his head out of the window and yells, "Wee-woo. Wee-woo!" at the dense traffic so they will make way. "Wee-woo. Wee-woo," he repeats. "Ambulance! Dead man in here. Make way!"

I pretend I never saw this happen, and gaze at the Pillar, who is genuinely amused by the corpse in the middle.

The Pillar cocks his head, sucking on a mini hookah with a sticker saying, *I know why a raven is like a writing desk.* He reaches for the corpse and inspects the deceased's head. It's also chopped off—probably a fresh dead kid sent to the morgue.

How in Charles Lutwidge Dodgson's name did that happen?

The Pillar is interested in the corpse's mouth, touching it and inspecting it. He hands me his hookah for a moment and uses both hands, trying to make the dead man smile.

"It's a shame you can't smile when on your way to meet your maker," he says to the dead. "You don't want to leave a bad impression when meeting Him. It will be the most important interview in your afterlife." He winks at me and pulls his hookah back.

"Hey," he calls his Chauffeur. "If I told you that this miserable corpse"—he stops and points at the deceased—"is too tired to fly up there and meet his maker, what solution would you suggest?"

The chauffeur takes off his hat while driving, scratches his three *hairies* on his bald, egg-shaped head, and then answers, "Help him with a drag from your hookah?" His eyes widen. "So he could get *high enough.*" He laughs and points upward and then sticks out his head out, blaring another "wee-woo" at the passing cars.

The idea of throwing myself out of the ambulance occurs to me. If this is how they talk in Wonderland, I might not want to be part of it. I am also dazed and confused with Jack's disappearance, but I know the Pillar doesn't like Jack, so talking to him about it will be of no help. I am afraid that my increasing attachment to Jack will only complicate things. Everything that happened to me tonight only worsens the way I feel about myself and the world.

"So, it was the Cheshire who pulled the toe tag prank on you?" The Pillar drags from his hookah, eyes sparkling.

"It's not funny." I scowl. "I feel like I am really going mad, having left the asylum again."

"You feel like you want to give up?" he asks. "You used to be so *much* more, Alice." He drags from his hookah again as if to distract me from what he is going to say. "Much more *muchier* in Wonderland. Have you lost your *muchness*?" He smirks.

I nod, although ashamed. But in all honesty, the incident with Jack wore me down a little. "Every time I feel I can do this business of saving others from Wonderland Monsters, I end up weakened, wishing I just stayed in my cell."

"Congratulations, then." The Pillar's face dims. "You just turned into what the Cheshire wants you to become."

"What is that supposed to mean?" I ask. "You have no

idea what I have been through tonight. You have no idea!"

"The Cheshire wants you to succumb to madness under his pressure," he says, dismissing my whining.

"Succumb to madness?" I blink in confusion. "I thought he wanted to see if I'm the Real Alice."

"Exactly," the Pillar says. "Do you think the Real Alice will 'succumb to his madness'?"

"You mean, other than giving me clues, he tries to see how much unbearable insanity I can handle?"

"Touché. You just described the human condition of everyday life." He seems pleased. "Can't you see that this is what's going on? People falter and succumb under the pressure of madness every day of their lives. Be it work stress, spouse and family, self-actualization, boredom, teen issues, old-age issues, you name it. Madness is all around us. It needs to feed on us." He spreads his hands wide. "But only..." He leans a bit forward and points a finger in the air.

"...Wonderlanders can stand it," I finish.

A generous, curvy smile adorns his face. It's one of the very few smiles I like on him. It's like seeing through a devil hiding in the dark, glimpsing a faint possibility of goodness in him. "You don't realize what kind of *madfest* Wonderland was, do you? It was beautiful."

I wonder what your real story is, Pillar? Who are you, and why are you helping me?

"Why is it so important the Cheshire makes sure I'm the Real Alice?" If giving in to madness will prove I am not Alice, I wish to know why it is so important he finds her.

"It's the only way to ensure he wins the Wonderland Wars, which I am—"

"You're not going to tell me what it is now. I get it. Just tell me why he can't win without me."

The Pillar hesitates. He looks down to his shoes and purses his lips. "You have something he wants. I don't know what it is. I might know what it *does*, but I'm not in the mood to tell you."

Although I have no idea what I have that the Cheshire wants, I nod. It makes sense. The Cheshire needs to make sure I am the Real Alice so he can get that mysterious thing he wants from me—whatever that is. It occurs to me that maybe that is what the Pillar is after, too. He is only helping me to get that *thing*.

"You see, this is why he will go to hell and back with you to make sure you are *her*," the Pillar elaborates. "There is no one else he thinks is the Real Alice at the moment, so there is no competition. He actually wants you to be her, so he will push you into the pits of madness like no one has ever experienced before."

"I don't mind." I take deep breath. "I need his madness."

"And why would that be?" A mix of admiration and worry flashes in his eyes, almost the same I saw on the Cheshire's.

"Because I need to know if *I* am the Real Alice."

"Understandable." He nods.

"I assume I don't know what it is he wants from me because I don't remember it, right?"

"I have no idea why you don't know, Alice," he says. "My intuition from the very first day is that it's you. Now, shall we not waste more time, as you have become a whining-fest yourself lately?" His tone peaks with enthusiasm. "We have a clue. A string of clues, actually. The Cheshire kills fat kids, chops off their heads, and stuffs them with Meow Muffins, then stuffs the head in a watermelon or a football. I really don't know how someone can stuff a head in watermelon, but it's a piece of art."

"These were exactly his words." I look straight at him.

"To know one's enemy is to read their mind."

"I agree. So what was the Muffin Man song all about?" I say. "He said it was a blatant clue, since we couldn't read any of the others."

"The Muffin Man rhyme definitely has to do something with Meow Muffins." The Pillar rubs his chin.

"I'd presume the Muffin Man manufactures the Meow Muffins or something. But I'm not sure."

"Isn't that a well-known nursery rhyme?"

"The rhyme was first recorded in an old British manuscript," he explains. "Presumably around 1820. Some say 1862, but it's all assumptions."

"Isn't that Victorian times?" I remember the vision I had of Lewis again. It happened 1962. I can't tell the Pillar about it. Lewis told me not to tell anyone.

"It is. I know it's tempting to link the rhyme with Lewis," he says. "Sadly, I never came across the 'Muffin Man' phrase in any of Carroll's works."

"Neither have I ever heard about a Muffin Man in Wonderland," I agree.

"Let's get back to the asylum," he says. "I always have a clearer head among the Mushroomers. We need to get going before half of the country wakes up with the heads of their kids stuffed in watermelons. We have a lot of work to do."

"One last thing." I raise a finger at him.

"We don't have time, Alice." He peeks at his pocket watch.

"This is important," I insist. "I won't have anything to do with this case if you don't listen to me."

"I get it." He shakes his head. "Jack."

"How do you know?"

"He's the only one who makes your eyes go so sparkly." He rolls his eyes, not fond of the idea of love. "What about him?"

"Who is he?" I demand. "I need an answer."

The Pillar purses his lips as if he is afraid the truth could spurt out against his will.

"Look. I met him inside—"

"Inside the morgue?" The Pillar squints. "Again?"

"Yes. And like always, he saved me."

"I am not surprised."

"I tucked him in a death bag to fool the nurse and the

officer so we'd leave the morgue," I say. "Outside, I discovered he wasn't there in the bag anymore."

"Don't tell me it's this miserable fellow you found." He points at the corpse, and I nod. "And I thought you began to pick up on Wonderland's nonsensical humor and brought me a sample."

"Do you know how this is possible?" I pray he has an answer. This is so important to me.

"I do." He closes his eyes for a second. What is it he knows about Jack?

"But you're not going to tell me?"

The Pillar says nothing. He glances briefly at the chauffeur then breathes back into his hookah.

"Look at me," I demand. "Is Jack a fig—"

"I will tell you who Jack is exactly when you finish this mission." He is strict, although not looking at me. I want to believe him.

"Deal." I stretch a hand across the corpse. Somehow, delaying the knowledge of Jack's identity is a relief to me, because I am so afraid there is no Jack in the first place. I wave my stretched hand again, but the Pillar isn't shaking it back.

"I prefer we don't shake hands." He looks irritated. "Germs and bacteria, Alice." He points at his gloves. "You just came out of a morgue, for Edgar Allan Poe's sake."

The rude son of a...

I take my hand back. I don't care. I need to solve the Muffin Man puzzle, stop the crimes, and maybe know if I am the Real Alice, and then my reward will be knowing who Jack is. *Please, God, give me a reasonable explanation to his existence.*

"You know it's not 'wee-woo,' don't you?" the Pillar says to his chauffeur with a tinge of disgust in his voice.

"Then what is it, Professor Pillar? Please help me," the chauffeur says. People driving by swear at him. Other London drivers fire back at him, saying things like "You're a nut!" and "Get your sorry ass back inside!"

"It's 'woo-wee,' not 'wee-woo,' you mousy fool!" The Pillar takes a drag and smiles at me. "Everybody knows that."

I try not to laugh and lean back, thinking of the Muffin Man puzzle. It occurred to me how crazy the journey has been. I mean, last week I met so many humans who turned out to be Wonderlanders. Who'd believe me if I told them? The thought opens a question in my mind. "Tell me, Pillar," I say in the same investigative tone he practices on me. "If Margaret Kent is the Duchess, Fabiola is the White Queen, you are the Caterpillar, and of course the Cheshire is the Cheshire, then I have to wonder how many other Wonderlanders live among us here."

"Oh, Alice," the Pillar says. "They are many, not mentioning those the Cheshire hadn't set free yet."

"I mean, Margaret Kent is a Parliament woman. Fabiola is the Vatican's most beloved nun. Does it get crazier than this?"

The Pillar leans back and smiles with beady eyes. "You have no idea."

Chapter 24

Queen's Chamber, Buckingham Palace, London

The Queen of England—yes, that Queen, whatever her name is in this mad book—awoke in the middle of night, furious and maddened, and slightly scared. She suspected an intruder had been into her chamber in the Buckingham Palace.

Of course, the Queen's chambers were immaculately secure, particularly after a thirty-one-year-old psychiatric patient had scaled a drainpipe and sauntered into her chambers a few years ago.

Tonight, laced in her expensive nightgown, she regretted sleeping alone without guards in her chamber. A few guards would have caught the intruder right away.

The Queen had previously caught her guards and footmen stealing from her at her son's wedding. And what in Britain's name did they steal?

The guard dared to steal the Queen's exotic nuts, exclusively imported from Brazil. She ordered all her precious nuts removed to her private chambers and prevented any of the guards inside.

The Queen's nuts drove everyone nuts.

The Queen was known to love two things dearly: Her five o'clock tea parties, which had been once exclusively hosted by the one and only Mad Hatter—but that was a long story she didn't want to remember now. And, of course, her nuts and munchies.

Right now, the Queen tiptoed as cunningly and slowly as a cat, her back slightly hunched, and proceeded to the corridor outside her enchanting bed—her bed was too high; she needed a small stepladder to embark it. Sometimes, she secretly jumped right off it when no one was around. Being a queen, with all of this etiquette she had to fake, certainly bored her sometimes.

The Queen tiptoed on her way to check her endless bowls of exotic nuts in the corridor. She had them set at five-meter intervals, adjacent to the corridor's wall. They were set on waist-high tables so she could reach them effortlessly. She considered it ridiculous walking back a few meters when the appetite for a nut hit her. A five-meter span between each bowl of nuts was just convenient. Also, laziness sounded like a brilliant hobby.

If queens didn't indulge in laziness, who would? she'd always asked herself.

She stopped in front of a bowl of nuts and dipped a hand inside. Even with her eyes closed, she could almost tell if a few nuts were missing from each bowl.

The Queen gasped. This bowl seemed to miss a few.

Who's been nibbling on my nuts?

The Queen's face tightened, and her cheeks began to redden.

"All right," she hissed. "I have to make sure before I punish anyone."

She continued walking ahead, targeting a few other bowls at the end of the corridor.

As she walked, one of her dogs came padding and panting toward her. It was a Welsh corgi. She had five of them. Meals were served for each dog in their own bowl, with Britain's flag drawn on the outer shell. The meals were usually readied here in the corridor, with a few precious nuts on the side. The dogs' diet had been meticulously approved by veterinary experts from all over the world. It cost twice the income of a middle-class citizen who had two children to feed on average. But those weren't just any dogs. They were the Queen's dogs—and, in many ways, Wonderland Dogs.

Sure, the dogs never attended the meetings at Parliament, nor did they have word in the country's economy. But they were important by law. Again, being the Queen's dogs was no joke.

However, nuts weren't allowed in the dog's diet. But

the Queen, being the *Queen*, broke the law and allowed them a few nuts as a gesture of love and pampering. Anything to make the Queen's corgis happy.

If the Queen didn't break rules and get away with it, who would? she had reminded herself.

"Sweet doggie." The Queen knelt against the pain in her knees to play with the dog. This one she called Bulldog—he looked weirdly like a bulldog and was excitedly funny. Her favorite dog, Maddog, wasn't here. Probably still recovering from constant constipation, which had been the reason why she couldn't attend the match at Stamford Bridge. "Are you hungry?" She ruffled Bulldog's ears.

Bulldog panted and gave her a sweet look.

"You haven't by any chance been nibbling at my nuts, have you?" she asked the dog.

Bulldog's smile widened.

"You terrible, bad boy." She squeezed his ears. "I told you to only eat those I personally serve you in your bowl." The dog lowered its chin to the floor and sniffed.

"But wait a minute." She rubbed her own chin. "You couldn't have eaten any nuts from those bowls." She pointed at the set of bowls by the end of the corridor. They were higher than the rest. To reach them, the dog had to roll the bowl over. "Let's check those. I have marked them."

She walked ahead with Bulldog and grabbed herself a small stepper, specially designed for her to stand up whenever she wished to reach something that was supposed to be out of reach. The Queen was slightly shorter than most queens.

She stood upon it and stretched her hands, pulling the bowl down. This time, she didn't need to dip her hand inside. She had these bowls previously marked with a yellow marker from inside, so she'd know when the level of nuts dipped below the mark. This was her perfectly planned trap for her nasty guards and footmen who were tall enough to get the nuts—if they had really sneaked into the chamber.

"Hmm..." The Queen's face reddened again. "So there *was* an intruder in the chamber a few minutes ago," she said to Bulldog, who nodded obediently. "Did you see the intruder?"

The dog shook its head with bulging Scooby-Doo eyes.

"Bloody traitors!" The Queen jumped off her stepper and plowed the bowl against a precious painting of Lewis Carroll that hung on the wall. The painting was called *Alice's Adventures Underground*, the original cover of one of very few initial copies that bore this name before changing it into *Alice's Adventures in Wonderland*. The painting, an older property of Queen Victoria, was signed by John Tenniel, Lewis' illustrator himself.

In the middle of the corridor, the angry Queen stood with clenched hands and stiffened feet, about to burst into tears like a child. Her shoulders were hunched but stiffened. Her hair thin and uncombed. Bulldog beside her had his tail clutched between his legs. The Queen's wrath wasn't to be underestimated.

"Something isn't right." She gasped again. "This can't be. The guards couldn't have entered and nibbled on my nuts." It briefly occurred to her that she sounded like the evil witch from Hansel and Gretel. "*Who's nibbling on my nuts, muahaha!*" But she flashed the thought away. "I am sure the chamber is locked. Only I own the remote control to lock it."

Bulldog nodded with approval, as long as it would calm her down. Dogs in general knew their owners were a bunch of cuckoos in the head. They had to pamper them and make humans feel good about themselves in exchange of charitable food and shelter. Nothing wrong with fooling a human to get what you want.

"So who's been nibbling on my nuts!" she screamed again from the top of her lungs, her voice echoing in the chamber. "*Nuts. Nuts. Nuts!*"

She tiptoed again, clenched hands again, and the thin

veins on her neck protruded outward. For another brief moment she felt like the Queen of Hearts in Lewis Carroll's book; that scene when she was upset about who stole her tarts. But then again, this wasn't the time for thinking about Wonderland. Her nuts mattered the most.

The anger showing on her face was gradually intensifying. It looked she could explode like a full-blown balloon.

The Queen's dog had no means to tuck his head inside his body like turtles did, or he would have not hesitated doing it now. The hair on his skin prickled like needles and pins.

Suddenly, the Queen's mobile phone rang.

Now she got really furious. Who dared to call her that late?

Maybe a citizen in need, Your Majesty, her inner voice told her. But she was sure that only a few selected people had her number.

Trotting back to her room, anger spitting out of her ears, she wondered if anyone knew about her secret Facebook profile, but there was no way she'd really give it a thought now.

She picked up the phone and read the caller's name.

Now, this is alarming.

She calmed down a little, as this was an unusually worrying call.

She clicked the answer button. "You know what time it is?"

"Yes, Your Majesty," Margaret Kent, the Duchess and revered Parliament member, said from other side. "But it's important."

"It better be." The Queen sighed impatiently.

"I know this will sound inappropriate if I ask, but..." Margaret hesitated.

"I hate the word 'but,'" the Queen said.

"Are you missing any of your precious nuts, My Majesty?"

The Queen was silent, and her knees felt wobbly all of a sudden.

"I see," Margaret responded to the Queen's utter silence. "So someone's been stealing from your nuts again. And it's not the guards, I assume."

The Queen nodded. Now, fear wrapped itself around her skin like a pale ghost. Bulldog was really starting to worry. Suddenly, it seemed apparent who took her nuts. The same man who broke in many years ago. *It couldn't be. After all these years?*

"Is it *him*? Is he back?" she asked, watching her dog's ears perk up. Of course, Bulldog must have been confused. What was so utterly scary about a thief stealing nuts from the Queen?

"I am afraid he is." Margaret sighed. "And it doesn't look good. He stole the nuts to remind you he's back. It's a message. A threatening message. We have to get rid of him. We can't handle him, not this time."

"You promised me last week's killings would be the last of Wonderland's nonsense," the Quern retorted. "I can't allow this in my country."

"I know. Don't worry. We'll contain the matter."

"Then do something about it!" The Queen's hands shivered. "Kill him. Do anything. Make sure I never see the Muffin Man again!"

Chapter 25

Director's office, Radcliffe Lunatic Asylum, Oxford

When we get back to the asylum, the Pillar and I separate so we won't be seen together by the guards. I still don't know how he is capable of escaping and returning to his cell, but I enter through the main door, as if the ambulance just dropped me back from the hospital I was sent to in London.

Inside, I have to pass by Tom Truckle's office.

"Before I let you in, I want to ask you something," Dr. Truckle says. He is eating his favorite mock turtle Soup, exclusively delivered from a famous restaurant called Fat Duck in London. Fat Duck is owned by one of the world's best cooks, Gorgon Ramstein. The restaurant is rumored to have stolen their amazing mock turtle soup from a Victorian kitchen in Oxford University's basement, supposedly the same kitchen that inspired Lewis Carroll's Mock Turtle character.

"And what would that be?" I ask flatly. He is mean, and he *means* nothing to me.

"Did Professor Pillar, under any circumstance, ever mention Houdini?" he asks after wiping his greasy lips on a napkin.

"Who's Houdini?"

"Harry Houdini, the most famous American magician of all time. The escape artist who could escape a box chained and submerged under water." He seems offended by my ignorance.

"Ah, that Houdini." Lately, no historical figure matters much to me. I am now all fixated on Wonderland Monsters. Who's Houdini compared to the Cheshire, really? "No, I don't remember him talking about him. Why would the Pillar mention him?"

"To cut it short, do you know how he escapes and sneaks back into the asylum without my cameras ever catching him?" Dr. Truckle points at the many new surveillance cameras in his office. "I've researched the matter, and only found one incident in history that matches the Pillar's skills."

I smile. It's amusing how the Pillar gets on his nerves.

"It happened 1819 in New York's Hippodrome Theatre, wildly known as the Disappearing Elephant event."

"Why are you asking *me* about his?" I am too tired to deal with his paranoia now.

"I figured you might know, since..."

"Since?" I tilt my head.

"Since you are an expert in escaping a straitjacket," he blurts.

I try not to shrug. I find it a plausible train of thought. Where did I ever learn to escape a straitjacket? I have no idea.

"You know how many people in the world are capable of escaping a straitjacket as tight as the one we used on you?" he explains, then makes a V sign with his fore and middle fingers. "You and Houdini."

I laugh. "Look, I don't know how I do it. I just know I can. If Houdini did it too, rest assured, I am in no way related to him. Besides, how did you ever connect those events together?"

"Because of this." He hands me an old copy of the *New Yorker* listing the honorable guests attending the Houdini event. I scan it, and among the names find the following:

> *Carter Chrysalis Cocoon Pillar,*
> *VIP guest,*
> *personal friend of Mister Harry Houdini.*

"Is that his real name?" I raise my eyebrows as high as I can. Dr. Truckle nods.

Although I am astonished, I don't know what to make of it. The documents could be forged. "Listen," I say. "I'm not friends with Professor Pillar, and I need rest. Can I go now?"

Sighing, he waves the path to the door to me, then asks, "Is he going to ask for you again tomorrow?"

"I believe so." We still have tons of work in the Muffin Man case. "Look!" I point at the surveillance camera behind him. "The Pillar is back."

Dr. Truckle turns around, looking like an angry turtle about to explode. He watches the Pillar smoking his hookah, leaning back on his sofa, and wiggling his feet. If you take the cell out of the picture, you'd think he was on vacation in Ibiza. When Dr. Truckle turns on the sound, there is a song playing in the background. It's "Crazy" by Seal.

I try my best not to laugh as I walk away, wondering if Waltraud would allow me a shower today.

Chapter 26

After dismissing Waltraud's insults and a few unnecessary chuckles by Ogier, I am back in my cell.

The first thing I do is check on my terribly insane flower. She seems to be enjoying the bigger crack in the wall and the sunlight seeping through. She isn't sleeping, nor talking to me. It's better that way. I already had my share of madness for a day. Still, I wonder why she means so much to me. It's not like she is a pet I keep home and come back to. Deep inside, I know she means more to me, but have no clue why.

I spend a few minutes staring at the six days I carved on the wall, wondering if I will live long enough to scratch the seventh diagonal stroke tomorrow. Next to the carvings, I glimpse the date, January 14th, still not knowing what it really means or why the number 14 keeps popping up everywhere.

Then there is the key, like the one Lewis gave me, drawn on the wall. I still have no idea who drew this key, but this time I notice the key is almost the same exact size like the real one. I take off the necklace and pick the key. Slowly, I near it to the drawing on the wall. I am right. It's the same size. I wonder if this means anything. Before I decide to give up on the crazy idea, the key on the wall glitters, so does the real one in my hand. I near it even closer, and then the coolest, and craziest, thing happens. The key in my hands dissolves into the one in the wall, still sticking out slightly so I can pick it up later. I realize I found a place to hide it, finally.

I wonder again: is it possible that my mind keeps coming up with such things?

I close my eyes and sigh, wanting to trust my mind. At least, I hid the key somewhere safe now. I don't have to hide it from the Pillar anymore, as Lewis had warned not to show it to anyone as well. This isn't just any key. It's is one of they keys to one of Wonderland doors, whatever that really means.

I open my eyes, and feel a bit relieved actually. Time to rest and prepare for a hectic day tomorrow.

Since Waltraud denied me a shower, I lie on the mattress on the floor, wishing for some sleep. They bought me a new one with the picture of a huge rabbit on it.

Waltraud knocks on my door again and tells me I will get my shower after I get my postponed dose of shock therapy. "No point in showering when you haven't sweated enough yet," she says, and tries to talk me into telling her where I have been. I tell her I am not allowed to say. She laughs and says they must be experimenting on me like a lab rat, because I don't even count as a human. It's interesting how insults don't count when you're in dire need of sleep.

Waltraud doesn't give up, though. She pulls the sliding window in the door and peeks in. "I just found a way to get you in the Mush Room."

"Huh?" I pull myself up and rub my eyes.

"I requested you for interrogation in the Mush Room tomorrow." She rubs her hands with childish enthusiasm.

"On what basis?"

"I requested I interrogate you about the patient who escaped last week, remember?"

"Yeah, I do. But I don't think my cell is close to the patient's."

"It's isn't. But I just remembered you acted strange that night."

"How strange?" What night was that, exactly?

"You asked me if I saw a White Queen enter your cell." She laughs. "I mentioned it in my report. Maybe you were distracting me so the patient could escape."

"I don't even know this patient."

"The patient never had a real name on his file," Waltraud says. "We call him the Muffin Man because he had an obsession with muffins." She shoots me with one last evil laugh and then shuts the window in the door, dimming my room into a mysterious darkness.

I take a few seconds to digest what I just heard.

Chapter 27

In the morning, when I am sent to the Pillar's cell, he is in one of those happy Caucus Race moods again.

I stand before the cell and watch him through the black bars. He is dancing in place, holding his cane up to the ceiling.

He is not alone.

Several of his favorite Mushroomers dance next to him. They aren't dancing to music, though. They're tapping their feet and drooling to the silly words of a nursery rhyme.

One of them faces the rest of the Mushroomers in their pajamas and chants:

"Do you know the Muffin Man,
The Muffin Man, the Muffin Man,
Do you know the Muffin Man,
Who lives on Drury Lane?"

Then the Pillar claps to the beat, the same way children would sing the song in a kindergarten. Then one of the Mushroomers facing the first chanter responds:

"Oh yes! I know the Muffin Man,
The Muffin Man, the Muffin Man,
Yes, I know the Muffin Man,
Who lives on Drury Lane."

The Pillar claps his hands and then rewards the Mushroomer by allowing him to slide over to the first one on the other side. Then both of them face the rest and start all over again:

"Do you know the Muffin Man,
The Muffin Man, the Muffin Man,
Yes, I know the Muffin Man,
Who lives on Drury Lane."

"Alice!" The Pillar's voice is barely audible across the chants and claps of the Mushroomers. "Come out and play!"

"Why are you doing this?" I cock my head, knowing most of the Pillar's actions are usually significant, not just a fool man's calling.

"It's the song the corpses were singing in the morgue."

"I know what it is." I raise my voice but control my temper. "Why are the Mushroomers singing it?"

"The same reason why the corpses were singing it." He winks. Now I am sure the song holds crucial information. Did he figure it out?

"Am I supposed to guess the reason now?" I ask impatiently.

Like a music conductor, the Pillar signals the Mushroomers to lower their chanting. He takes a few steps forward, holding the bars with his gloved hands. I wonder if he sleeps with that elegant blue and gold striped suit he wears. "You forgot to tell me the Cheshire paid you a visit," he says in a blaming tone. "Why did you do that, Alice?"

"I..." Stuttering isn't helping. I don't really know why I didn't tell him. "I think because I wasn't sure it really happened."

"That explains the random occurrence of events," The Pillar says. "All the clues he sent you were based on him trusting you would tell me he paid you a visit a week ago, the night the patient called the Muffin Man escaped the asylum."

"I don't understand."

"If you'd told me he paid you a visit, I'd have dug deeper behind the reason why." His tone is still blaming, but also calm and assured. "I'd have easily known from Dr. Truckle that the Muffin Man escaped the asylum that night."

"You knew the Muffin Man was a patient in the asylum?"

"No, I didn't." The Pillar laughs and abandons the bar, straightening up. "Anyway, now we know the Cheshire helped the Muffin Man escape the asylum. That's why he visited you."

"So he wasn't really here for me?"

"Of course, that was part of the plan. Helping the Muffin Man out to commit the crimes was his first priority, though."

"Are you saying it's not the Cheshire who committed these murders?"

"The Muffin Man!" the Mushroomers interrupt us.

"Who is he?" I grip the bars myself now, curious about the mysterious killer. "Why is he so important the Cheshire got him out? What's going on? Who is this Muffin Man?"

"I know who he is now." The Pillar pulls out a file with *The Muffin Man* written on it. It's his file at the asylum.

"You read it?"

He nods.

"And?"

"He is pretty terrifying, I have to say. He admitted himself to the asylum many years go. The asylum rejected him on the basis of 'no apparent insanity.' It's laughable. So he climbed up to the Queen of England's chamber and threatened her," the Pillar says.

"*The* Queen of England?"

"Yes, the only one who's allowed to drive without a driver's license or license plate." He rolls his eyes. I never knew that about the Queen of England before. "The Muffin Man managed to sneak up the Queen of England's chamber a few years ago and threaten to kill her. And *voila*, his wish is granted. He is finally admitted to the Radcliffe Lunatic Asylum."

"He threatened the Queen herself so they'd know he was mad?"

"It's pretty plausible," the Pillar says. "Who'd do something like that if he wasn't mad?"

"How old is the Muffin Man?"

"Mid forties," the Pillar says. "He's been in the asylum for some time, and no one ever complained about him."

"He must have wanted so badly to hide in an asylum.

Why?"

"My humble guess is that he was running away from something," the Pillar says. "The real question is why he would prefer to stay locked in here over the real world outside."

"You're the one holding his file."

"There is nothing here more that what I just said." He hurls the file away. The Mushroomers collect the scattered pages behind him. "The file doesn't mention his real name." He stares sharply at me. "It's doesn't even mention an address, a next of kin, or what kind of conversation took place between him and the Queen, although she'd been his hostage for more than half an hour."

A few moments of silence drape on me. I need to re-evaluate the situation. "Why did the Cheshire help him escape, and why is he killing kids?"

"That sure escapes my caterpillar brain cells," he says. "But here's a good one. You know what the Muffin Man's answer was when he was asked where he was from?" He lowers his head a little and whispers, "Wonderland."

"This is truly puzzling now." I let go of the bars. "We need to know who he is so we can stop him from killing again."

"He isn't waiting for us, Alice. Another fat boy's head with a muffin stuffed inside was found in a dumpster yesterday." The Pillar purses his lips, playing his games with me.

"And what are we supposed to do now? We don't even know where the Muffin Man lives."

"That's not true." The Pillar winks.

"You just said he has no address in the file."

"Alice, Alice, Alice." He step backwards slowly and rolls his cane in the air. "Didn't we agree that Wonderland's puzzles aren't ever solved in earthly grounds?"

The Mushroomers begin hissing the rhyme again:
"Do you know the Muffin Man,

The Muffin Man, the Muffin Man,
Do you know the Muffin Man,
Who lives on Drury Lane?"

I listen to the chanting and want to kick myself in the head. How didn't I figure it out sooner? I near the cell again and say, "The Muffin Man lives on *Drury Lane*." I spell the name slowly, not knowing if it's a neighborhood, town, or city. I am not sure it even exists in our modern world. Most nursery rhymes are products of the Victorian era, about two centuries ago. "Where is Drury Lane?"

"London." The Pillar purses his lips. "The Cheshire's puzzles are really intricate."

"Don't tell me it's close to the morgue."

"Very close, and we need to get going now. Drury Lane is a culturally important place in the world," the Pillar says. "Shall we take the ambulance from yesterday or my limousine?" he ask the Mushroomers.

They prefer the ambulance because it makes a "woo-wee" noise.

"You're still keeping the ambulance? That's property of the health institution."

"I'm only borrowing it for the greater good. I'm sure the *institution*, and Parliament, won't mind." He carefully rubs his suit clean.

"Well, it won't be the first time we've broken the law since I've known you," I mumble, morally compromised.

"Knowing me *is* breaking the law, Alice." He smiles. "Funny how you never worried if I buried the corpse of the dead man you stole, instead of caring about the *health* institution."

Chapter 28

On the way to Drury Lane

The drive to London should take an hour and half. We're taking way longer than that.

The Pillar orders his chauffeur to stop at every junk food store we come across. Whether it's Dr. Nugget's Wingless Chickens, Banned Burgers, Pizza Pinge, Wacko's Tacos, DoNuts Bogus, or Muffit N Puffit, the recent American franchise that bought he rights to the Meow Muffins. Insanely, and for all the wrong reasons, smoking inside Muffit N Puffit is mandatory!

Each store we stop by, the Pillar enters it with his chauffeur, dressed as doctor and nurse. The chauffeur halts the ambulance sideways with a screech like a mad driver in a Need for Speed game. Then he intentionally parks the ambulance in spots reserved for handicapped drivers. Finally, they dash into the store.

At first, they look weird, but then, skipping rows of waiting citizens at the counter, they pretend they have a dying woman in the ambulance.

I watch from the passenger's seat with bulging eyes, unable to gaze back at the corpse in the back of the ambulance. How did the Pillar turn into such an irresponsible whack? Moments like these, I have no doubts he killed those people for reasons of utter and undeniable insanity.

"Please," the Pillar says to the girl over the counter, his hands stretched out. "In the name of the Three Stooges." He flashes the sign of trinity in the air, so fast no one even registers he said "the Three Stooges." His dramatic acting distracts disbelievers from what's going on, and entertains those bored with their lives, looking for entertainment. "I'm Dr. Marshmallow Nuttinghead, and this is my male nurse assistant, Fourgetta Boutit. We are from the Queen's Renowned Hospital for the Deliberately Poor and

Forsakenly Unhealthy Disease Center." I don't even know how no one laughs or comments on his nonsense. I guess he has crept in with such a sense of urgency and panic that he entranced the whole smoking crowd of Muffit N Puffit. In particular, the girl over the counter. Come to think of it, they are as mad as the Pillar, eating in here in the first place. "We have a dying woman in the ambulance." I slide deeper into my seat as the crowd turns their heads my way. "She is divorced, pregnant, and dying of loon cancer." The crowd sympathizes deeply. "All she asks" — the Pillar holds the girl's hands and looks pleadingly into her eyes — "is to have one last Meow Muffin and Spit Burger before she dies."

Instead of the crowd laughing, or thinking this must be some *Candid Camera* joke, they start urging the girl to grant the loon cancer victim her last wish.

"What is loon cancer?" an old woman with glasses and a cane asks.

"It's the cancer you get in the loons," a middle-aged man in blue overalls informs her. "How can you be so insensitive? Does it matter which cancer you have?"

"I'm sorry." The woman lowers her head but stubbornly feels the need to ask again. I can't blame her. She might be the only sane person in there. "But I didn't know I have a loon organ. What does it do?"

"It's in a sensitive place, old lady." A middle-aged woman punches her to save her the embarrassment from not fitting in the crowd. "It's right down near the..." She whispers in the old woman's ears. Her eyes widen.

As the counter girl prepares the meal for the Pillar, the store's supervisor offers it for free. The Pillar kisses the girl's hand. She blushes as he prays the Three Blind Mice to reward her a place full of "Danish cheese with no holes" in heaven.

And so, the Pillar and his chauffeur did the same at every food chain we stopped by for two hours, until the back of the ambulance was stuffed with every snack or junk food available in Britain.

Speechlessly, I watch the Pillar gorge on every high-calorie, unhealthy, and greasy sandwich he obtained. He and his chauffeur eat, chew, and spit like the Cookie Monster from *Sesame Street*.

"Can you pass me the ketchup, Alice?" the Pillar asks with a mouthful.

"Why are you doing this?" I manage to put a sentence together.

"The food is delicious. Addictive. Frabjous. Remember the way you felt addicted to the muffin in the morgue? I feel the same about this." He points at the snacks in his hands. "Besides, I'm a caterpillar. In order to become a cocoon, I have to eat. A lot!"

"Are you deliberately stalling our visit to Drury Lane?" It's the best conclusion I can put together.

"Of course not," he says. "We're on our way. But first, we have to stop at Harrods to buy you a dress."

"Why a dress?" I neglect the fact that we have to stop again. I haven't worn a dress like a normal girl since...well, I don't remember since when.

"We're going to see an important play in a theatre." The Pillar wipes his mouth and stops chewing. It's time to tell me what's going on. "When I researched Drury Lane, I found nothing of interest that could lead us to the Muffin Man. All but the Theatre Royal on Catherine Street in Westminster, London. Also known as the Drury Lane Theatre. It's one of the most prestigious theatres in history. A dress code is required. That's why you need a dress."

"Why do we have to go?"

"Because the Muffin Man will be there."

He has my full attention. "And how do you know that?" I inquire.

"Because the only thing in Drury Lane connected to Lewis Carroll is the Drury Lane Theatre." He swoops what's left over from his sandwich out of the window, then he claps his hands clean. The leftover glues with its sticky mayonnaise on the front shield of a silver Bentley driving by. An elegantly dressed lady rolls down the window and swears at us. It's surprising how vulgar she is. The Pillar ignores her, and wipes mayo from his lips.

I wait until he finishes his childish acts, thinking about how he refused to shake hands before when he was worried about germs. Whether he is simply messing with me, or all this food binging is some kind of message I am supposed to read through, I can't seem to understand the contradiction. I lean forward in my chair, fishing for more answers. "You're serious about that, right?" I lace my hands together. "How is Lewis Carroll connected to the Drury Lane Theatre?"

"That" — he raises a mayonnaise-stained finger — "I will explain to you in detail after we get the dress." He licks his finger and sits back. "Now be the insane girl you're supposed to be and stick your head out of the passenger's window."

"Why would I?" I grimace.

"To say, 'Wee-woo, wee-woo,' since my chauffeur's mouth is stuffed with carbs, sweets, and saturated fats."

"No, I won't." I muster an expressionless face like he does most of the time, and lean back again. I even cross my legs to feel relaxed.

"And why would that be?" He is curious, and excited with my behavior.

"Because it's 'woo-wee,' not 'wee-woo,'" I tease, then I start to wonder if there is actually a real science to nonsense, like Jack said before.

Chapter 29

Lady's department, Harrods, London

The Pillar stands outside my fitting room, fluff-talking to the young girls selling all kinds of expensive outfits. I am inside the booth, resisting the urge to pull the curtain and warning the infatuated girls of him.

The working girls are all ears. They are so into his stories.

He is dressed in his regular blue tuxedo with horizontal golden stripes. His gloves are a shiny white, and he is wearing a magician's hat with a golden ribbon on his head.

Although he looks much paler, and his skin seems to be worsening—slightly peeling off day by day—the girls don't pay attention to such turn-offs. I understand they are young and naive—I am young myself, though days spent in an asylum make me feel older—but I am amazed at their infatuation with the short, sneaky man.

The Pillar enjoys entertaining them, messing with their heads. He starts by predicting what they like the most, and what kind of guy they would love to date. His predictions are always right.

The girls ditch most of the customers at Harrods and circle the Pillar while he brags about his adventures in the Queen of England's palace. The Pillar, unbeknownst to me, claims he'd been the one of the many personal advisors to the Queen of England at some point. With a doctorate in philosophy, he says he had been very useful.

My guess is those girls never read newspapers, or it would have crossed their minds that he is Pillar the Killer, one of Britain's notorious murderers. Maybe, like he theorized before, people are really in love with villains like him.

"So, the Queen of England really counts her Brazilian nuts each night?" a giggling girl says.

"She is obsessed with her nuts." The Pillar points a finger to the girl's skull. "If you know what I mean." The girl laughs. "Bowl after bowl, the Queen marks them with yellow marker to see if the nuts have dipped." He is conspiracy-talking now, making the girls feel special. "It started years ago when she'd imported a set of exotic nuts for her son's royal wedding. The guards, having never tasted such amazing peanuts, had to dip in sooner or later. A big mistake." He waves his forefinger.

"Why?" a bright-eyed, but not bright-minded, girl asks.

"Yes, why?" her friend follows.

"The Queen's peanuts are addictive," the Pillar says. "The guards couldn't stop nibbling on them."

"But then the Queen must have been mad," the giggling girl says.

"I heard she took the matter to the Supreme Court of the United Kingdom," another girl suggests.

"True," the Pillar says. "It was on Parliament's most important discussions a few years ago."

I pull the curtain and peek from behind it, hoping there is a point behind this conversation.

"Parliament granted the Queen immunity from her dishonest guards." He purses his lips with sarcasm. "They granted her a first-class security system she can install in her chamber to keep away the guards while she is asleep. The Queen's nuts are a matter of national security now."

The girls laugh hysterically. I do, too. I admit it. The story is insanely amusing. I heard it on the radio on our way to Harrods. A few ladies nearby were talking about it too. It seemed like an impossible story spread by a cheap newspaper, but it is a true story.

"You know what I really think the Queen did?" the Pillar whispers to them. The girls step in closer. I almost fall semi-naked out of the booth, eavesdropping. "I think the Queen brutally punished her guards, regardless of the word from Parliament."

"Punished them?" The girls exchange Barbie-like

worried looks. "How do you think she did that?"

"I think she went, 'Off with their heads!'" He pantomimes a knife cutting through his neck with his hand.

"Like the Queen of Hearts in *Alice in Wonderland*?" The not-so-bright one's doe eyes widen.

The Pillar nods and leans back. "Just don't tell anyone." He pantomimes zipping his mouth.

The girls are horrified. They can't tell if the Pillar is joking or not. Nor can I. Is he suggesting the Queen of England is the Queen of Hearts? I don't even want to consider the possibility.

"One more thing," he says, breaking the tension. "Do you have any idea who paid for the Queen's expensive security system?"

The girls shake their heads.

"You." He points at each of them, mustering a serious face.

"Us?" The girls are genuinely puzzled.

"From the taxes you pay." He rubs a thumb against his fore and middle fingers, indicating money.

"Really?" The girls' hands snap back to their mouths. This time they manage to show anger. I would.

Did I pay for the Queen's security system, too? Do insane people pay taxes?

"The Queen's nuts are *that* important." The Pillar ends his lesson with a bang, pulls his chin up, and turns back to me. "Alice!" He raises his cane, leaving a set of middle-class girls almost teary behind them. One of them actually quits her job on the spot. "Have you found an appropriate dress yet?" he asks.

I stare at him. Really stare at him. All kinds of thoughts flicker in my head. I want to punch him. I want to bring back time to a point where I have never met him. I want deliver him to the authorities. But I also want to laugh with him. As he approaches me, a flash of Wonderland sparks before my eyes. It's a short one about me talking to a caterpillar atop of an immense mushroom.

The flash disappears in a *flash*.

"Who are you?" I ask the Pillar approaching me in Harrods. I am sincerely wishing for an answer. A fragment of an answer will do. "I mean, really, Pillar, who are you?"

He laughs. "I used to ask *you* that question in Wonderland." He stops before me, knocking his cane against the floor. "And I actually do it with style. *Hoo aaare yoooh?*" Hookah smoke swirls out of his mouth as he ends his sentence. He hasn't even brought his hookah with him. I cough, closing my eyes, not wanting to get sedated again.

If close my eyes and open them again, will my world ever change for the better?

When I open my eyes, the Pillar is gone. No wonder Dr. Truckle connects him to Harry Houdini.

Chapter 30

I sigh at the Pillar's disappearance and get back in the booth. Surely he will come back again.

I pull the curtain back and try on the new dress. I try not to overdress. Nothing too fancy, although I'd love to. A merely noticeable, but moderately proper dress should work just fine. I am not going to the prom. It's just a play at the theatre. A great bonus for a girl locked in an asylum, I must admit. Besides, whatever I wear usually ends up spattered with blood.

I have already chosen a fitting room with no mirrors — the Pillar pretended he had broken it accidentally, and the staff had to remove it when we first entered Harrods. I told them I didn't mind using a mirror-less dressing room. The Pillar covered the rest of the mirror on the wall with a veil he borrowed from an older woman and told me, "What's the use of a dressing room without a mirror? It's just like a book without pictures." He winked and closed the curtain to talk to the girls.

When I look at the dress I chose, I like it on me. Not bad for a mad girl. I think I can look like normal girls, ones who have a few friends, loving parents and siblings, a girl who lives in a nice suburban house, awaits a bright future, and, above all, has a solid memory of her past.

I also think I look like a girl who could have a boyfriend. At least, a mutual interest with a boy. I wonder if this is could be my life when all of this is over — if this is ever going to be over.

The accumulation of thoughts reminds me of Jack Diamonds. How is it possible he always appears when I need him? He never complains, and is always positive about his energy. I should be flattered he always wants to have a date with me.

Now that I know Jack is Adam J. Dixon, my dead boyfriend, I understand why I am so into him. My feelings are justified. I am not a love-hungry girl fresh out of the asylum, *insta-loving* the first boy I meet. I am in love with the boy who has been my boyfriend since two years ago. The same boy I killed *two years ago*.

But how is Adam alive, calling himself Jack?

I shrug and silence my overworking mind. Better pull the curtain and ask he Pillar who's going to pay for my dress. I know he hasn't fully disappeared. He was just playing games with me.

When I pull he curtain, I am surprised someone is standing right behind it. Not the Pillar. Someone I miss dearly, but haven't expected to see here.

Jack Diamonds flashes one of his smiles with cute dimples at me. It's a sexy smile.

Chapter 31

"Are you wearing this dress for me?" He has his arm resting on the doorframe, a seductive gleam flowering in his eyes.

"Jack!" I tiptoe like a young girl meeting her loved one after he has been away for long.

"With a dress like that, I could get on my knees and propose."

I am sure I am blushing, so I lower my head and lace my hands. Slowly, Jack's finger nudges me back to look at him. "You know I am poor and can't afford a ring, right?"

"You're just silly." I am blushing red roses out of my cheeks.

"I'm not silly. I am mad."

"You're not mad. Trust me." I wrap my fingers around his wrist. I feel as if the world is slowly disappearing all around me. No one's left in it but him and me. "I'm the mad one. I have a Certificate of Ins—"

"I'm mad about *you*," he says. I don't think he heard what I just said. "I would go to the moon and back for you. You have no idea, Alice."

"Mad enough to die for me?" I shrug. In the name of Mushroomers, why did I say that?

"Alice." He leans in, still smelling of a deck of cards. Normally, a smell like that would spoil a moment like this. It doesn't. I'm in love with all the nonsense aces, spades, hearts, clubs, and diamonds he brings to my life. "You can kill me anytime you want. I won't complain," he whispers.

A sticky tear threatens to seep out of my eye when he says that. Now, why did he say that? Should I tell him that I killed him? Should I tell him I have no idea how he is standing in front of me?

"Who are you talking to?" The Pillar waves at me from an aisle of dresses a few feet away.

"It's Jack," I reply. "I have never had him appear in

your presence before."

The Pillar says nothing as he walks silently toward me. He briefly checks out the crowd around us before he stops and says, "Jack who?"

"Jack Diamonds," I insist, poking Jack at his chest.

The Pillar looks behind him and then back to me, a suspicious gaze in his eyes. Almost pitiful.

"Look." I sigh. "I know you don't like him, but it wouldn't hurt you to say 'hi.'"

"I would if I could," the Pillar says. His gaze starts to worry me.

"What is that supposed to mean?"

"It means I don't see a 'Jack' in here."

"It's Jack, Pillar," I stress. "Adam, my boyfriend. Don't play games with me."

Slowly, the Pillar closes in, standing right behind Jack. "Alice," he almost whispers. "You need to calm down. There is no one here but you and me. Behind us, everyone is taking care of their own business. But right here, there is no Jack."

"You're lying," I say. "I'm not imagining him."

"I didn't quite say that. I just don't see him."

"Nonsense!" I look back at Jack. "Say something, Jack."

"Like what?" Jack looks uncomfortable with the Pillar's proximity.

"Tell him you're not a figment of my imagination," I plead. "Tell the Pillar you're real."

Jack sighs and walks away, brushing against the Pillar. I see the Pillar slightly make room for him. Why is he saying he can't see him? Where is Jack going?

"I am real, Alice," Jack says from afar. "I just don't like this man." He points at the Pillar. "I think he doesn't like me. And honestly, I think you shouldn't be around him."

"Pillar?" I dare him. "You heard Jack. Is that true?"

"What did Jack say?" The Pillar purses his lips, but looks in the direction I am looking at.

"He says you're playing games with my mind."

"Please, Alice," the Pillar says. "Let's forget about Jack. I will tell you who he is when we catch the Muffin Man. You gave me your word."

"And what is that supposed to mean?" Jack protests.

"There is no Jack here, Alice." The Pillar holds me gently by the shoulders.

"He is standing right there!" My high-pitched voice catches the customers' attention. The Pillar looks like he doesn't want anyone to notice me.

"All right." The Pillar sighs. "Ask Jack to talk to one of the staff girls. Let's see if they can see him."

"Don't listen to him, Alice," Jack says.

"Do as he says, Jack," I beg him. "Please."

Jack slowly walks toward a girl in the staff and stretches out a hand. She smiles and shakes it back. No one can resist those dimples. They start chatting.

"See? He is real." I pout at the Pillar. "He is talking to the girl."

"No, he isn't," the Pillar says. "What girl?"

"I can't believe you." I push the Pillar away. I am about to pull my hair and scream. I feel like I want to hide back in my cell. Something isn't right. It's like a hidden truth that I feel but can't put my hands on. I return to the dressing room, away from the Pillar, and grab my clothes so I can leave. "I don't understand why you are doing this," I shout at the Pillar in public. The hell with people. I am a mad girl. I can do as I please. "I've had it with you!" I walk away with Jack.

It's time to end this.

Furious, I pull my clothes and accidentally catch on the dark veil covering the mirror. My heart almost explodes at the horror, realizing what I have done. I reach for the veil before it curls down to the ground.

But I am too late.

Once the mirror flashes like summer rays at my eyes, I see that scary rabbit inside it again. My fear of mirrors prickles every hair on my skin. This time, I am too furious and fragile to deal with it.

I faint and drop to the floor like an empty satin dress, devoid of its owner, swirling lonely to the ground.

Chapter 32

Theatre Royal, Drury Lane, London, 1862

I am standing in front of Theatre Royal in Drury Lane on Brydges Street—renamed Catherine Street two centuries later. It's 1862 again. I am back in Lewis' vision, only we're in London this time.

There is a coach and a small crowd waiting outside the theatre's façade. All in all, a few people. Hiding at the edges of my vision I still see a lot of homeless people and beggars, scattered all around like invisible diseases. Those waiting by the theatre pretend they don't see the poor.

A man with a pipe tells his wife about the theatre's history. How it had been mysteriously burned down in 1809. How Richard Sheridan, Irish playwright and owner of the theatre, watched the fire from a coffee house with a bottle of wine. The man laughs and takes another drag from his pipe, which smells of the exact flavor the Pillar smokes.

With all the poverty, mud, and stinky smell of open sewers, these few aristocrats manage to wait outside the theatre, demanding entry to a famous play. Whenever a poor girl or boy in tattered clothes approaches them, they shoo them away like a annoying fly buzzing near their ears. They drink their wine, tell their stories, and talk about the dinner party they should attend after the play.

Not sure if I am invisible in this dream, I keep approaching the rich, wanting to listen to them. They argue whether last night's turkey wasn't cooked properly, whether they should fire their cook. The man's wife, wearing a lot of jewelry, wishes they could afford hiring Alexis Benoist Soyer, a French celebrity chef. Her husband can't agree more. He jokes that their cook, although they pay him decently in such filthy times, probably steals all his meals from a book called *Mrs Beeton's Book of Household Management.*

My mind flickers when I hear the name. I think I have seen a copy of the book in Lewis' private studio when I entered it through the Tom Tower a week ago.

But all this interest in food, whether in this vision or the real world, confuses me. Am I supposed to read between the lines and learn something about food?

The world around me here is all filth and dirt, aggressively ignored by a few rich men and woman waiting to enter the Drury Lane Theatre.

Still vaguely listening to the man and woman speaking about food, I see the man interrupt his wife and raise his glass of wine at someone in the crowd.

Someone almost dressed like a priest.

Lewis.

The men and women greet him as he steps down from the theatre's entrance. They hail his name and seem to love him, but he looks absent and disinterested. He walks among them, nodding politely, and tries to step away from them. A big suitcase with clothes showing from its edges is tucked under his arm. The other arm is hiding a package wrapped in a newspaper.

"Excuse me," Lewis says, and vanishes into the filthy dark. London is so dirty that the moon refrained from shining through tonight.

I follow Lewis into the dark. I even call for him, but he doesn't return my call.

This must be it. This must be why I am here.

I trudge through the muddy dark. Smog is the only guiding light for me.

"Lewis!" I finally see him kneeling down to talk to homeless kids. They gather around him as if he were Santa Claus. He unwraps the newspaper and offers them loaves of bread.

The kids nibble on the bread with their dirty hands. If a loaf drops down in the mud they pick it up again and eat it right away. Some of them fight for it, but Lewis teaches them how to be as one, promising he will bring them more.

I stand in my place, watching. The kids are too skinny, even when wearing layers of tattered and holed clothes.

I step closer. No one seems to see me.

It baffles me to realize the kids are much older than I thought. Their faces suggest they are about fifteen years old, although their contracted bodies look no more than nine years old.

One of the kids asks Lewis what he keeps in the suitcase. Lewis' smile shines like a crescent moon absent in the sky, but I can't hear what he says.

"Lewis!" I call again.

He doesn't reply.

"Lewis." I feel dizzy.

Otherworldly voices are calling my name from the sky.

"Lewis!" I repeat before they wake me up in the real world.

But I am too late.

As I leave my vision, my eyes are fixed on Lewis' suitcase. Why are clothes tucked inside? They look like costumes.

Then the vision is gone.

A peculiar smoke invades my nostrils. I surrender to sneezing, opening my eyes. The Pillar stands over me in the ambulance, saying, "Wonderland hookah smoke never fails to wake up anyone. It's even better than onion."

Chapter 33

*Theatre Royal, Drury Lane, Catherine Street, London
Present day*

The play we're attending in the Theatre Royal is *Alice Adventure's Underground*. It's a new play that has only been running from a week ago, when the killings started. I think the Pillar might be right. There is too much coincidence here. We should meet the mysterious Muffin Man tonight.

"The '*Pig and Pepper*' chapter where Duchess appears is hilariously funny," the Pillar reads from a local newspaper. Behind us, the chauffeur buys our tickets.

"Really?" I am stretching my tight dress a bit. I am not used to this kind of intimacy on my skin. Neither am I comfortable with my heels. What's wrong with sneakers, or better, being barefoot?

"That's what the papers say." The Pillar looks at the billboards showing "previous attractions." "Damn," he mumbles. "We missed *Shrek the Musical*."

"And 'Coraline' by Neil Gaiman," I point out.

"Who's your favorite, Lewis Carroll or Neil Gaiman?" He points his finger playfully at me.

"Carroll." I don't hesitate. "Lewis Carroll or J. R. R. Tolkien?" I shoot back.

"Carroll." He doesn't hesitate either. "Lewis Carroll or C. S. Lewis?"

"Hmm." I love the Narnia books. "Nah, Carroll." I can't resist. "Lewis Carroll or *Charlie and the Chocolate Factory*?" I am starting to love this game.

"Can't compare an author to a single book, Alice," he says. "Here is a good one: who has a better sense of absurd humor, Lewis Carroll or God?"

I raise an eyebrow. I can't answer that. "Who do you think?" I feel eerily playful.

"God, of course." He waves hi at his approaching mousy chauffer, panting with the tickets in his hands. "Just look at what he has created." He secretly points at his chauffeur. "It can't get *absurder* than this."

"There is no such word as 'absurder.'" I bite my lips at his blunt sense of sarcasm.

"Who said it's a word? Absurd is an emotion." He winks and welcomes the tickets the chauffeur gives him.

"Eight tickets, like you ordered," the chauffeur remarks.

"Eight?" I grimace at the Pillar.

"My seat and yours." The Pillar counts on his fingers. "Two seats to our left and right, two behind us, and the two front of us."

"Why?"

"Precautions, Alice," the Pillar says. "Who knows what might happen inside? I have a bad feeling about this."

"All seats are also right in the middle of the theatre," the chauffeur elaborates.

"Evil people, such as terrorists, are dumb." The Pillar spares me the burden of asking. "They usually start bombing the back seats if they've intrusively entered from outside. Or bomb the front seats if they're sleeper cells. Middle is just fine."

"Not if the theatre's chandelier falls on your heads in the middle." My knack for opposing him grows in me.

"If something hits you in perpendicular line straight down from the sky, that's not a terrorist," the Pillar says while he hands a piece of his portable hookah to hide in my dress. "That would be God's sense of humor."

"What is that for?" I look at his Lego hookah.

"They don't allow hookahs inside, and I have a bad feeling I will need it."

I tuck it under my dress, counting on the Pillar to deal with security on our way in.

"So, let me be your guide for tonight, Miss Edith Wonder." He requests I engage him, and I do. "Pretend I am your father," he hisses between almost-sealed lips as we stare at the security gate. "A smile will do wonders, too."

We both smile, but I have to ask, hissing, "Why did you call me Edith?"

"In case something horrible happens, I don't want them looking for you," he says, not looking at me. "Also, your sister has been mean to you. Let's get her in trouble." We keep on smiling at the guards. "Tell the security man on your side that his taste of clothes is exceptionally *très chic*. That'd be a good distraction."

"But he is wearing a boring uniform," I hiss through my plastic smile.

"And he happens to be in his mid-forties, not wearing a ring, and probably desperate to hear a compliment from a beautiful young lady too," the Pillar says as we close in. "Make him think this a special conversation between you and him, behind daddy's back."

I do as he says when we enter. The man blushes and doesn't bother checking the tickets. I emit a seductive laugh and turn to the Pillar when we're inside, "It worked. How did you pass your guard? You haven't promised anything you can't keep?"

"Nah." He raises his chin and greets a few ladies he hasn't seen before. "I puffed hookah smoke in his face. It hypnotized him long enough for me to pass."

"Just like that? You didn't show him anything?"

"Of course I did." He smiles broadly at he crowd. "My middle finger."

Chapter 34

"The theatre is on the eastern boundary of the Covent Garden area of London," the Pillar says, pretending to guide me through as we eye everyone around us, looking for a clue to the Muffin Man. "It runs between Aldwych and High Holborn," he continues. "Not to be confused to the many other so-called Theatre Royals in the world."

"I'd prefer you tell me what Lewis Carroll has to do with all of this," I say as we enter the auditorium.

The Pillar gently holds my hand as if I am a princess and ushers me to my seats. "No farting, I promise," he says to the seating crowd we pass in the row.

We finally are seated.

"Lewis Carroll used to work briefly with the theatre," the Pillar says, holding my hands between his. "They used a few plays he'd written long before he got mad; I mean, long before he wrote *Alice in Wonderland*."

I sit and listen, not telling him about my vision of Lewis.

"You have to understand that these Victorian times were harsh," the Pillar says. "We're talking about London's filthiest, cruelest, poorest, and hungriest times. You couldn't tell people's real ages. From their unnaturally skinnier and smaller sizes, you'd think they were dwarves." He asks me to hand him the hookah piece, and begins preparing his weapon. "Food was so scarce that poorer people went down in size and length. It's true. Look at me. I am not that tall. And I lived these times."

"Proceed, please." I try to pose like someone who's accustomed to being in theatres.

"Carroll wasn't in any way fond of London. He loved Oxford, with all its books, grand halls, and studios," the Pillar continues. "He had also been a priest for a brief time; the Oxford Choir in the church will never forget him. But then Lewis developed a great interest in photography, particularly kids, like Constance's photograph."

The light in the hall dims, preparing for the start of the play.

"As you might have heard, photographers will tell you a camera never lies," the Pillar says. "In Carroll's case it was exceptionally true. The poverty his camera caught was heartbreaking. If you'd ever paid attention to his photographs, mostly of young homeless girls, you would understand his obsession. Poverty, hunger, and unfair childhood screamed out of every photo."

"I could imagine Lewis like that."

"Before writing books and puzzles, Lewis directed small plays in Oxford to entertain the poor, skinny kids with tattered clothes. He did it because there was not enough money to buy them food. In all history, art has been food of the poor, Alice. Remember that." The Pillar seems lost for a moment. I wonder what memory he is staring into. "Carroll called his intentions 'saving the children.' He wanted to save a child's *childhood*. He wanted to save their memories from being stained by the filth of his era."

"*I couldn't save them!*" Lewis' words ring in my ears.

"Those plays he directed for them introduced Carroll to the art of nonsense," the Pillar explains. "Kids are nonsensical by nature. A lame joke would make them laugh, because they are at ease with who they are. Unlike grown-ups, who are weighed down by the years."

"I still don't understand his connection to the Drury Lane Theatre, where we're supposed to find the Muffin Man."

"That's the easy part," the Pillar says. "The plays needed funding for production. Carroll was smart and resourceful. He gave his plays for free to the Theatre Royal, which was struggling after being burned down a few years back and couldn't afford to pay for new plays. In return, the theatre provided Carroll with costumes for his plays."

"That was why he held the suitcase and smiled when the kids asked him," I murmur.

"Excuse me?"

"Nothing," I say. "So that's his connection to Drury Lane Theatre?"

"My assumption, with the Cheshire's clues, is that Lewis Carroll met the Muffin Man in Drury Lane," he says. "Only, Carroll never felt the need to mention the Muffin Man in any of his writings."

"Maybe Carroll wrote the nursery rhyme?"

"That's farfetched, and we have no evidence to back it up," he says. "All I know is that after all those connections and the fact that an *Alice in Wonderland* play took place here the day the murders started, I believe the Muffin Man wants us to be here. He will probably want us to witness something."

"Something like what?"

In this moment, the Pillar cranes his neck upward at the higher balconies in the theatre. An unusual look startles his face. "Something like this." He points up.

I look and squint against the faint light in the theatre. I see an important woman arriving in the balcony, accompanied by a number of guards.

"What brings Margaret Kent here?" I ask.

"The Duchess is in the house." The Pillar sighs. "This is getting curiouser and curiouser." He lowers his head, ready to watch the play. "I don't feel guilty using her credit card to pay for your dress now."

"What?" I crane my neck at him in surprise. "You did what?"

"We used it to book the theatre's tickets too." He shakes his shoulder. "She is a charitable woman." Then a huge smirk invades his face. "Which reminds me..."

Chapter 35

The Duchess' presence provokes the Pillar. Consequences are both absurd and hilarious.

"Take this." He passes me his hookah again, spits in his gloves, and says, "This is going to be fun."

The Pillar stands and faces the crowd. Sitting right in the middle of the audience, the crowd is watching us from every direction.

"Sit down!" someone says.

"Ladies and morons of the Theatre Royal." The Pillar's welcoming hands masquerade his insults. The smile on his face is overly sincere, like those self-help lecturers. "Tonight isn't a normal night. It's the kind of evening remembered in history books. You know history, which only winners write, and forge it the way they like?"

Someone chuckles among the crowd. A few still demand he sits. A couple swear at him, pretty vulgar words you're not supposed to say in a theatre. And to my surprise, the stage's curtains hang half open.

"Are you part of the show?" a kid asks.

The Pillar nods. "So, like I said, ladies and monkeys, all you silly Wonderland lovers." Another couple of spectators chuckle. "Tonight is the night. We're here in the presence of an extraordinary woman." He points upward at the balconies. The Duchess' guards keep calm, but reach for their guns. The light technician, thinking the show has turned elsewhere, directs the spotlight at the balcony. That's where everyone is looking now. "The one and only Margaret Ugly Kent!" The Pillar's theatrical act deserves an Oscar.

"Is that really her middle name?" I hiss.

He dismisses me with a wave of his hand and talks to the theatre's orchestra. "This wasn't really the bang I was looking for." He looks annoyed. "This is the most important woman in Parliament."

The orchestra musicians seem to suddenly think he is the man in charge. One of them suggests he welcome the Duchess again, so they could play a great musical introduction.

The Pillar sniffs and repeats his welcome: "The one and only, woman of the year, whom all you morons are secretly afraid of, Margaret Kent!"

This time, music and light overwhelm the place. The crowd, either pressured or on their own will, stand up and clap for the Duchess.

Margaret Kent feels the pressure to stand up and greet her fans, her pursing lips growling at the Pillar. I don't think she wanted to be seen. She sneaked in, last minute. Is she looking for the Muffin Man too?

"Flowers!" the Pillar demands of the theatre's staff. "Where are the flowers?"

No one offers flowers. Why would they have flowers in a play? The Pillar changes strategies.

"Be seated, citizens," the Pillar says. They do so. "Now, do you think that our beloved Duchess—ah, I mean Parliament lady—is here for the sake of art? Of course she doesn't care about art," the Pillar continues. "She doesn't even care about theatre." The crowd's faces go red. Some of them sink deeper in their seats. "But she cares about you." Some of them rise back in their seats. "She loves you. She really does. And you know what she has in store for you?" He laughs. "Oh, no, don't be absurd. She's not going to chop off anyone's heads today. That would be the Queen of Hearts we're about to see in the play." The Pillar signals to the orchestra's drummer to hit the cymbals for effect. Most of the crowd laughs, uneasily. "Our beloved Margaret Kent has a surprise for you. And you know why? Because you are all sheep—I mean, obedient citizens who pay taxes and vote for her." His smile never weakens. "And because of that, she, on behalf of all prestigiously obnoxious members of Parliament, and on behalf of the Queen of England, and of course let's not forget Roman

Yeskelitch, the man who lost his children's heads to an evil watermelon last week. On behalf of all of those, you're rewarded a lifetime's free meals at Duck N Donald's Trashburgers." He raises his hands, and a few kids clap. "And lifetime free drinks." His voice pitches even higher. "From Drink Dishit soda drinks." People stand up again and clap. "Lifetime free meals! Can you even imagine?"

Praises, claps, and moans as if they all won the lottery. The crowd goes crazy. What's with people's unconditional appreciation for food?

Again, the Duchess feels the need to comply and smile to her fans.

"And who do you thank for this?" The Pillar points up at the Duchess, who forcefully waves back to the appreciative audience. "You've gotta love Britain!" The Pillar's voice is barely audible among the crowd's praise. The Drury Lane Theatre turned into one great chaotic food market.

"Enjoy all the food you can eat." The Pillar raises his voice as much as possible in this *madfest*. "Enjoy all cholesterol, all the bad crabs, all the sugar and saturated fat! Get fat, people of Britain. Sugar your bellies. Beer away your minds. Forget about your Bill of Rights. Here is your Bill of Disease. Buy a ticket for your loon cancer. It's awesome to be insane!"

The Pillar, out of breath, taps his hat at the Duchess, who smiles in the face of the enemy. That fake politician smile.

The Pillar sits down, adjusts his clothes, and says, "Well, that was something." He smiles at me. I have to admit, I smile back. He might be a killer. He might be devious, and plagued by a lot of conspiracy theories, but I can't help but laugh. "So why were we here, again?"

Chapter 36

The play is actually entertaining, full of laughs and quirky moments. The acting is superb, very believable, and the production is top notch. They start with the "Down the Rabbit Hole" chapter where Alice meets the rabbit who is chubby and small and very funny. I have to admit the costumes are excellent enough that if you just buy into the fantasy, you wouldn't think of them as human actors portraying animals anymore.

I do squirm a bit in my seat when a mirror comes into the scene. Thank God we're sitting in the middle of the auditorium, far enough that the mirror has no effect on me.

"That Alice is horrible," the Pillar mumbles. "In the real book, she wore yellow, not blue. Blue is Disney's doing."

"You hate Disney."

"What makes you think that?" he whispers. "Jafar from *Aladdin* is my hero."

The next chapter, "The Pool of Tears," is superbly portrayed. There is an actual flood of water taking place on stage. I have no idea how they do it. The Pillar raises a suspicious eyebrow, as if telling me something is fishy here.

Still, the acting is amazing. The songs are enchanting. I like how the play is presented in a comedic way, not the morbid Alice world I live in.

The "Caucus Race" chapter follows. It's hilarious. When they start to dance in place, the Pillar can't resist moving his feet and cane to the music.

When the caterpillar chapter plays, the Pillar squirms in his seat. "That's not me," he mumbles. "Absolutely not."

Then he sits back and watches chapters four and five without much interest. He says he never liked those chapters.

Midway, the curtains pull to a close, announcing a break. Lights turn on again. A few sellers offer drinks during the break. There is a loud ice cream boy walking around, offering it for free. He isn't much welcomed by the elders, but the kids adore him.

A few people hurry to the Pillar's seat, asking for autographs. I think they believe him to be the Duchess' spokesman. I tilt my head up; the Duchess is gritting her teeth, although cameras aren't giving her a break to breathe.

The curtains pull open again, and now we're in for the much-loved "Pig and Pepper" chapter.

I don't know what is supposed to be so great about it. It's lame and boring. The Duchess, portrayed by an actress with brilliant makeup, is mad at her cook in this scene. Her cook, a peculiarly tall actor, even taller with the toque on his head, loves pepper in the strangest ways. He keeps adding pepper in the food and enjoys watching the Duchess' guests choking. Then he throws pepper in the air, chanting, "Peppa! More peppa!"

The crowd finds it amusing, actually.

Maybe I am not just in the mood, now that we have waited too long with no appearance of the Muffin Man. I look to my left, and the Pillar is as bored and puzzled as me. Are we here just to watch a play? It looks like we followed a wrong lead all along.

I take a deep breath and continue watching the performance on stage. Suddenly, someone is sitting on my right side. He grabs my hand and squeezes it, but I don't panic. It's a warm hand that I know and trust.

It's the ice cream boy. It's Jack Diamonds.

Chapter 37

"Hey," he whispers, sliding down in his chair and tightening the ice cream cap on his head. "I was thinking."

I say nothing. I am happy he is there. It's illogical. It doesn't make sense, but I can't fight the feeling.

"About what I said about marrying you," he says. "I can't."

"Why?" I raise an eyebrow, whispering, pretending to be surprised.

"It's not because I don't like you," he says. "I told you I am mad about you."

"You said that before, Jack."

"Saying it every morning won't express how I really feel." He squeezes my hand. "But it's just...I'm not ready for marriage."

I act upset. "You think you're too young?" I whisper.

"I am too poor, but that's not the reason," he says. "They fired me from Oxford University today, so I practically have no future now."

"Why did they fire you?" A smile sticks to my face and promises not to leave me as long as Jack is nearby.

"It's silly," he says. "They said I was dead. Can you believe that?"

I shrug and pull my hand away. I feel guilty when I hear this. Why does he keep bringing up the subject?

"No." His eyes moisten when I pull my hand away. "I'm not really dead. They just think that. How can I be dead? I am here talking to you. What bothers me is that they said that my name isn't Jack, which is really absurd."

"Then you're not fired. They can't fire you without getting your name right," I suggest.

"I know. I am not giving up, trust me. I will do my best to become a great man and deserve you."

"Selling 'Ice Scream' sounds like a start," I tease, easing my aching heart.

"I did try racing in France, but it didn't work," he says. "It's like I don't know what I really want yet."

"I know the feeling." I pull his hands back. He seems the happiest boy on earth.

"Alice." His voice gets softer. "Don't bother with me. It's you that matters."

"Why do you say that?"

"Just listen. I don't think you know what you are capable of." He holds both of my hands, and his look in my eyes intensifies. "Trust me. You have no idea. I know it's a bumpy road, but you will be all right." His eyes sparkle as his gaze scans every part of my face adoringly. I think he is about to kiss me.

Just before he does, the Pillar interrupts and asks whom I am talking to.

"It's Jack." I sigh. Bad timing, Pillar. Very bad timing.

"Who's Jack?"

"You know who," I grunt.

"Ah, the boy who is not there," the Pillar says, watching the show with interest. "I assume he is on your right side now."

"He is."

"Tell him I said hi, because I can't see him," the Pillar says. "Tell him I wonder if he'll still be there when the light turns on."

"I will be," Jack says, finally confronting him. "You shouldn't walk with this man, Alice." Jack squeezes my hand.

Silence steals my breath away. I am still confused about the Pillar's reaction to Jack. I am also heart-warmed by Jack wanting to become a better man to marry me.

Then the silence breaks when the glaring spotlights from the stage are directed toward me. When I look up, the man hosting the play is talking to me.

"Hey, miss," he says in the echoing microphone.

I say nothing, freaked out by the sudden and unexplainable attention.

"Yes, you." He points my way. "Are you even watching the show?"

The crowd laughs.

"We've chosen you to kindly approach the stage," the host says. "I believe you haven't heard us."

"Why?"

"This is the part of the show the reviewers said is the most refreshing. The 'Pig and Pepper' chapter," the man explains. "We select a girl from the crowd to portray Alice for a short scene. Amateur improvisation. You haven't had any kind of acting lesson before, have you?"

"No." I shrug.

"Fabulous," he says. "It's really going to be fun. Would you mind approaching the stage?" The man stretches a welcoming arm.

The crowd encourages me to go.

"No thank you," I say. I am not going to do some acting improvisation on stage on my fifth day out in the real world.

"Yes!" The Pillar stands up and encourages the crowd to clap their hands. "She will come." He pulls me up, sneering at me.

Finally, I get the message. The Pillar thinks this is the part where we meet the Muffin Man. Come to think of it, he might be right. Why would the host choose me to get on stage? It's too much of a coincidence.

"I'm her uncle," the Pillar says. He needs no other introduction to the crowd. "She doesn't go anywhere without me, which means I will approach the stage with her."

"Hmm..." The host sighs. "If she is going to play Alice, who do you suppose to play, then?"

"I'll play the doorknob," the Pillar says.

The crowd goes nuts, laughing.

"I always wanted to be the doorknob." The Pillar smiles like a child again. "You know, the doorknob Alice has to talk to when she is crossing the Pool of Tears."

"And I am her husband." Jack appears. "I mean, her boyfriend. I mean, I am Jack. I could play...hmm...Jack. Jack of Diamonds," he stutters, uncomfortable with the many faces looking at him.

I take my time to hear the crowd's reaction to Jack. They see him, or no? Come on. They saw him as an ice cream boy before. Why not see him now?

A long, long moment passes before the host says, "Why not. You may approach the stage." The man turns his back to us and waves his finger.

My heart drops to the floor. I want to know if he sees Jack.

A few steps in, the man turns back, annoyed by our slow reaction. "Hurry, we have limited stage time. Come on stage, the three of you."

Chapter 38

Performing stage, Drury Lane Theatre, London

I hold Jack's hand as we get on stage. The Pillar walks behind us, avoiding my sharp looks. I still don't understand why he wants me to think Jack doesn't exist. All those audience members can't be wrong.

Once on stage, I am dazzled again with the accurate reality up there. It's a huge stage, but everything feels so real. The trees leading to house of the Duchess, where we're supposed to meet her and her insane cook, smell just like normal trees do. When I reach out to touch them, the host offensively slaps my hands and tells me to concentrate on the play. He also orders the Pillar and Jack to wait by the curtains until he figures out their roles.

"My uncle could play the Cheshire Cat," I tell the host, grinning with joy at the Pillar. If he still pretends Jack doesn't exist, this is my chance to get back at him. I know it's childish, but I'd rather call it mad.

"Don't be silly, Alice." The Pillar tries to keep his posture.

"Actually, it would be fun," Jack says to the host. "With the right cat costume, the audience will love it."

"Agreed." The host hands the Pillar the cat costume. The Pillar squirms at even thinking about wearing the skin of his cruelest enemy.

I can't help but smile. A little revenge would make him not lie to me again.

"If you come near me, I will kill you, cook you, and eat you with a whole lot of pepper," the Pillar growls. "Give it to the brilliant Jack," he says, still not pointing at him.

"So, you *do* see Jack," I say.

"Of course. Of course," he mutters. "Now get going with the play."

Jack wears the cat outfit, thinking maybe acting is the career he should try. The host gives me a blonde wig to wear to play Alice. When I ask him what I should do exactly, he says I could improvise on the scene in the book where Alice enters the Duchess' house and meets her pepper-obsessed cook.

"But if you want to stay true to the book, there is a baby in the scene as well." The Pillar's inquisitive tone is unmistakable. He does believe something bad is going to happen in this scene.

"Well, we did have a baby," the host said. "But human rights groups prohibited kids under seven acting on stage until the Watermelon Murders are over."

"Understandable." The Pillar peeks upward, probably at Margaret Kent's balcony. The curtains block the view from where we stand.

I think about the actress who'll be playing the Duchess' part. Does she have any idea the real Duchess is watching the play?

Is that why Margaret Kent is here?

"Shall we begin?" The host talks to the actors, including the Duchess actress and the tall cook actor, whose long black hair is blocking his eyes. He seems very obedient and calm, though. "Outstanding," the host says as he orders the curtains pulled. "Let the madness begin."

Chapter 39

The pulled curtain permits the bright light pooling in. Here on the stage, all I see is an infinite source of brightness, almost blinding my eyes. It feels like each actor is entering a new world of fantasy all of a sudden. It's almost like another realm.

My eyes shut for a moment. I can't see the audience's faces with this kind of light. I merely see wavy silhouettes sitting down there. I take a deep breath and open my eyes. The stage reminds me of the Mush Room somehow. I think this is what they call stage fright.

But it actually works. The actress portraying the Duchess, wearing a silly oversized hat, plays her part well. Obnoxiously entertaining. The crowd loves her.

I start saying all kinds of nonsense, partially memorized from the book. I act freely without intimidation. The stage has a certain magic to it. It's like singing alone in the shower and letting the trickling water camouflage your horrible voice.

My inner fear spreads from something else. Something I can't explain yet. It's probably the Pillar's fear that worries me. I peek at him, standing askew near the curtain, like a detective looking for a lead to a crime that will happen in the future.

What in God's name could go wrong on the stage?

I keep on acting. People don't respond much to my sentences, as if I am not there. But I am not complaining. They are immensely entertained by the Duchess. It's also funny how I am not supposed to be acting. The scene we're portraying supposedly has happened to me in Wonderland.

Oh, my. Oh, the paradoxical madness.

Jack jumps in the scene, curls his flexible body on the cook's table, and meows the Cheshire part. Jack is hilarious, like always. I hear the audience clap. My hand itches, wanting to clap too. Jack's ease with nonsense is charming, and he seems to have the talent for acting.

Then comes the cook's part.

He is a tall, interesting guy, different than as portrayed in *Alice in Wonderland*. Other than being tall and having his black hair fall down and cover his eyes, he is a bit scary for such a comedic event.

Uniquely dressed, I must say.

I turn back to the Pillar to see if he has his eyes on the cook. The Pillar does stare at him. He doesn't like him at all. I look back to see what's so odd about the cook.

Then I see it.

The cook wears a double-breasted white jacket, like all cooks do. Except this one looks like a straitjacket backwards.

Chapter 40

I swallow hard when I see the straightjacket. Is it supposed to be an artistic touch from the costume designer? The cook was mad in Lewis' book, obsessed with pepper and having a bad temper.

But the straitjacket also implies the possibility of a man who's just escaped an asylum.

The Pillar rushes onto the stage and interferes with the scene. Since this is the most improvised chapter, it's no big deal. He nears me and talks in my ear. It's obvious he wants to tell me something about the cook. I can't hear him, and I don't know how to weave this into the act.

"And who are you, strangely dressed man?" the Duchess says obnoxiously.

"Shut up, ugly lady," the Pillar says. "I'm the doorknob. Everyone knows that."

The audience laughs and claps hysterically. It buys the Pillar time to tell me, "The Cook!"

"I know," I say. "There is something wrong about him."

"Let's see what he is up to." The Pillar points his cane. "Why is hiding his eyes with his hair?"

"He might be the Cheshire," I shriek.

"That's not the Cheshire," the Duchess says, thinking we're acting. "That's my cook. He has an obsession with pigs and pepper."

"Shut up, hag!" I say. "We're trying to solve a crime here."

Why doesn't anyone laugh at my jokes?

"Peppa!" The cook acts furious, pulling jars of pepper from under the table. "More peppa!" He starts pouring ridiculous amounts into a boiling cauldron.

I realize the boiling water in the cauldron is real. Shouldn't this endanger the actors? The cook is definitely the Cheshire. I look at the Pillar for confirmation, but he is in a haze of confusion.

Maybe we're both just paranoid.

As the cook pours the pepper, a few kid actors run into the scene and ask the Duchess for food. I know for sure this isn't part of the real script of Alice in Wonderland. But nothing has exactly followed the book so far.

"Go away, you obnoxious, filthy children!" The Duchess kicks one of kids away. The boy rolls on his stomach, aching. Those guys act brilliantly. It's so believable.

"Pigs for the children," the cook announces, and holds a baby pig in one hand. It's a real pig. "Do you want me to cook it for you, along with some spicy peppa?"

"Yes!" the children plead. "We're hungry. We haven't eaten in days."

Suddenly, I can't help but notice the children's clothes look exactly like in my vision. But it makes sense. The play portrays Victorian times, so I shouldn't be suspicious about it.

The Pillar still watches the cook closely.

Another unexpected thing happens when a woman, acting as the Queen of Hearts, bursts onto the stage. She is short and chubby and wears a joker's outfit. She holds an axe triple her size.

"Off with all your heads," she shouts. "Horrible children eating the food in my kingdom."

Even the Duchess acts horrified by the Queen.

"Pardon me, my Queen," the cook says. "Could I use the axe to chop off my pig's head? I need to cook it for the children." Then he says, in an unnecessary way, "Peppa! More peppa!"

"What is this?" the Pillar asks me. I have never seen him offended by nonsense like this before. But honestly, this is way crazier than I thought it would be. "What's going on?"

We're hardly part of the act anymore. The crowd loves every bit of this mishmash of characters.

"I can't give you my axe," the Queen of Hearts tells the

cook. "But I can chop the pig's head for you." The grin on her face is deeply disturbing to me. Of course, none of the audience can see it this far.

Is the Cheshire also the Queen of Hearts?

The cook holds the pig heartlessly from its feet. The poor animal struggles with its head upside down. It sneezes painfully because of the pepper.

"Put the pig down!" I shout. This not acting anymore. What the heck is this? "This play is over. Put the poor pig down!"

Instead of backing me up, the crowd boos at me.

"Show it to me," the Queen of Hearts orders the cook. He nears the kicking pig down to here so Her Majesty's short existence can reach it.

And then...

Then...

The unbelievable happens, the sort of thing that breaks all barriers between real and unreal.

The Queen of Hearts swings her axe and chops off the pig's head.

My head processes the scene in slow motion. It's too horrifying for my mind to digest it in normal speed.

The axe chops off the pig's head, which blobs down into the hungry boiling water in the cauldron.

I have never witnessed a crowd love such a performance.

Mouth agape, I feel something hot splash at my face. I felt it once the Queen chopped off the head, but I only register it when it trickles down my chin. I rub my face with my hands and raise them in front of my eyes.

It's the pig's blood.

This stage show is happening for real.

Chapter 41

I am stiffened, cemented, and chained by the cruelty of what looks like normal people, be it actors or the crowd.

The Queen of Hearts grins and starts to chop off the kids' heads. The kids start to stab the Duchess. The cook doesn't hesitate to boil whatever ends up in his cauldron—pig, heads, and even the Duchess' leg, chopped off by a kid.

Still stiffened, Jack holds me tight. Whatever he says is scattered into a million pieces. I think I lost my hearing.

I am pulled away by the Pillar and Jack. They are getting me off the stage. When I try to peek back over their shoulders, the Pillar grips my head tightly between his hands. He doesn't want me to see what's going on there. The shock value might be too high for me to tolerate.

We hurry down the steps and run away. The crowd doesn't understand yet. The crowd praises and hails. They are all standing in ovation now. I wonder how they will feel when one real spatter of blood reaches them. They still think it is all acting.

As I look at them, my hearing comes back. Their sound is deafening.

"Come on," the Pillar says. "We have to go!"

Near the exit door, I try to make any sense of what just happened. Why would the Cheshire do this? Just to drive me mad? It's not holding up. Something huge is missing.

The answer comes to me faster than I thought.

The crowd suddenly stops clapping, and some of them shriek.

When I stop the Pillar from exiting and turn around, I see them all staring with trembling bodies at the stage. It's the cook they are looking at. He is standing tall on the stage. All alone now. His double-breasted jacket is almost completely red from the blood of all those he killed.

It seems like he killed everyone, bearing two glinting

knives his hands. I haven't noticed before that his trousers are a black and white pattern, like a chessboard. His eyes are still covered with his wavy hair.

The cook isn't talking, but his presence is strong. I am not sure if the crowd realized what's going on yet.

Silently, the cook pulls out a few jars of pepper. Those are different from the one he used before. He sets them in order at the cauldron's edge, like a scientist meticulously preparing for an experiment.

An epidemic of sorts comes to my mind. My heart pounds to the realization that the stage massacre, with all its gore, isn't the epic finale to his work of madness yet.

The crowd's breathing is almost absent; they have finally registered the reality of what is going on.

"Pepper," the cook says. This isn't his theatrical voice from the act. It's a hoarse voice, coming from someone who doesn't speak much. Someone who has kept to himself for years, locked in an asylum, awaiting his chance to break loose. "This pepper in my hand will make you sneeze."

A few forced chuckles scatter across the crowd, stopped immediately by the rise of his hand and the pursing of his lips.

This man isn't the Cheshire. This man is pure darkness. Why is he doing this?

"This time you will sneeze differently," the cook lectures. The hollowness of his voice fills the auditorium. It's like talking to a god. There's nothing you can argue with. "Please approach, madam."

A woman in the front row is pushed by the rest of the crowd toward the cook. One sheep sacrificed for the safety of many.

The cook tells her to stop a few feet away from him. He opens his jar of pepper and pours some in the air near her.

There is a long moment of waiting before the woman sneezes.

Once.

No one is laughing this time.

Then twice.

No one utters a word.

Then she can't control it. She sneezes and sneezes until she starts shivering and collapses to the floor.

"Sneezed to death," the Pillar murmurs.

Before the crowd panics, the cook holds the jar up high. "All doors in the theatre are locked." His voice still fills the place. "Everyone here is going to die here tonight. This isn't a warning. It's a fact that the theatre's surveillance camera will witness it for the world to see."

Everyone goes silent again. Me too. Running and knocking him down crosses my mind, but he already has the jars open in his hands. All he needs is to give them a little shake and dance.

I look for Jack, but he is gone again. Maybe he was never there really. It still isn't fair.

Behind me, the Pillar holds my hand. I am perplexed. Are we really going to die? Is this the end to the whole madness? Death by pepper?

"Of course, your beloved Margaret Kent is gone." The cook points at the empty balcony upward. "People like her always get away," he says. A bitter smile curves his lips. I notice a tinge of sadness in his last words. Is this cook the Duchess' real cook from Wonderland, now used like a puppet by the Cheshire to create chaos in the world?

"Before you have to die, you need to see this." The cook kicks a few things from behind the cauldron with his foot. Something rolls down before the stage.

A watermelon.

Finally, we realize who he is. We're staring at the Muffin Man himself. The mysterious man responsible for the watermelon murders.

The Muffin Man turns his head toward me and the Pillar. "You fell for the bait, Professor Pillar," the cook says. "You and your Wonderland apprentice are going to die too. Only the Real Alice would know her way out of this."

The shock value reaches its zenith. Although he hides his eyes, the smirk on his face is made for us. Somehow, he sees us. Even the Pillar next to me feels like a fool.

"He tricked us into coming here to die?" The Pillar is as shocked as me. I never thought I'd see that day.

The crowd around us begins running aimlessly, like in a Caucus Race.

The cook, I mean the Muffin Man, puffs his pepper in the air, like a madman would spread the Black Death's disease onto the world.

Everyone sneezes around me. The effect is fast and abrupt.

One sneeze.

Two sneezes.

Three sneezes, and if you last long enough for the fourth, you're already eligible for a death certificate.

Am I really going to die? Didn't Jack promise he'd die for me? Aren't I supposed to find a way out if I am the Real Alice?

It saddens me that those who haven't died from the sneezing yet are about to die under the scrambling feet of others trying to escape. Some people try to break the locked doors, but they are made of steel and locked with digital codes from outside. I wonder if the guards know about what's happening here inside the auditorium. Is it possible they are involved in the crimes, or did the Cheshire possess each one of them?

Now, I'm left waiting for the first sneeze to hit me, wondering why I ever left the comfort of my cell in my asylum.

I admit it. There is comfort in madness.

Unexpectedly, my moistened eyes meet the Pillar's. I never thought I'd see that look on his face. He is no less shocked than I am, staring at the endless sneezing people all around us. Dying by sneeze is as humiliating as it is terrifying.

"Well." The Pillar considers his last words. "It did cross my mind that I would die of hiccupping, but sneezing?"

He looks angry that he has been fooled by the Cheshire and the Muffin Man.

Suddenly, I realize I have a last wish. "Pillar." I grab him by his collar. "I need to know who Jack is before I die."

"Don't worry about your boyfriend, Alice," he says, still looking over my shoulder. "You're going to meet him in a few minutes when we die."

My hand drops like a dead thing from his collar. I'm not really sure of anything. This is another Catch-22, I guess. If I die now, I haven't been mad at all. What a way to prove one's sanity.

"We have been seduced to solve a trail of puzzles that only lead us to our own deaths," are the Pillar's last words, just before I experience my first sneeze.

Chapter 42

Queen's chamber, Buckingham Palace, London

The Queen of England sipped her five o'clock tea while sitting in a bamboo chair in her private garden among her Welsh corgis. She wore her solid red coat, matching her red hat with white feathers and few flowers wrapping it. She didn't like her tea much though.

A few hours earlier, she had been bored to death, taking selfies of herself back in her chamber. Selfies sucked when you barely knew how to smile, she had thought. So she took snapshots of her bowls of Brazilian nuts, which looked even more delicious in high-resolution photos.

Now, sipping her tea in her balcony, she was waiting for someone. The Queen hated waiting, but things had gotten out of hand. She needed to fix them by meeting a few people.

Another sip reminded her of how she missed the Mad Hatter's tea. This Twinings tea she was sipping was nothing compared to his genius invention—and oh, those mad parties.

But those were times gone past. She wasn't even sure if the Mad Hatter would be on her side if the Wonderland Wars really took place.

She wondered if the wars were necessary. But then, people loved wars, whether they admitted it or not. Wars were always profitable and a great release for years of suppressed anger, and the gushing of blood.

But the Wonderland Wars weren't going to be like that. Blood and gore were merely the background of their war. It was a war of minds. A war of truth. More than anything, a war of insanity. Those who'd stay sane long enough usually won these kinds of wars.

The Queen sipped that poor tea again and spat it out on the floor near one of her dogs. Not Bulldog. It was Maddog, her favorite female corgi. She had been cured from her constipation and was in good health again.

Maddog licked the tea obediently from the floor, then panted pleadingly. Maddog had eyes the color of pale pearls.

"No more nuts today," the Queen declared. "They're addictive and they cost me a fortune. And you get constipated."

Maddog looked disappointed.

"I apologize for being late, Majesty." Margaret Kent arrived in her grey business suit. She wore a twenty-four-carat blood-diamond ring on her left hand today. It didn't distract from the grumpiness in her surgically enhanced face today. The beautiful Parliament woman looked overly exhausted.

"Apology denied." The Queen merely waved her white-gloved hand. "You're lucky I can't chop your head off," she muttered with fake, super-white teeth. "I still need you."

Margaret Kent sat next to her, unable to look Her Majesty in the eyes. "I know the situation got out of hand," she began. "I never thought the Cheshire would go that far."

"He wouldn't if he hadn't gotten his grin back." The Queen poured herself another cup of tea, knowing she'd eventually spit it out like the last. "That was a terrible mistake. You should have stopped him."

"It's all because of Alice Wonder," Margaret said. "She gave the Cheshire his grin back to save some poor girl's life."

"That's not *the* Alice." The Queen reached for a spoon, disgusted by a little stain on it.

"How do you know, Majesty?" Margaret asked. "Are you sure?"

"I am sure." The Queen stared at the spoon, thinking of chopping some servants' heads off.

"But Carroll's potion left us oblivious of her looks," Margaret reasoned. "He protected her from us this way."

"True." The Queen called for Maddog to come lick the spoon clean for her. "But Carroll's potion didn't leave the Real Alice unable to recognize who *we* are." Maddog licked the spoon religiously and the Queen put it back in the cup, stirring two cubes of sugar inside. "If she was *the* Alice, she'd have recognized us and killed us all."

"It's a plausible assumption," Margaret said. "But there is the incident of this Alice killing her friends in a school bus. She might have lost her memory because of it."

"If she did, she should have already regained her memory under the Pillar's influence." The Queen sipped her tea.

"I doubt the Pillar doesn't know what he is doing," Margaret said. "If he picks a girl and thinks she is Alice, he has enough evidence to back it up."

"Of course, the Pillar knows what he is doing." The Queen wondered why her tea had dog saliva in it this time. "He is playing games with us."

"I am not following, Majesty."

"Damn this tea!" The Queen spat the tea back on the ground. Maddog licked it. "The Pillar needed to have a powerful weapon against us. What better to draw us to the illusion that he has found Alice?"

"You mean he picked just any girl to play us?"

"Not just any girl." The Queen poured tea in a newer cup again, hoping it had no dog saliva in it this time. "He was very smart about the girl he picked. Think of it: an insane girl who killed her friends and used to think she was Alice from Wonderland. Almost every poor girl in this country dreams of being Alice so she could eat big mushrooms and grow stronger and bigger. Pillar picked a troubled, friendless, mad girl, then used her complicated history and insanity to make up a cute little story. Also, he needed to find a lonely and confused girl so he could persuade her that she is the Real Alice."

"So, we shouldn't worry about the Pillar?"

"You should worry about the mess happening in this

country!" The Queen reached for the same spoon but stopped. She decided it was better to use a newer spoon to make sure everything was clean this time. "A head stuffed in a football in front of millions of watchers? Then watermelons stuffed with kids' heads? And now a mass murder at Drury Lane Theatre?" She stared at the new spotless spoon and saw it was definitely clean. A smile filled her face as she started to use it to stir the sugar. "A murder by peppers?" she asked Margaret. "What the bloody bollocks of hell!"

"It won't happen again, I promise," Margaret said. "The Cheshire helped the Muffin Man escape the asylum. He taught him all the dirty tricks and backed him up with the killings. He used the Muffin Man's anger against him, and against us."

"The Muffin Man has always been angry since what happened to him in Wonderland." The Queen said.

"Not just Wonderland, Majesty," Margaret began, but was cut off by the Queen's waving finger.

"Enough," Apparently, the Queen didn't want to delve further into the subject. "I don't want to remember any of this." She decided to sip her tea when she met Maddog's pleading eyes again. The Queen lowered her hand and let poor Maddog sip from the teacup. If she couldn't give her more nuts, maybe a few sips of tea would make her favorite dog happy. "You should have killed the Muffin Man, I mean your cook, back in Wonderland," she told Margaret as she leaned back in her chair.

Margaret sighed. "I should have." She tried her best to avoid the Queen's blaming eyes.

"The Muffin Man has to be stopped this time, Margaret." The Queen said.

Margaret nodded twice, saying nothing, looking at her feet.

"Killing people is merely the worst he can do. You know what the real threat of the Muffin Man is." The Queen elaborated.

"I know." Margaret said. "He could expose — "

"Shhhh," the Queen warned her again. "I said I don't even want to talk about it. That's what the Cheshire wants. He wants to expose that secret you were about to discuss. The people of Britain, and the whole world, shouldn't know about our secrets."

"Damn the Cheshire!" Margaret sighed. "I shouldn't have used him as an assassin, or he wouldn't have known so much. But I had a lot of dirty work to take care of. Sudan, Libya, and — "

"I said enough." The Queen began to lose her patience. "You make it sound like we're the only ones who take care of our dirty business. You think the Americans don't do the same? You think all those third world countries don't do the same? If you want to rule, you have to sacrifice a few things."

"You're right." Margaret pantomimed zipping her mouth. "It's just that I'm sometimes confused which side the Cheshire is on. Which side are *we* on? And the Pillar, whose damn side is he on?"

"We don't need to know any of this now." The Queen sipped her tea with unmatched delight. "No Wonderland War is possible without the Real Alice being found. All we need to do is catch the Muffin Man. I have a clear idea how." The Queen licked her lips, offended by the dog saliva present in the tea again and again.

"How, My Majesty?"

Disgusted by the taste of tea, The Queen stood up and threw the teacup against the wall. Margaret ducked to avoid the flying cup and its saucer while Maddog ran to lick the tea. "Bloody awful tea, smells of dogs all the time!" The Queen roared.

Margaret wondered if she should have better left. But then Queen took a deep breath and calmed down a little. "To stop the Muffin Man, you have to find the Cheshire. Let's make a deal with him. Let's promise him a piece of the pie."

Chapter 43

Alice Wonder's house, 7 Folly Bridge, Oxford

The girl at the door had tears in her eyes. She faced Alice's mother, unable to utter the words coherently.

"What happened?" Alice's mother shook her, almost predicting what the girl was about to say.

"I'm sorry, but your daughter, Alice Wonder, died yesterday," the girl announced. Alice's mother sank to her knees, holding on to the girl's hands, as if she had always feared her daughter would die this young.

"How did she die?" asked Edith, Alice's older sister. Her tone was inquisitive and disbelieving. She stood a few steps shy of the threshold, unimpressed by her mother's sentiments.

"She was present in the Drury Lane Theatre when the audience died of pepper poisoning."

"There is no such thing as 'pepper poisoning,'" Lorina, Alice's other sister, grunted, smoothening her fingernails behind Edith. Her sister's death seemed unimportant to her. She wanted to know, though. "The audience were poisoned with something that *looked* like pepper."

"It's not like that." Edith tapped her sister's hand so she would stop smoothening her fingernails. The sound of it made her go crazy. "They died from sneezing."

"You can't die from sneezing, Edith." Lorina rolled her eyes. "That's like saying a person could die from too much makeup."

"If you can die from hiccupping and laughing, you can die from sneezing," Edith said, not taking her eyes off the stranger girl at the door.

"Shut up!" their mother yelled. "Your sister is dead."

"Hallelujah!" Lorina rolled her eyes again.

"We're not sure, Lorina. Don't go on celebrating yet," Edith said. "Why wasn't Alice in the asylum? Did she escape?" she asked the girl at the door.

"And where to? Theatre?" Lorina felt the urge to roll her eyes for the third time.

"Unless she was the crazy cook who sneezed the audience to death." Edith snickered and high-fived Lorina.

"She wasn't the cook," the young girl at the door said politely. "She is dead. I'm sorry."

"Are you here to send us a death certificate?" Edith asked.

"No, I'm afraid that is something you will have to do yourself after you confirm her death at the morgue."

"I'm not going to any morgue," Lorina said. "I just had my hair done."

"I have an appointment to...get my hair done," Edith said.

"I will go." The mother stood up feebly.

"But I'm not here for that, madam," the girl at the door said. "I'm here to collect a photo of Alice Wonder for the obituary, which the Theatre Royal will take care of."

"I will get you one," the mother offered.

"I'd prefer to fetch one myself, if you don't mind," the girl said. The two sisters threw her a long, suspicious look. "There is a hefty compensation for you if I pick an appropriate photo that lives up to the standards of our theatre," the girl added.

"Oh," Edith said, neglecting the absurdness of the girl's request. "Why didn't you say so? Please come in. Do you happen to know how much the theatre will pay us?"

Chapter 44

Alice Wonder's room in her mother's house

The mysterious girl asked to be alone in the room. To ensure the two sister's compliance, she gave them a reward ticket: a lifetime of free food stamps at most of Britain's junk food stores and a sincere apology on behalf of the Theatre Royal for the death of their daughter.

Edith, who was a bit chubby, with a few freckles on her face, couldn't hide her excitement. Food for life? Now she wouldn't have to worry about the budget she spent on Snicker Snacker double bars, Queen of Hearts Tarts, or the latest Meow Muffins.

Lorina, on the other hand, said she couldn't use the ticket much, since she had to take care of her figure—and, of course, her delicate fingernails. She said she would invite all of her friends and make them owe her. She believed it was always good to have her friends owe her.

Alice's mother said she would use the food to give to the poor and ask them to pray for her dead daughter.

"Insane daughter," Edith corrected her mother. "The fact that she is dead doesn't mean she wasn't insane. If bad people go to hell, and good to heaven, where do the insane go?" She thought it was a funny line, and she laughed at her own joke.

"Was she really insane?" the girl from the theatre asked.

"Since she was seven years old," Lorina said, unsatisfied with the stain the ticket caused on her fingertips.

"Really? What happened?" the girl asked, about to enter Alice's room.

"We lost her when she was a kid," Edith said. "When she returned, she said she was..."

"Was what?" The girl was unusually curious.

"She thought she was Alice and said she had been to

Wonderland and back," Lorina replied. "She is insane, no doubt about it."

"You're not telling it like it is," Edith said. "Why are you hiding the best part of Alice's return?"

The girl from the theatre almost tiptoed. She definitely had to know about that part. "What was the best part?"

Lorina shrugged. Edith looked at her mother and back. Her eyes scanned the house as if to make sure there was no one listening. "When she returned, her dress was stained with blood." She craned her neck forward and almost whispered, "She also held a glinting kitchen knife, spattered with someone's blood, in her hand."

The girl's eyes widened. Either the sisters really hated Alice or they were telling the strangest truth. She decided she'd had enough of this family. Her mission here was precise. All she had was to accomplish it and get out of this madhouse as fast as she could.

Inside Alice's room, the girl didn't look for a photo of Alice. She looked for anything that had to do with Alice's friends, the accident, or Adam J. Dixon.

A few moments later, the girl was outside Alice's house, standing before the famous Iris Lake, which streamed out of the River Thames. It was famous for being where Lewis Carroll was inspired to write *Alice in Wonderland*.

The girl didn't know any of this. She had been paid to come here and fool the Wonder family so she could enter Alice's room. Mission accomplished. She picked up the phone and dialed a number.

Chapter 45

Tom Quad Garden, Christ Church, Oxford University, Oxford

Listening to the girl on the phone, I nod a couple of times and thank her. I hang up and lean back in the bank I am sitting on, gazing at the Tom Tower at Oxford University. The sky above is a grayish blue. Rain is trickling like hesitant tears on my face. I take a long breath as I fiddle with the sleeves of the pullover I had exchanged with the girl on the phone. She gave it to me, along with her shoes and pants, in exchange of my bloodstained theatre dress. *The dress is beautiful,* I remember her saying. *Blood can always be washed away.*

The rain keeps drizzling in Christ Church.

The few students in the garden shade themselves under the safety of the university's halls, leaving me almost alone in the middle. I am not going to move. I like the feel of trickling water on my skull. It helps me contemplate the things the girl on the phone just told me.

"Sometimes I ask myself, what if the door to Wonderland is hidden here inside the university?" The Pillar's voice resonates behind me. I didn't invite him, but he found me. "Imagine if the real rabbit hole were right beneath our feet." He sits next to me and leans forward. He rests his chin on his cane and stares at the Tom Tower like an obedient dog.

"How did you find me?" I ask.

"People tend to go to certain places when they feel lost," he says. "Places that resemble a god in many ways. Be it a father, a mother, a mentor, a lover, church, mosque, synagogue, or even a real god." He rubs his nose to resist sneezing, an aftereffect of the infinite amount of pepper we were exposed to in Drury Lane. Thank God we didn't sniff a lot of the pepper. "For a girl like you, who is in many ways a character in a book, your god is definitely the man who wrote it."

The Pillar is right, and I hate it when he is. I came here hoping I could meet Lewis through the small door in the Tom Tower. I came here to ask him about the meaning of the vision of Victorian England, and why he *"couldn't save them."* And if possible, I'd like to know how he managed to stay whimsical and optimistic in hard times like these. Maybe I could use his advice to face the cruel world I live in now.

"How did we escape the theatre?" I break the silence without looking at him, still staring at the Tom Tower.

"It depends on the last thing you remember." He leans back, both hands on his cane.

"I remember sneezing and then you puffed hookah smoke into my face. Then I think I..."

"Blacked out, that's right."

"What happened after I blacked out? How are we the only ones who managed to escape a locked theatre?"

"The same way I escape my locked cell in the asylum." I sense pride in his words.

"That's not an answer."

"It's not meant to be," he says. "The same way you weren't meant to escape my limousine after I saved you."

"I woke up in a dress stained with pig blood," I explain. "I felt awful and wanted to get away from everyone."

"Even me?"

"Especially you."

"Although I saved you from sneezing to death?"

"You're not doing it for me. There is some plan you have, and I don't care to know it anymore. I'd just like know how I am still alive."

"Why is it so important to know how?"

"To make sure I am not insane." I shrug. "To make sure all of this is really happening."

"The way I escape closed rooms is meant to stay a secret," he says. "I can't help you with it."

Dr. Truckle's assumption about the Pillar and Houdini seem plausible now. "Are you a magician, Professor Pillar?" I can't help but turn around and face him, chuckling at my own nonsensical question.

"What's magic but facts humans are oblivious to see?" He utters the words as if he were a poet quoting Shakespeare.

"Another one of your vague answers." I sigh, frustrated. "I should stop getting my answers from you. I know I will find them elsewhere if I ask the right person." I look back at the tower.

"Is that why you sent a girl to your mother's house to gather information about the bus incident?"

I am not surprised that he knows, but I don't care. I decide to keep silent.

"Did she find anything useful?"

"Photos of my friends, some of which she sent to my phone."

"Recognize anyone?"

"None. She also found endless scraps of paper with my handwriting."

"Special phrases?"

"'I can't go back to yesterday...'"

"'...because I was someone else then,'" he finishes.

"Over and over again. You want to tell me what that's about?"

He shakes his shoulders nonchalantly.

"What really bothers me, she found no evidence of my Tiger Lily in my room," I say. "I mean if I feel so attached to that flower, wouldn't she at least find a photo or a book about flowers?"

"Forget about your flower," he says. "Did she find any photos of Jack?"

"Yes. Very nice photos. We were in love." I hold a single tear back, pressing harder on the phone.

"How do you know you were in love?"

"The way we looked at each other. It's the way only

lovers do."

"Just that?"

"You wouldn't understand," I say. "There is one photo where Jack and I are at an *Alice in Wonderland* event, somewhere in Oxford, I believe."

"It's called the Alice Day," he says. "Usually celebrated on the 7th of July for a week. People wear everything Alice and eat a lot of tarts. The parade starts right there by the Alice Shop you visited last time down the street." He points beyond the gates of the university. "What about it?"

"I'm wearing an Alice outfit in the photo. Adam is wearing a" — I shrug — "Jack of Diamonds outfit, pretending to be one of the Queen's cards."

"I see." He drums his cane on the grass.

"Is that why I'm imagining Jack?" I turn back to face him. "Is the memory of that day so important to me that I imagined Adam resurrected as Jack? Is that true?"

"I thought you were sure he existed. A lot of other people saw him, too, didn't they?"

"But you never admitted seeing him."

"I pointed at Jack in the theatre and asked the host to make him wear the Cheshire costume, didn't I?"

"You may have been bluffing." I am guessing. "To get rid of the Cheshire's costume. Even so, why did you pretend you didn't see him before? Why did you say I was going to be with Jack in a few minutes if I died in the theatre?"

"Knowing Jack's true identity isn't going to make your life easier, Alice." He says it with all the confidence in the world.

"But you will tell me when this mission ends?"

"I can tell you now, if you want." He turns and dares my eyes.

I don't stare back. I didn't expect him to say that. My jaw drops. I have too many mixed feelings orbiting in my chest.

"I thought so," the Pillar says. "You're not ready to

know. It's typical of people to keep seeking answers they can't handle yet. Questions are easy. Everyone's got many. Answers are hard, and usually unlikable."

Again, I hate it when the Pillar is right. I close my eyes and take a deep breath. Delaying the truth a day or two isn't going to kill me. I am so afraid Jack is a figment of my imagination. I can't handle it if he is. Who has their boyfriend return from the dead? It's such a blessing, I can't deny.

In the darkness of my closed eyes, I glimpse a faint image of the homeless children in Victorian England. It urges me to open my eyes again and ask, "Now, tell me why you're really here."

"I know who the Muffin Man is, and the reason behind his killings."

I lean forward and stare directly at him. "I'm listening."

Chapter 46

"I didn't know the cook—I mean the Muffin Man—personally in Wonderland," the Pillar begins. "I didn't even know his name back then. It still puzzles me why they call him the Muffin Man. I think the Pepper Man fits better." He pauses. "Frankly, he was some nobody to me; a third-degree citizen, a middle-aged man with many kids, if I remember correctly."

"Third-degree citizen?"

"The lowest rank in Wonderland. We called them 'Galumphs.' Bloody mean, if you ask me," he says. "There was a rumor he had been one of the Queen's advisors, specializing in crops and farming. But I can't confirm that.

"My assumption is the Queen punished him, *galumphed* him, and sent him to work with the Duchess, who had always been Queen's favorite. But I'm not sure. I never visited the Duchess in Wonderland. I had always been friends with my mushrooms and hookah more than anything. Whatever the Muffin Man's story is, I believe Lewis knows it better."

"Do you at least know why he was obsessed with pepper, like it was mentioned in the book?"

"I have no idea," he says. "But what I'm about to tell you is a complicated story, so you have to bear with me and listen carefully." He stands up, stretches his arms, and enjoys the drizzle on his face. "Let's take a walk outside the university. I'd hate for you to spend your time out of the asylum sitting."

I comply. He reaches for my hand. I don't comply.

We walk slowly outside on St. Aldate's, saying nothing. It's as if he wants to enjoy the simple things in life for a few seconds. It does help me feel at ease.

The Pillar stops by some kids eating chocolate bars and asks for one. I notice most of these children are overweight, like the ones who died and the ones I saw in

Richmond Elementary School. I look up at other kids walking by. Most of them are a little overweight for their ages as well.

A young girl gives the Pillar a chocolate bar, but he returns it and asks for the *double bar.* "I want the Snicker-Snackers double bar. One for me, and one for my friend." He points at me and ruffles her curly hair.

We keep walking.

"You see this chocolate bar?" he asks. "This is a Snicker Snackers bar, just like Happy Tart Bars, Bojoom Bars, and all the other *Alice in Wonderland* candy products infesting the world lately."

"The Meow Muffin among the list," I remind him. "What about them?"

"Don't you think this bar is a little too big in both size and portion?"

"You're answering a question with a question. I'm not following."

"Right answers are found if you ask the right questions," he says, unhappy with me interrupting him. "Did you ever stop in front of a junk food store and wonder how many disadvantages this kind of food has?" He is dead serious. "All the exaggerated carbs, the saturated fat, and the oil used over and over again until it has lost its elasticity and natural color? Did you ever think this kind of food isn't much different from slow-poisoning yourself?"

"So?"

"So?" He asks this as if I am a dumb student, unable to understand the professor's lecture. "Did you ever research the ingredients of the hamburger you just ate, or ask what they inject into chickens to make them look so fat and delicious? Why the meat you bought feels so plastic you can't bite through it?"

Having known the Pillar for a while, I'm aware that he never talks in straight and clear sentences. I need to focus and read the truth between the lines. I am hoping this is leading somewhere.

"Actually, I did," I say. "Waltraud Wagner, the asylum's warden, gorges on such stuff all the time. Snacks, sweets, and stuff. She rarely eats a *real* meal of fruits or vegetables."

"I'm glad you did." He waves his cane higher and walks on. He glances at people as if he was sent down from heaven to inspect human stupidity. "Did any of the questions I just posed ever make you wonder about the government's role in all of this? How is it allowed to sell unhealthy food to a youth whose body desperately needs vitamins, healthy fat, and proteins, not an endless source of glucose and corn syrup?"

"I never thought of it, but now that you've mentioned it..."

"How about why there are only few commercials about vegetables, fruits, or natural foods?" He is like a train of unstoppable questions. "Why mostly chocolate, crackers, and fizzy drinks?"

I pull him by the hand and stop him. He complies. "What has any of this to do with the Muffin Man? What are you saying exactly?"

"This bar in my hand. Why is two pieces, Alice?" He taps it on his hand, a bit violently.

I read the cover. "Because it's for two people, not one."

"When was the last time you shared your Twinkie, Alice?" It's a rhetorical question, just like all the others. "The answer is 'almost never.'"

"Are you saying the Muffin Man is punishing us for allowing our children to grow fat at a young age, for letting them eat food that hurts them more than it helps them grow healthier?" I try to skip the lecture and get to the point.

"If you want to know the Muffin Man better, you need to study his surroundings." He holds me by the arms as if wanting to wake me up from sleepwalking. "Every killer, terrorist, and corrupted person you meet is a reflection of society. Look into the world around us and you will understand his insanity," he says. "You know why most terrorists and those who cause human destruction are never caught, Alice?"

For the first time, this isn't a rhetorical question. The Pillar expects me to answer it. It explains why the Wonderland Wars are beyond the reach of the police — the police who only follow physical evidence and logical procedure, dismissing the core method of catching a lunatic: knowing who he really is.

"Because in order to catch those madmen, we have to..." I look the Pillar in the eyes. It's a moment of epiphany to me. "We have to step into their shoes and live their insanity to know how they think."

The Pillar lets go of my arms and smiles. I am his smart and dedicated student now. He is a satisfied professor. He adds, "And be willing to live with the consequences of being exposed to such horrible minds."

"Are we done with the lecture now? Are you going to get to the point?"

He nods with closed eyes.

"Then tell me something," I say. "Tell me something that is an actual lead in this case."

"Gorgon Ramstein." The Pillar opens his eyes.

"What?"

"Professor Gorgon H. Ramstein."

Chapter 47

"Isn't that the man who owns the Fat Duck restaurants that are most famous for the mock turtle soup?" I ask, remembering Dr. Tom Truckle's obsession I with that soup?

"Yes, but he is much more than that," The Pillar says. "Gorgon Ramstein is an Oxford University professor who challenged a Fortune 500 company a few years ago, one of the world's biggest food manufacturers, to be precise."

"Go on."

"Years ago, trying to quadruple their profits, this high-profile company released this double chocolate bar," he says, pointing at the one in his hand. "One huge piece of hard candy, double its previous size, which had been big enough already that doctors advised against eating it a few time before."

"And?"

"Gorgon, specializing in Global Health and Development, scientifically proved this bar's drawbacks. Gorgon's proved that eating this bar for a whole year, say a bar per week, is nothing less than slow-poisoning yourself, and a strong reason for obesity for children. Thus, a slow death for the youth of Britain."

"I'm not getting —"

"Gorgon also proved that this bar messes with kids' brain cells and gets them to want more; they're addicted to the high amounts of sugar in it. These kids are just growing up; they are sensitive to everything."

"Did any one specialized authority look into Professor Ramstein's research?" This begins to interest me.

"Academically, everyone found his research plausible. The government, on the other hand, treated him as if he were the invisible man," he says. "Professor Ramstein filed a case against the food companies, based on his academically approved results."

"What was the verdict?"

"The court was persuaded by scientific research, and ordered the production of the huge bar to be stopped. They also fined the major company a hefty amount of millions of pounds," the Pillar replies. "A year later, the tycoon company tricked the court and re-released the sugar-infested bars as a *double* bar, half for each person," the Pillar says. "It was a clever way out, and legal. There was no conclusive evidence that half of the bar did any immediate damage. But we all know that once a kid gets his hands on that bar, he will eat it from head to toe. The double was only a hoax."

"And the older verdict?"

"It meant nothing," the Pillar says. "We were practically talking about a new product."

"What happened to Professor Ramstein?" I suppose all his should tie together in the end.

"He didn't give up. He filed a few other cases, but they were all useless because the older court's members had been replaced. The newer ones seemed to favor the food company all the way. The case was lost."

"Even though Britain scientifically backed up the dangers of the portion of the bar?"

"Of course not," the Pillar says. "Ramstein's research was noble, and most probably accurate, but in the insane world we live in you can't even prohibit smoking. Hell, there are countries in the world were killing hasn't been prohibited yet."

I can't seem to connect all of this to the Muffin Man, but I am sure the Pillar will eventually. Also, I find myself genuinely interested in the story. "Where is Professor Gorgon Ramstein now?" I ask.

"Where do you think, Alice?" The Pillar tilts his head and imitates the Cheshire's grin.

"Dead?" I resist clapping my hands on my mouth. "Assassinated by the Cheshire Cat?"

"They killed Ramstein's lawyer in a fabricated car

accident first," the Pillar says. "You know who ordered the assassination?"

"Margaret Kent." The words force themselves out of my mouth. The Pillar nods and I let out a long sigh, connecting the dots. Every awful thing is always threaded to the ugly Duchess somehow. "But why? Who is Margaret Kent protecting?"

"The same people who hired the Reds to chase us in the Vatican. The same people who protect and stand behind corruption in the world. The same people who profit from wars, famine, and poverty," he says. "I don't have a name for them, but The White Queen likes to call them 'those who walk the black tiles in the chessboard of life.' 'Black Chess' for short."

I take a moment to digest all of this. Is this really how the world outside works? Are all the bad guys connected and intertwined in a spider web of cruelty and deception? Are the few good ones who try to oppose them — I imagine Fabiola leading them — helpless and weakened? Of course, whose side the Pillar is on will always baffle me, but it seems irrelevant now.

"I have another question," I say. The sun is sinking to the weight of the Pillar's revelations. "Before I ask you what all of this has to do with the Muffin Man, I want to know the name of the company that sold the bar."

"Who else?" The Pillar straightens his back and rolls his cane a full vertical circle around his hand. "Muffit N Puffit, the same company that produced the Queen of Hearts Tarts and Meow Muffins."

"That's a lame name for an evil corporation that is almost secretly ruling the world."

"Of course," he agrees. "Muffit N Puffit are only a branch of the mother company, which is rarely mentioned and I think is operated by the most evil Wonderland Monsters, but that's way too soon to get into."

"Does the major corporation have a name?"

"What else, Alice?" he says. "Black Chess."

Chapter 48

"So, how is the Muffin Man related to all of this?" I manage to ask, finally.

"The Muffin Man thinks he is doing the world a favor," the Pillar says. "Like I said, I don't know his full background, but he is persuaded by the Cheshire to do this, so they expose us."

"Expose us?" I laugh.

"By us, I mean humans," the Pillar says. "The Cheshire wants to expose us to ourselves. Never heard of serial killers trying to wake up the world against committing the seven sins? A man bombing innocent civilians to prove a point? The world is full of this kind of madness."

"But the Cheshire didn't say anything about that—nor did the Muffin Man."

"I'm sure we will hear from them soon," the Pillar says. "Somehow they will explain the crimes and maybe ask humanity to repent or something. Who knows what goes on in this cat's head?"

Replaying this conversation in my head, I wonder about some of the Pillar's behavior. "Frankly, I don't trust you, Professor Pillar," I say as it starts to rain heavily. "You have been eating like crazy the past two days, doing crazy things related to food, and now you tell me the Muffin Man is punishing the world for letting their children eat deadly food." I spit some rain out. "Then you tell me all you know about Gorgon Ramstein, and I have no idea how you knew about it. You sound like you care about humanity while I know you don't give a damn. Are you expecting me to believe that you care about people?"

"Not at all," he says. "I don't give a Jub Jub about the world." He summons a buff man walking by, trying to shade himself from the rain. "Do I look like I give a Jub Jub about the world?"

"Jub Jub this." The man shows him the finger and

walks.

"You asked me about the Muffin Man and why he kills. I am just telling you, Alice." The Pillar turns to me, his eyes catching too many people staring at their phones at the same time. The activity makes me suspicious as well. But I have a conversation to finish.

"Prove it, then." I step forward. "Prove that all you just told me is true!"

"I don't need to," the Pillar says as he pulls his phone from his pocket. At the same time, my phone buzzes.

What's going on?

I click a link sent to me in a message. I am transferred to a video. I click it to open it. It's a live-stream, the same one everyone else, including the Pillar, is watching now.

It's the Muffin Man, aka the cook, aka the watermelon killer is live online, talking to the world.

Chapter 49

The Muffin Man's presence on TV puts everyone to silence. The people on the street are watching their phone screens with the utmost attention.

The Muffin Man heartlessly streams a photo montage of the killings: the head in the football in Stamford Bridge, children's heads discovered by the police inside watermelons, the sneezing crowd in the Theatre Royal. The carnage is streamed worldwide.

The camera then shows a headshot of the Muffin Man. He is sitting in what looks like a huge Victorian kitchen with an oversized fireplace behind him. The scene is surreal. The uniqueness of the kitchen suggests he is almost broadcasting from the past. It can't be. There must be another explanation.

The Muffin Man still wears the cook's uniform; his double-breasted coat is turned to show the straitjacket's side. On his head, he wears a French toque. His hair, like strands of a bending palm tree, covers his face, all but his scarred lips. Next to him, two glinting kitchen knives are visible.

"Good day, citizens of Britain," are his first words. He talks slowly, confidently yet carelessly, and inhumanly. "I would like to make this short and to the point." He clears his throat. "Like my friend, the Cheshire, warned you before..." People around me shriek at the mention of the Cheshire Killer. "Any interfering by any of your 'authorities' will be annihilated immediately. I ask you to stay away, as this is a matter of the Wonderland Wars."

In any other scenario — in another, saner world, maybe — this would be a laughable phrase.

A matter of Wonderland Wars?

But it isn't. This the real life, as insane as it's *exposed* to be.

"I am not a ruthless serial killer," he begins to read

from a paper. "I am what you'd think of as a 'wake-up call.' My so-called 'killings' have a greater purpose," he confesses. "I kill children..." Britain gasps in one breath. "Fat children," he elaborates. "Fat children who aren't supposed to be as overweight and unhealthy as they are today." He stops and holds one hand up to stop himself from sneezing. It makes him look a little vulnerable. Just for a fraction of a second. He must be immune to the pepper or has unprecedented control of his sneeze. "You filthy, ungrateful caricature of a society," he continues as a strand of hair shifts, briefly giving way to one of his eyes. Or should I say the vacancy of one of his eyes, and a darkly hollow socket instead.

He surely doesn't look vulnerable now. A woman faints on the street next to me.

"Here are a few facts you should know to understand why I do what I do," he reads on. "One person in every four British people is overweight." He takes a short breath. "The average person in Britain is nearly three stones heavier than they were twenty years ago. Your children are a generation of overweight and unhealthy lads who have the highest rate in history for being diabetic and seriously sick at the age of ten."

The Pillar folds his hands next to an old woman and whispers, "I don't care. I'm on the Dr. Oz diet. Not the wizard, the doctor."

The woman dismisses him, her eyes glued to her phone.

"The food industry is as imposing a threat as the cigarette industry." The Muffin Man sounds far more educated than a Victorian cook for the Duchess. "The food industry is slowly murdering our nation. I know you are worried about an apocalypse, but believe me, you won't even live long enough to see it if you keeping eating their food." He reaches for a glass of water, sips slowly, and clears his throat. The way he holds the glass of water suggests a man of a different caliber than what I thought he'd be. Who are you, Muffin Man? I feel I should know but can't put it together. "The companies spend millions of pounds on marketing their products. They make triple that money by seducing our children to force their parents to buy it. The child grows up and gets sick. The medical industry profits from the same person, now a patient. Then doctors prescribe us medicine that promises to make us better—and never does—so we spend even more money. It's a vicious circle that never ends."

"That's a Catch-22!" The Pillar clicks his fingers together. A few people shoot him piercing looks. He puts his fingers back in his pocket. "Sorry, I should've known finger-clicking is rude."

"You have to ask yourself who benefits from this." The Muffin Man faces the camera, abandoning the paper. "People wake up and ask how they became this fat and sick and penniless, and if it ever was their fault."

"Of course it's their faults," the Pillar says. "No one forced them to eat that much."

People eye him again. The Pillar pantomimes zipping his mouth shut.

"We live in the age of 'buy one, get one, get one free,'" the Muffin Man says. "Nothing in this world is for free."

"This Muffin Man rather reminds me of Willy Wonka in *Charlie and the Chocolate Factory*." The Pillar can't help himself. "He used to scare the panty pants out of my oranges."

No one eyes him this time. I think they can't even hear him. The Muffin Man's message demands attention whether they believe in his theories or not.

"Now that I have your attention, here is what I want," the Muffin Man says. "First, the easy part." The killer makes the rules now. "I want a personal apology from the Queen of England and Parliament toward the people of Britain for allowing the food industry to manipulate us and deteriorating our children's health." He pauses. "The second part is that I want a thorough investigation about the food industry, backed up with Professor Gorgon Ramstein's research, and have those responsible thrown in jail. I demand their profits divided among the poor citizens of Britain equally."

"Pretty noble demands from a man who stuffs children's heads in watermelons," the Pillar muses. "Would he be kind enough to show us how he actually stuffs heads in watermelons?"

The Pillar is mostly talking to himself.

"If these demands aren't met by five o'clock tomorrow," the Muffin Man announces, "I will poison most of Britain's children with the same candy that made them fat." This time his pause is longer, as if he is contemplating what he is going to say next.

I look around me. Everyone is holding their breath. They know they are about to see something they aren't ready for, but are forced to experience.

"In case there are still any doubts after all those killings," the Muffin Man says, "here is a footage of Mudfog Town, which is about seventy miles from London, a few minutes ago."

The broadcast shows the town of Mudfog as silent and dead as the most abandoned place on earth. Then the camera zooms to show everyone dead on the ground, white foam spurting out of their guts. Closer, the camera shows endless packages of Snicker Snackers, Queen of Hearts Tarts, and all other kind of food and drinks open and dropped to the floor. The footage then changes to "one hour earlier." It shows the few citizens of Mudfog nibbling on these snacks everywhere. Then suddenly, a kid begins to vomit uncontrollably, holding his stomach with one hand, a Wonderland snack in the other. And the rest of the town of Mudfog follows one by one.

"It only took a few minutes to kill a town of seven hundred citizens." The broadcast returns to show the Muffin Man. "If you have suspicions about my ability to poison all your food, ask yourself how I was capable of stuffing heads in watermelons."

"See?" the Pillar says.

"It shouldn't take me more than a few hours to kill everyone in London," the Muffin Man says. "And then I will poison your water. Give back to the people you cheated or you will die." His warning tone is confident and unmistakable. "Even if you live, ask yourself this: if I can poison all food, what will be left for you to eat?"

The broadcast ends abruptly with the Cheshire Grin logo on the screen. Silence crawls on every building and soul in Britain.

Chapter 50

The silence is only present for a few moments. It's like the few seconds the runners of the Olympics stand by before all hell breaks loose. The world around me explodes into people running in every direction. People debate theories, others panic, and the rest watch those who panic, contemplating if they should panic too.

The sun has sunk into darkness. We missed the sunset. No one is guaranteed to catch another one tomorrow.

"By the time the Queen of England sips her five o'clock tea tomorrow, all those people might be gone," the Pillar says, shakes his head, and then walks away.

"Where do you think you're going?" I run after him, avoiding a few pedestrians ready to step over me already. "We have work to do!"

"You have work to do." He doesn't stop, and keeps walking.

The panic around us intensifies. People are arguing if it's possible to poison all food. Others say only snacks will be poisoned. Others suggest only one brand of the snacks will be poisoned, so they could sacrifice a few people testing which brand is poisoned and which isn't. Then they wonder if they should buy food and stock it at home in case the panic gets out of hand tomorrow. A few educated people argue that the Muffin Man is bluffing, that it's impossible to poison the food of the companies he is actually opposing. Another few claim all of this is only propaganda to sell more Queen of Hearts Tarts.

I can't stop listening to all kinds of theories as I snake through the crowd, looking for the Pillar. I hear people standing by the Muffin Man and calling him a hero, saying that food companies are no different to the toxic waste factories produce. Children are denied another delicious Meow Muffin by their parents. Then I finally see the Pillar. I pace faster and hold him by the shoulder. He stops, sighing, but doesn't resist.

"What do you mean by *I* have work to do?" I ask.

"Do I look like an Alice to you?" he says.

"What is that supposed to mean?"

"It's you, Alice, who has to confront the Wonderland Monsters," the Pillar says as someone bothers him, running around. He tries to stabilize himself and avoid the panicked runner. "I've been trying to tell you this for more than a week, and all you do is whine about Jack, who you really are, and if you really killed your friends." He grits his teeth, still bothered by the man running in circles around us. "Don't get me started on you whining about what's real and what's not."

"Are you saying only *I* can stop this?" I am afraid he will confirm my suspicion. I don't think I can handle this.

"Yes!" He knocks the annoying citizen down with his cane, and then pierces through me with his direct look.

"I—" The truth is that I am speechless, and very much wish this was all in my imagination now. I would love it if this is a nightmare and I could wake up from it. But I don't seem to wake up. The fear and panic of the people around me is too real to be imagined.

"You are the Real Alice," he says. "*Alice.*" He rolls his eyes. "And I am just a caterpillar. A special one, though." He seems vain about it. "But I can only guide you, teach you, and sometimes save you. I just can't confront the Muffin Man."

The panicking people around are still there, but I feel as if they have disappeared. I am all in my head now, trying to find the words to say and live up to their consequences. Lewis' vision seems to prove to be significant at every passing moment. It's mostly about Lewis struggling with the kids' poor health in Victorian times. The Muffin Man's case is all about the same, but in modern times. It can't be mad, because I couldn't have predicted it. Should I tell the Pillar about the vision?

"Professor Pillar," I say.

"Yes?" He cranes his neck forward.

"What is it I have to do to stop the Muffin Man?" I take a deep breath, my heart racing.

"From what I see, there is nothing you can do." He raises his voice against the crowd's shouting. "Not in *this* life."

For a moment, I am taken aback, upset that he would be playing games again. He knocks someone else with his cane and says, "Remember when we wanted to stop the Cheshire to save Constance? Remember what I told you before we knew his motives?"

"That a man's weakness lies in his past."

"Clever student." He nods.

"How are we going to know about he Muffin Man's past now?" I ask. "He has no name. His has no records. His file in the asylum doesn't say much. He has his face concealed."

"I know his past in this world, but trust me, it's irrelevant."

"Don't confuse me like that," I say politely. "We don't have enough time."

"Time." The Pillar flashes his cane in the air and circles me, knocking off whoever gets in his way. "Time, Alice! You have to go back in time." He acts like a performer on Broadway about to sing a finale song.

"To Wonderland?"

"Not exactly, but kind of." He continues circling, moving like Gene Kelly from *Singin' in the Rain* while the world is falling apart around us. "To know the Muffin Man's real motives, you will go back and try to stop whatever happened to him and turned a cook into a serial killer."

"Is that even possible?"

He stops in front of me. "Only if you're the Real Alice."

"And if I am not?"

"You will die, somewhere in the past," he says bluntly. "Frankly, who needs a mad girl who isn't Alice?" He is nonchalant about it.

"I am ready to do it," I say.

"It's not going to be easy."

"Don't!"

"I won't." He smiles. "So let me tell you how you could time-travel back to yesterday to save the world today." He signals for me to follow him. "And by the way, Alice, who said the Muffin Man has no name?"

"He has a name?"

"Of course. If he hadn't just popped up on national TV, I would have had time to tell you."

"Why am I going back in time if we know his name?"

"Because his name is Gorgon Ramstein."

Chapter 51

Wolsey's kitchen, Christ Church, Oxford University

Gorgon Ramstein, dressed in his cook's outfit, was chopping carrots on a metallic kitchen table in Wolsey's kitchen. He wasn't really cooking, or preparing to. Chopping carrots was his personal meditation to calm himself down and cope with the urge to kill again.

Every now and then he accidentally cut himself. He didn't mind. Blood spattering had stopped being a distraction years ago.

And now?

Now nothing mattered as long as the Queen didn't publicly apologize, as long as his demands had not been met.

Gorgon cut himself again. This time, the anger was too strong. He hurled the heavy kitchen knife at the wall and roared at the empty kitchen.

The knife plowed against one of the two turtle shells hanging on the wall. He looked at them through the haze in one eye. *That turtle shell,* he thought.

Only a few people knew that this turtle shell was Lewis Carroll's inspiration for the Mock Turtle character. Fewer people knew about the historical significance of the rarely visited kitchen underneath Oxford University.

Wolsey's kitchen. Oxford's legendary kitchen since the sixteenth century, where so many secrets were buried and hidden.

Gorgon was taught the art of cooking in this kitchen. He learned about the passion for cooking. That there was a rhythm, a tempo, and a song and dance to it.

Who were Auguste Escoffier, Alexis Soyer, or Isabella Beeton compared to him? They might have been great names carved in Victorian history books, but Gorgon knew he was something else. He was legendary. An icon to be remembered. He wasn't just a cook. He was a scientist turned cook. His approach was detailed and meticulous like no one else's.

But all that was gone now. And not because of what Margaret Kent did to his lawyer and his family in this world. His anger and hatred, although suppressed for years in the asylum, began when he was in Wonderland.

He pounded a heavy fist on the table, remembering what the Queen of Hearts did to him in Wonderland. The spoons and knives shook all over and bowls slipped to the floor. The pain was so strong that he fell to his knees from his own impact. And then a tear trickled like a drop of olive oil down his face. A tear that came out of his empty socket.

Slowly, Gorgon stood up and went to a side table, where he swallowed a muffin whole without even chewing it. Gorgon loved muffins — and pepper. He loved them because his kids were crazy about them.

Gorgon washed blood off his hand, staring at his reflection in the mirror.

It wasn't like he hadn't seen it before, but his image seemed to shock him this time. He had turned from victim to a ruthless killer, and he didn't know if he should like it.

The Cheshire certainly liked it.

Gorgon stood six feet four. His hands were lanky and very useful in cooking. He wore his double-breasted white jacket, which was actually the asylum's straitjacket. The main idea behind cooks wearing double-breasted jackets had been the possibility to reverse it many times and hide the cooking stains. In the past, when this kitchen was still proudly called Wolsey's kitchen, there was no time to change before presenting the food to the obnoxious and pretentious Victorian rich who had enough money to pay for it. They had to flip the working side of the jacket and present the cleaner side within minutes.

To Gorgon the idea was almost the same when he committed his murders, except he used it to hide the bloodstains of previous victims. It allowed him to kill two victims in the span of minutes before he had to change the jacket. Kill, reverse, and kill again. Or better: kill, reverse, escape while looking clean.

No one ever thought of the cooks to become serial killers.

Still, Gorgon's jacket had many other purposes. The thick cotton cloth of his jacket protected him from the heat of the stove and oven back then in Wonderland. Victorian kitchens weren't as safe as today's kitchens. Cooking was a dangerous profession back then; you were exposed to the insanely large stoves and not really protected from the splattering of boiling liquids. A good jacket had been a must. In present times, it helped him hide from his pursuers in a heated place that people usually avoided.

Under the jacket, he wore specially tailored trousers. They had black and white patterns. In the past, cooks wore patterned trousers to hide minor stains. Gorgon used them to mock the White Queen's belief in what she called the Chessboard of Life, where good people walked on white tiles and bad people walked on black. Gorgon believed he had walked both tiles evenly.

Gorgon stared at the *toque blanche* he wore on his head on his head, the kind of hat once worn by kings like Philip II. Some liked to simply call it a toque, as it had been the traditional headgear for magistrates—an officer of the state. In modern usage, the term usually referred to a judge.

Looking at it in the mirror, it seemed like an ironic coincidence. In his psychotic endeavor to correct the world, he was in many ways playing judge.

He didn't laugh at the thought. He rarely laughed at his thoughts. Gorgon, unlike other delusional killers, knew what he was. He knew his head wasn't buzzing to the right frequencies. But he just couldn't help it. What the Queen of Hearts did to him had shattered every single molecule of humanity inside him.

"Portmanteau." Gorgon tipped his toque, looking in the mirror. A French word, and one of the rare things that brought a smile to his lips.

Portmanteau was the art of combining two words or their sounds and their meanings into a single new word. Lewis Carroll loved that. That was how he invented the words like "slithy," which meant "lithe and slimy."

Gorgon loved hearing it from Lewis back then. Those were the lovely days. Still, Lewis couldn't save him from the Queen.

Sometimes, it struck him as funny being thought of as just a cook for the Duchess, like it was mentioned in the "Pig and Pepper" chapter in the book. He despised people thinking he was fired for using so much pepper and making the Queen sneeze when she was dining at the Duchess' house.

He reached for a copy of *Alice's Adventures Underground*, one of the few original copies of the book—he knew the Pillar owned one of them, and that it probably drove him mad that the cook had killed many people, but he didn't care the slightest about the Pillar.

The Muffin Man opened the book to a part in the "Pig and Pepper" chapter where it said: *There was certainly too much of it in the air. Even the Duchess sneezed occasionally. The only things in the kitchen that did not sneeze were the cook and a large cat, which was sitting on the hearth and grinning from ear to ear.*

"Well, here we are." The Cheshire appeared out of nowhere behind him. Gorgon could see him in the mirror showing his real face. "Me and you, immune to the sneezing pepper." He had a horrifying and ugly grin, which even Gorgon wished to avoid.

"You didn't knock." Gorgon hated surprises.

"I'm a cat, Gorgy." The Cheshire's grin widened. "We sneak, never ask for permission. Ready?"

"The Queen didn't apologize?" He knew she wouldn't, but still wished she would.

"You knew it was never going to happen," the Cheshire said. "That's part of why we're doing this."

"I thought we were doing this to expose her to the world," Gorgon said, still preferring to talk to the mirror.

"Well, that's part of it." The Cheshire sniffed for food in the kitchen. "But we're also showing her we're as strong as she is."

"Why would we need that?"

"The world is complicated, Gorgy." The Cheshire picked a fish's spine and sucked on it. "The Wonderland Wars are coming. The Queen and her followers will have the upper hand. And since the likes of me and you aren't really considered the good guys, we need to find our place in it."

"How so?"

"By proving how badass we are." He licked his paws. "I love that word, 'badass.' People really like it in this world."

"Are you saying part of us doing this is for her to stop underestimating us so she would have us join her league?" Gorgon turned around, anger flushing his face. This wasn't part of his plan. Under no circumstance would he join the Queen's army.

"Of course not," the Cheshire lied, and threw the spine away. He clapped his paws clean and said, "I was joking. We're doing this to expose the Queen, of course."

"I knew I shouldn't have trusted you," Gorgon grunted. "But I have to take my revenge."

"We all have our dark ticks, Gorgy." The Cheshire patted him. "Don't be hard on yourself. You just killed a few kids, that's all. Kids die every day in the world, be it starving, be it underage soldiers, or dying from diseases. No one ever makes a fuss about it."

"I don't feel good about it. I only did it for—"

"I know, I know," the Cheshire said. "To expose the companies working for the Queen and the Duchess. We already said that."

"I still need to know why you are helping me," Gorgon said. "We haven't been really close in Wonderland."

"I'm after the Pillar and Alice. I'm sending them a message they will eventually catch on. A terrifying message. But what does it matter? You're on my team now. Look at you." The Cheshire spun Gorgon around to look back in the mirror. He pointed at his reflection with pride and enthusiasm. "Look at the glory of what you have become. From a nobody cook for the Duchess, hardly remembered by any child who read the books, to a lame scientist in this world, to one of the scariest villains on earth." The Cheshire was proud, and Gorgon felt hypnotized by the words. The Cheshire had a way of making everything sinister and bad sound so good and endearing. For a damaged man like Gorgon, it was just an admired trait. "From nobody to a proud Wonderland Monster," the Cheshire repeated. "Now let's show the world your magnum opus. Let's make some humans suffer!" He rubbed his paws together. "Mass-poisoning London. How beautiful."

Gorgon nodded, angry veins showing in his eyes.

"We need to give it a word, though," the Cheshire said. "Something catchy. You know, how people like marketing and stuff."

"Something catchy?"

"Yeah, the same way they have catchy names for their products: Snicker Snackers and the like. I got it!" He flashed one of his claws. "We'll call it an 'Epidemic of Tarts.'" The Cheshire laughed.

Chapter 52

Graduate Common Room, Christ Church, Oxford University

Fourteen minutes past midnight, the Pillar guides me through the empty, dimly lit corridors of Tom VII in Christ Church, Oxford University. He is supposedly going to show me into a room that has the ability to help me travel back to Victorian times. Given all the madness I have seen, I am still skeptical about the concept of going back in time. If it were possible, and relatively easy, why wouldn't all Wonderland Monsters use it?

"Are we there yet?" I whisper.

"Patience, my dear Alice," he says, counting the doors left and right. "It's been a long time since I've been here. They always change things in the university," he uses his pocket watch as some kind of compass. I don't bother to ask. "A few years ago they made a mess out of the university to shoot Harry Potter movie," his voice shows he really disliked it. "But I'm not feeling like I am Dumbeldore now. Thank you very much."

"Until you find that door, I am still wondering why Professor Gorgon Ramstein, a.k.a. Muffin Man, is doing this," I say, neglecting any silly side jokes of his. "I mean, I know the government dismissed his research, killed his lawyer, and he feels responsible to expose the food corruption of companies. Is that enough reason to massacre all those people?"

"Of course not." The Pillar is still looking for the door leading to the time travel room. "The Muffin Man, like all of us Wonderlanders, took a new identity in this new world. He became a professor. He even got married and had three kids. Margaret Kent ordered his kids killed."

I stop in my place. The Pillar notices and turns to look at me. I can feel silent anger creep up in my veins.

"Shocked?" He raises an eyebrow. "Well, do you want to know how his kids were killed?"

"I think I have an idea." Although I am beginning to get used to shocking deaths, I don't want to say it.

"Margaret seduced his kids to eat a great amount of expired Queen of Hearts Tarts," the Pillar says. "Enough to get them poisoned...slowly. When Gorgon drove his kids to the hospital, the nurses were ordered to conspire with Margaret and look away until the kids died."

"The same way he wants to kill everyone in the country," I lament. "And you still think something more sinister happened to him in Wonderland?"

"I am hoping so," the Pillar says. "Because if the Muffin Man is only fueled by his present-day anger, I don't know of any way we can stop him. To be honest, the man has been squashed like cockroach in this life. And I don't know how to use this time machine to go back a few years. It's a Wonderland time machine. It only goes back to Wonderland. Let's hope we find a trigger point in his past and stop the story from the beginning." The Pillar turns the knob of the door next to him and pushes it open. "Welcome to the time-travel room."

I read the sign on the door as I enter. "The Graduate Common Room?"

"Formally known as Professor Einstein's Room." The Pillar follows me in and closes the door behind us.

The room is modernly decorated with a notable fireplace and a huge desk with old English carvings. There are a few souvenirs here and there, looking as if transported from the Museum of the History of Science. A couple of couches colored red and black are set on one side. There is a table with magazines in front of a large window looking out into the garden. One thing stands out: a blackboard with mathematical writings on it.

"Albert Einstein?" I ask.

"He lectured in Oxford for a while, and was given this room in 1930." The Pillar takes off his suit's jacket, which he rarely does. "I suppose you know Einstein is in many ways the father of the concept of time."

"I'm insane, but I went to school," I say, eyes on the blackboard. "So Einstein really knew how to time-travel?"

"Of course he did. Einstein was as mad as Lewis. While Lewis Carroll stuttered, Einstein was actually autistic, but few people know that. Einstein was a great fella—bad haircut, though." The Pillar pulls the blackboard to the middle of the room. He does it with care and respect. "This same room had been Lewis Carroll's room for five years when he studied here."

"Wow." I like the connection. Didn't know about it. "That's about seventy years before Einstein came."

"Seventy years, and no one discovered Carroll's secrets but a madman—a.k.a. Professor Einstein himself." The Pillar rubs the blackboard clean. The chalk doesn't come off.

"Secrets?"

"Technically, Carroll discovered time travel." The Pillar looks at me. "But since he wasn't sure a Wonderland Monster would end up using it, he kept it a secret."

"And Einstein discovered that secret seventy years later when he entered the room?"

"Along with other things, like the Zebra Puzzle, but that's irrelevant now. Lewis Carroll wasn't just anyone, Alice. He was an artist, photographer, writer, priest, and mathematician. Have you ever met anyone like that?" the Pillar chirps. Suddenly, I remember Lewis telling me about Einstein the last time I climbed up the Tom Tower. I believe the Pillar isn't lying. "Einstein reinterpreted Carroll's work by staying in his room in Oxford many years later. Do you know his messy hair was an aftermath of repeatedly using the time machine in this room? It rather fried."

"Why didn't Einstein tell the world about it, then?"

"Are you kidding me? You know what those lunatic politicians and businessmen out there would do with such a device?" He stops and looks at the blackboard. "Besides, the time-travel machine has never been fully functioning."

"Are you saying it doesn't work?"

"I never tried, myself," the Pillar says. "I only read about it, and Carroll used to hint at it. It works for only fourteen minutes, and I believe it has certain limits."

"Fourteen?" I grimace. "What's with this number popping up everywhere?"

"It only popped up once on your wall in the cell. This is the second time," the Pillar says, and then shoots me a suspicious glance. I know it shows up all he time. "Did it show up somewhere else?"

I shrug. Lewis' vision was on the 14th of January, but he told me not to tell the Pillar about the vision.

"Aha." His tongue plays with the insides of his cheeks. "Little Alice has been having visions." I try to act oblivious of what he says. "Are you sure Lewis didn't give you anything last time when you met him through the Tom Tower?"

I hesitate, thinking he knows about the key to one of Wonderland's doors. I am glad I hid in the wall.

"It's okay." The Pillar doesn't push it. "We'll talk about that later. Now, we need you to go back in time to meet the Muffin Man."

"Which we will do how?" I crane my neck and squint.

The Pillar says nothing, and points at the blackboard with sticky chalk. "This is called Einstein's Blackboard, the one he used for lecturing when he was here. It's one of the world's most valuable artifacts. Historians will claim the original one is in the in Museum of the History of Science, and that this one here is a replica. Actually, it's vice versa but they don't know it. Originally it was Carroll's blackboard, and it is used to time-travel."

"And how is that possible?"

"It's easy," he says. "You write the date, time, and name of person you want to meet, and then use it as a doorway to the past."

The blackboard is actually tall. Hypothetically, it looks like a door a mad girl like me could walk into. But unless the board's surface turns into rippling water or air, I don't see how.

"So I just walk into it?" I give up and assume fantastically.

"Oh." The Pillar's lips twitch. "Of course not. Don't be silly."

Chapter 53

The Pillar paces toward the red curtain by the window and looks for something behind it. "There it is," he murmurs, and looks back at me with a smile that soon shifts to a serious straight line again. "Now, before I show you how, you need to know what you're getting yourself into."

"I was waiting for you to say that."

"This time-travel method lasts for only fourteen minutes." He pulls out his pocket watch and tucks it in my hands. "It's very close to my heart. Use it with care and bring it back to me—along with you, of course. It's an old watch, so there is no timer. You have to memorize the fourteen minutes."

"What else should I know?"

"There are two possibilities where you won't come back and probably die." He has that piercing look again.

I pretend I am not afraid, and hold a shrug.

"The first one is if something happens to you in the past, you get killed, set back, or simply stay there more than fourteen minutes. I can't help you if any of that happens."

"And the second?" I feel I can deal with the first one myself.

"If you're not the Real Alice," he says. "Which I believe you are."

"Believe or know?"

"Believing is knowing," he says. "It's up to you if you believe in yourself or not. You still can walk away from this."

"And stay for what?" I say. "The death of millions tomorrow?"

"I thought you'd say you could never live without me." He musters a sad face.

"I'd rather succeed, come back tomorrow, and find you gone," I tease.

"I'm hurt." He puts a hand on his heart and blinks twice. "Which reminds me." He pulls out a small piece of paper. It looks like it was an A4 size and folded repeatedly to become that small. "I've got a present for you." He doesn't hand it to me but squeezes it in my front jeans pocket.

The sincere look on his face worries me. "What is it?"

"It says who Jack really is."

The urge of pulling the paper out and reading it now tickles my finger. There is this burning sensation of anticipation in my chest.

"I thought if something happens to you there, or you're about to die, you get to know what you desire the most," the Pillar says, walking toward the red curtain before the balcony. "Not that I am fond of Jack, not one little bit."

"I think I should thank you," I say.

He shakes his head, lips pursed. "No, you don't," he says, and looks peeks behind the curtain to check on something. "Because the only way to walk into Einstein's Blackboard isn't going to be pleasant." He turns back to me.

"I'm ready to know how." I straighten my back.

"No, you aren't." He is sure of himself. "Think of how no one else all these years was able to figure Carroll's time traveling secret. I mean, the blackboard was here, right in front of them. Carroll and Einstein's writings fill the university's archives. Still, no one ever found out about the secret."

"Tell me how, Pillar," I say. I am both impatient and worried at the same time. "I'm not afraid."

"You can only time-travel through the one thing you're scared of the most."

I shriek immediately. There is no question about it. A lot of things scare me and intimidate me, but one is the *one*, and only that brings to my knees.

"A mirror," the Pillar says, confirming my fears. "I have one behind the curtain. If I lay it opposite to the blackboard, you will be able to step inside through the—"

"Looking Glass." It all starts to connect now. "Like Alice did in Lewis' book Through the Looking Glass." I remember clearly how in one chapter she entered Wonderland through a mirror. Lewis wasn't over-imagining or fictionalizing. This was true, except the mirror had to be entered while set opposite to Einstein's Blackboard.

"The book is called Through the Looking Glass, and what Alice Found There," the Pillar lectures me again. "Now it's more of an Einstein's Blackboard Looking Glass now." He tries to sound funny, but he isn't. He knows the gravity of my fears.

"Is that why only the Real Alice can do it?"

He nods.

"But I am unimaginably afraid of mirrors," I say. "I will faint like in the fitting room."

"You can close your eyes, Alice, and I can guide you inside, hold your hand until you step inside," he offers. "The problem will be on your way back."

"How am I supposed to come back?"

"The same mirror and blackboard should be in Carroll's studio on the roof of the university, next to the Tom Tower."

"But there is no one to help there with closing my eyes."

"I know," he says. "Maybe Carroll could help."

"Why can't we just use the Tom Tower like last time?"

"The Tom Tower is the Bridge of Realities," the Pillar says. "It's like dreaming or crossing realms. Whatever you change there isn't going to change the future."

"But I gave Lewis the idea to write the *Alice in Wonderland* book last time."

"You might have, but it's not necessarily the real reason. Who knows why he wrote the book, really?" The

Pillar pulls his hand back from behind the curtain. "Like I said, we still can go back to the asylum and be happy, insane people. You don't have to do it."

"If there is no one who can do it but me, then I have to do it." I rub the pocket in my jeans, right over the folded paper with Jack's identity. It's insane how safe it makes me feel.

I walk to the blackboard and write the date of January 14th 1862, the place of Lewis' study—because I don't know how to reach the Muffin Man if not through him. With my back to the blackboard, I close my eyes and ask the Pillar to bring the mirror and guide me through it.

As he pulls it close, I feel the walls closing in on me, because how good am I at closing my eyes and making sure they won't disobey me by just opening up?

Chapter 54

Lewis Carroll's studio, Oxford University, 1862

The transition to the past isn't as complicated as I thought. Once I step into the mirror, I feel the creaking wooden floor underneath me. I am in Lewis Carroll's studio. The air smells of violets and a scent called Fleurs de Bulgarie. I don't know how I know it. I just do, although it's not sold in the modern world.

I am afraid if I open my eyes, I'll find another mirror in front of me. Logically, it should be behind me, but I am too scared to run into the scary rabbit again. There is one thing I am sure of, though. I am back in my seven year old body like last time when I met Lewis through the Tom Tower.

"I need more costumes, Alice." Lewis' voice eases my worries. "I don't think I bought enough costumes from Drury Lane."

I open my eyes slowly. There is no mirror in front of me. I let out a sigh of relief, and check the pocket watch in my hand. It's fourteen minutes to seven in the evening. Time is definitely different than back there in Oxford, where it should be a little after midnight right now.

I look at Lewis standing before a large pile of costumes. His rabbit is standing atop it, nibbling on a carrot and scratching its head. Both are staring at the costumes, hoping to solve some problem. The piled costumes are cut and sewn back again together in smaller sizes after being redesigned. I wonder why Lewis would do this to the precious outfits.

"Why did you cut the costumes?" I ask, supposing I just fit in the scene as if I hadn't just reappeared out of nowhere. Who knows how this time travel really works.

"I told you, Alice," Lewis says.

"He told you, Alice," the rabbit repeats.

"Each costume had been designed for an adult," Lewis explains. "Cutting them in half makes each costume available for two kids instead of one."

"You want them to act in your plays?" I ask.

"Not the plays." Lewis sighs, still staring at the pile. "In the beginning, I used the costumes for entertaining the poor and homeless children. But then I discovered they needed the costumes themselves as shelter from the cold."

The more I know Lewis, the more I admire him.

"Maybe we could cut the costumes in three parts," the rabbit suggests. "The children are all smaller in size than normal children their age already. I think it could work."

"Why are the children smaller than their usual size?" I ask, wondering about the differences between past and future. Nowadays children are slightly oversized.

"Malnutrition, poor health, and the cold," Lewis answers. "These times are harsh, Alice. Look outside. The children are homeless and hungry. And this is only Oxford. Filth and poverty in London is much worse. It breaks my heart, Alice. I have to find a way to save them."

The words ring in the back of my head. *Save them*, he said. So those are the ones he couldn't save? Can I change the past and help him save them?

"We could build a shelter in the university's church, Lewis," the rabbit says. "Maybe give them some of my carrots." The rabbit shrugs, and its ears fall to the sides. It realizes the luxury of living with Lewis and having enough carrots to eat. It lowers its eyes and cuts the carrot in two halves. It puts one aside for later and nibbles slower on the one in hand.

"We need to find a way to get them food." Lewis looks as if he is responsible for their hardships. "And we need to educate them. Most of them don't know how to read."

As much as I want to help with the issue of kids, I need to ask them to help Gorgon. "Lewis," I utter. "We have to save the Muffin Man."

Lewis senses my unusual intensity and turns to me. "Who is the Muffin Man?"

"The Muffin Man. The Muffin Man. Who lives in Drury Lane," the rabbit sings.

"That Muffin Man." I point at the rabbit.

"You mean the nursery rhyme?" Lewis asks.

"No, I mean the Muffin Man," I insist. "Hmm...the cook. Yes, I mean the cook."

"The cook?" Lewis exchanges puzzled looks with his rabbit.

"The one who works for the Duchess." I didn't expect it to be this hard.

"The Duchess has no cook," the rabbit says. "She is looking for one, but she hasn't found a cook yet."

"I mean the Queen's cook." I remember that the Muffin Man used to work for the Queen, like the Pillar said. "The Queen of Hearts."

The rabbit slides back into Lewis' pocket and says nothing. I can hear its teeth chatter inside.

"You scared him." Lewis laughs. "The Queen of Hearts scares him. I think you mean Gorgon, the Queen's crops handler?"

"Yes, that's him." God, I lost so much time talking already.

"What about him?"

"He is in danger," I say. "We have to help him."

"What kind of danger?" Lewis stutters. This is the second time I've heard him stutter. I wonder if he was born that way.

"I don't know, but we have to help him before something happens to him."

"You're not m-making any s-sense." He seems embarrassed by the sudden stutter. He rubs his forehead. I think he has a migraine.

"I know, but please, Lewis. Let me see the cook."

"Ah," Lewis says. "Y-y-you are using Gorgon as an excuse to go back to W-w-wonderland." He seems to refer to a prior conversation I don't remember. "Like I said. I locked them and am not planning to open its doors anytime soon."

"But we have to." I grip his arms. He doesn't understand. "You have to save him. Don't you remember the vision when you said you 'couldn't save them'? I think it has to do with the cook."

"You had a vision of me?"

"Please, Lewis. You're not one to leave someone in need behind. Trust me."

"All right. All right," he says. "Let's see what's wrong with Wonderland again. Close your eyes. I will walk you to one of the doors to Wonderland." I nod and close my eyes. So the doors to Wonderland are really through the university, like the Pillar suggested? "You can't open your eyes until I tell you."

I nod again, although I am tempted to open them and know the door's location. Still, I can't. What if I mess something up? The Muffin Man is my priority.

I sense Lewis take my hand, and we walk for a while. Almost a minute. We descend a few stairs and then I hear the sound of the turn of a key. Does my key open a door to Wonderland? Is that why he gave it to me before?

After we step through something—I am not sure it's a door—he asks me to open my eyes.

Chapter 55

It's the same Wonderland I saw in my vision. Enchanting and with an endless variety of colors. Sizable fruits acting like huge trees. There is a huge arching rainbow in the distance and a few mushrooms nearby. Unfortunately, there is no time to explore it now.

Lewis seems to look around cautiously, avoiding some kind of threat. I notice he has brought his sword along.

"We need to act faster, Lewis," I say.

"Don't be fooled by all the beauty, Alice," he says. "Wonderland isn't what it used to be."

"It doesn't matter." I look at my watch. It's ten minutes to seven. "Please, we have to find Gorgon."

"Wait." Lewis pulls his rabbit out of his pocket and orders it to run fast and ask if anyone knows where Gorgon is. The rabbit hesitates but then hops and disappears into the forest.

"Can't we just go to his house?" I ask.

"I don't know where Gorgon lives."

The rabbit hops back with the news. "She is right, Lewis. The Queen of Hearts has Gorgon imprisoned," it says. "She is punishing him for stealing pepper and muffins from her kitchen."

"Why would he do that?" I have to investigate.

"He was eating with his children and they asked him to buy pepper for their food, and muffins for dessert," the rabbit says. "Gorgon lives in a poor neighborhood, so he went out, but no one agreed to give him pepper for free. He ended up borrowing a handful from the Queen's kitchen. The Queen was upset and sent the Reds to bring him to her. They say she is in a bad mood today, just like last year, and the year before."

"The children in Wonderland are as poor as the children in London," Lewis tells me. "We have to stop the Queen from hurting him." Lewis holds my hand and starts running. "Gorgon is a good man. His wife died giving birth to his last child, and he takes care of them, working hard to raise them properly. I am sure the pepper issue was just a slip of faith on his behalf. The Queen's wrath is lethal."

I pant as I run with Lewis. He seems to be taking a longer route, trying to avoid whatever scares him in the forest. I can't complain, as long as we're getting there.

We arrive at a great castle, which I have no time to look at long. We're standing behind hordes of Reds circling the Queen and Gorgon. Both are too far away. I can't see their faces in detail.

"Go see what's going on," Lewis orders his rabbit.

The rabbit hops again. We duck, afraid the Reds will see us. As we wait, I feel the need to ask, "Lewis, is there any chance we could use None Fu against the Reds?"

"Not a chance, Alice," Lewis replies. "I haven't developed the art of it yet."

So Jack wasn't bluffing. There is such a thing as None Fu, the warrior's art he told me about in the Vatican. But how does Jack know about it?

A minute later, the rabbit comes back with fear bulging its eyes. "The Queen of Hearts is torturing Gorgon in front of all her acquaintances," the rabbit says.

"Is she planning to chop off his head?" Lewis asks.

"Worse," the rabbit says. "She intends to torture him for embarrassing her in front of the elite visitors she had invited over to taste her delicious tarts. She's stuffing his nose with tons of pepper now, until he wouldn't be able to stop sneezing."

"She is going to make him sneeze to death," I murmur. But in my mind I can't see the harsh punishment that changed the Muffin Man from an ordinary father into a killer. All of this seems nonsensical and irrelevant.

"She has her guards holding him by the arms, and vowed he will not be freed until he sneezes so hard his eyes pop out." The rabbit finds it kind of funny, but tries to hide it.

"That Queen." Lewis sighs. "I don't want anything to do with her, but it wouldn't be right to leave him behind."

"Are you sure that's it?" I ask while staring at my pocket watch. It's six minutes to seven.

"Why are you asking, Alice?" Lewis says. "The man will have one of his eyes popped out from sneezing. Isn't that enough torture?"

I don't answer, because as horrible as it sounds, it doesn't seem like enough reason to turn an ordinary man into a beast. Why would he go on killing innocent kids later? "I'm sorry. I expected worse," I say. "Let's save him, then."

Gorgon's screams are audible now. They must have started to torture him.

"All right." Lewis sighs. "I guess I will have to do this. You stay here, Alice." He turns to his rabbit. "You will distract the Reds. Make them chase you for a while so I get through. I know how to fight the guards and free Gorgon. He should be able to run, right?"

"I don't think he is hurt much," the rabbit says. "Except for his eyes, if he loses one."

It's only a moment before Gorgon screams louder and we hear something pop like a cork out of a bottle. My eyes widen, and the rabbit digs the ground to hide its head.

There is no stopping the nonsense factor in Wonderland. I hear the Queen laugh loudly and happily, as if she has been told a sincerely amusing joke.

It gets even weirder when Gorgon's eye comes rolling before us and stops in front of me. The rabbit sticks its head out and stares at the eye, with ears flipped straight and goose bumps all over its arched back.

I know it's gory and unfair, but I still can't think of it as reason enough to transform him into a child killer. I think I have become slightly indifferent toward all the blood spilling around me.

"Help them!" someone screams from inside the circle I can't see past.

"Who is saying this?" I ask.

"It's Gorgon!" the rabbit says.

"Why is he shouting, 'Help them'?" Lewis asks.

"Help who?" I say.

"Maybe he lost both his eyes and is calling for them." The rabbit pulls out a bag and tucks the lost eye in, looking away as it does it.

"That's it." Lewis' anger peaks. He stands up and doesn't even wait for his rabbit to distract the Reds. He starts chopping the heads of the Reds army off.

Chapter 56

I am astonished at how skilled and agile Lewis is. Did he learn to fight because of Wonderland? What happened here and made him lock them all away?

My watch says I only have four minutes left.

I pick up my fragile seven-year-old body and run through the Reds as Lewis fights alone.

"Queen of Hearts," Lewis shouts. "I demand you free this man."

"Help them, please!" shouts Gorgon.

For the first time I am able to see him. He is held by the Reds, unable to free himself. They have his hands and legs roped and tied to trees on four sides. The Queen, although I can't see the details of her face, is pouring pepper onto him. Gorgon sneezes, risking his other eye popping out. She loves torturing him. She doesn't look worried about Lewis fighting her guards behind her.

"This will teach you to never steal my pepper again," she growls. "This will teach everyone in Wonderland to fear me forever." She laughs like an evil witch.

I use my small figure and keep chugging through the red cloaks all around me. I have to reach Gorgon. Maybe it's not about what will happen to him now, but later. If I help him escape the Queen now, it should divert the course of events in the future and save him from turning into a killer.

I stumble over something tiny, and fall on my face. The watch says three minutes. Looking for what I stumbled upon, I find a few croquet balls scattered on the ground. No mallet, though. I pick up a bunch of croquet balls and carry them in my yellow dress. Before I can use them, two Reds hold me by the arms. I kick and moan in this child's body, but it's all in vain.

"Help them, please!" Gorgon begins to cry out of an eyeless eye socket. I wonder how a big man like him isn't capable of freeing himself from the Queen.

And who is he, asking us to help? I don't get it!

I kick the Reds in the faces, but it doesn't help much. Behind me, Lewis starts calling for me. "I told you to stay away, Alice!" He slashes at the fighting Reds with his swords, but he can't get near me or Gorgon. Lewis Carroll in a priest's outfit, fighting the Reds in Wonderland, is a scene that will stay with me for a long time.

"Please, Majesty," Gorgon says. "Let me go, or they will die."

"I want them to die," the Queen growls. She has such a scary growl for such a short person. "Children have small heads. I can use them as croquet balls for my games." She sneers and pours more pepper on him.

Finally, I realize what Gorgon means. Someone has to save his kids from something in his absence. I pull out a ball and hit one of the Reds in the back of his head. It works, but I need to free myself from the other one.

"He wants us to save his children, Lewis!" I yell. "He probably left them back in his house when he went to get the pepper."

"I don't know where he lives." Lewis sounds exhausted from fighting.

I kick the other Red with the ball, but it doesn't hurt him enough to fall. So I try to kick him in the balls with my fragile legs. Oddly, this works fine. His red cloak falls to the ground and whatever was inside it disappears.

On my feet again, I run ahead as I throw balls at each every one of them. If they have swords, I have balls—pun intended.

From afar, I aim one ball at the short Queen's head. Bull's-eye. She gets dizzy, birds chirp around her, and then she falls slowly to one side like a chopped-off tree. I run at Gorgon and try to free him. The knots are too tight for my stupid small body. He has been tied from all fours to different trees in the garden.

My pocket watch says two minutes left.

"Where are your children?" I ask.

"They are trapped in my house." He can't stop crying, trying to free himself, as we don't have a sword or a knife handy. "I live in a mushroom house, and have them *locked* inside."

"What?" I hold my head with my hands. "Why lock up your children?"

"There is a beast who eats children, roaming in Wonderland. They asked me for pepper. Thee little one asked me for muffins. I paid the Duchess for the muffins, but she ate them in front of me after she took my money. She said Galumphs like me shouldn't eat muffins, as it's considered a luxury to eat them in our times. I have always tried to fulfill my children's wishes after their mother died. I made a mistake and stole from the Queen's kitchen. She caught me. Save my children, please. They are locked in the house."

"It's okay," I say, trying my teeth on the strong rope.

"What?"

"I mean, it's all right," I say, not quite believing myself. "If they're locked, we will get to them once Lewis kills the Reds and frees you."

"It's not all right," Gorgon protests. "I left them three days ago. The food in the house isn't enough. They will die of starvation."

"Three days ago?" My whole world tumbles around me when I hear this. I have to go and save them myself. Maybe take Lewis with me.

"Tell me where you live, Gorgon," I demand. "Where is your mushroom?"

And right before he utters it, the answer already rings a high note in my ears.

"I live on Drury Lane!"

Chapter 57

I run as the nursery rhyme rings in my head. The nursery rhyme was made after him. Because the Muffin Man, captured by the Queen, was never able to go back to Drury Lane and save his children. That's why Lewis told me, *I couldn't save them,* in my vision. I wonder if I will be able to save Gorgon's children.

I tell the rabbit to show me the way to the Drury Lane of Wonderland.

I have only one minute left.

Lewis picks me up, having learned we need to save the children. He takes me by hand toward another blackboard he hid in the forest for immediate escape when he couldn't fight the beast everyone feared by himself. Lewis has many Einstein Blackboards with mirrors hidden everywhere so he could easily escape Wonderland to his office in Oxford when needed.

"Listen to me, Alice." He kneels and grabs me by the arms. "There is a mirror right in front of this blackboard. You will walk into it back to Oxford. I can't risk you being here longer. You have done well already. I fear the Reds will hunt us and hurt you. You mean so much to me, Alice. And you're still a child. I don't want you to die young by the Queen's guards," he says, not knowing that I can't stay much longer anyway. If I do, I will die without any of the guards even laying a hand on me. "I will save the children."

"But he said they have been there for three days—"

"Have faith, Alice." He shushes me. "I will save them. Hopefully they're still alive."

"I hope so," I say, staring at my pocket watch. I almost have no time left. I don't even know how I am going to go back through a mirror I fear. But Lewis is Gorgon's only hope to save his kids and save him from becoming the

Muffin Man. Hell, Lewis is Britain's only hope against mass food poisoning.

Lewis turns me around to face the mirror. He does it so fast I have no time to resist. When my eyes meet the glaring reflection of the mirror, I shriek, thinking I will see the scary rabbit right away. But I don't.

Lewis kisses me on the forehead and runs away to save the children, his loyal rabbit following him. I wish him all the luck in the world, regretting that I have to go back now — that is, if I am not already late.

As for the mirror, I get it now. I get why I am not scared of it. I think it's because I am seven years old. Whatever made me fear mirrors happened later when I was older.

I look at the pocket watch and realize I broke the fourteen-minute deadline. I begin to feel dizzy. Something urges me to dig my hand in my pocket to read the Pillar's note about who Jack is. If I am not going to make it, I think I deserve to know that, at least. I dig my hands into my pocket but I come up empty-handed. There is no paper inside. How is this possible? I think it's because I am wearing a different dress in this world. If I die, I will never know who Jack is. I use the strength I have left to walk through the mirror before it's too late, hoping Lewis will save the Muffin Man's children.

Chapter 58

I am lying on my back again. This time I am on a comfortable leather couch. The room's temperature is just about right. The smell of flowers fills the room, which is dimmed except for a faint yellow lamp next to me. I feel tired, but I feel cozy. I think I just woke up from sleeping.

Where am I? Why am I not waking in Einstein's room in Oxford University?

"You realize nothing of what you said makes any sense," a man tells me. I can't see his face, dimmed by a curtain of darkness. I can smell the tobacco from the pipe he is smoking. It has a certain flavor I can't put my hands on. "The Pillar, the Cheshire, The White Queen; you realize they are only characters in a book," he says as the chair he sits on creaks against the parquet floor.

I am too tired to look deeper or stand up. It feels better lying on this couch. Does this place feel familiar? Have I been here before? Why don't I feel the need to resist the man's voice? His voice is soothing, and I like it.

Where am I? Who am I?

"I see you'd prefer silence," the man says. A tinge of pity is lurking in this voice. "Would you like to end this session now?"

My hands are too lazy to move. Was I sedated? Am I being hypnotized? Why is this man saying the Pillar's existence doesn't make sense? Have I not returned to the right time?

"We've reached a great point in your story," the man says. "Usually patients need to let their imagination go wild." He drags from his pipe. What's that flavor he is smoking? "We encourage patients to let their imagination go wild because, however creative, it always goes too wild and hits against the walls of absurdity." He pauses, and I don't feel the need to speak. How can you speak when you're not sure whom you're speaking to? When you don't know who you are. "Absurdity is good for patients. It makes them start to realize they are hallucinating. Because, frankly, some stories can't be believed, even by the most delusional patients. Like the story you just told me about entering Wonderland through Einstein's room in Oxford University, then trying to save this Gorgon from the Queen of Hearts. A man who has his eyes pop out when he sneezes? You don't really believe this. Do you?"

I feel like I have no mouth, and I want to scream. My arms are still numb. I have no idea where I am or who this man is.

"I'd say we stop the session today," the man says, and scribbles something on a paper. The scratching of his pencil is annoying to my ears. "I'll prescribe you a new drug called Lullaby. It will help you let your imagination go even wilder. I need you to stretch your mind as far as you can so you can see and realize how none of this is true. How none of it is but a production of your overactive imagination influenced by a book you read as a child." He pulls the paper out. "I will also tell Waltraud to stop any shock therapy for a while. See you next week?" He sounds like a gentle doctor smiling at me, but I still can't see his face in the dark. "Great." He stands up. I hear footsteps walk out of a nearby door.

I crane my neck to take a look at my numb arms. They aren't numb. Nor is there anything seriously wrong with my arms, except that I am wearing a straitjacket that this time I can't free myself from.

Chapter 59

Alice's cell, Radcliffe Lunatic Asylum, Oxford

Waltraud and Ogier enter the room and help me to a chair. At first I tell them I don't need a wheelchair because I can walk. But then I discover my legs are even number than my arms. I let them wheel me through the corridor underground. Patients are holding their cell bars without saying a word.

Not even Waltraud or Ogier talk to me. They roll me into my cell, which terrifies me when I enter it. Nothing is really different but a mirror stacked on the wall right in front of me.

I shield my eyes and shout, "What is this mirror doing here?"

"Relax," Waltraud says in her German accent. "The mirror won't bite you."

You don't understand," I press my eyelids tighter. "Get it away from here."

"You have to face your fears," Waltraud says. "Doctor's orders."

"I can't," I plead. "Please take it away."

"I can't too," she says. "Your doctor said you have to look in the mirror. Nothing bad will come out it, but he truth. And it's time to face the truth, Alice. You can't keep denying what happened to you. Face your fears and you might be out of here sooner than you think."

"Deny what happened to me?" I have no idea what she is talking about. Then a thought occurs to me and rather changes my mind.

I am mad. Totally bonkers, hallucinating a whole world in my mind. Then I wake up on a couch and a doctor tells me I need to push my imagination to the limit in order to heal. I WANT TO HEAL. Maybe I should push it further and look in the mirror. What do I have to lose? Vomiting or fainting again when seeing the scary rabbit?

I take a deep breath and open my eyes.

Nothing happens—just like in Wonderland. Maybe I am finally cured from my phobia.

The mirror in front me has no rabbit in it. There are only a few dirt stains on its surface and a cobweb on the frame's upper left. But no white rabbit sneering at me.

It doesn't mean I shouldn't panic. In fact, I might cry for hours. Days. Years.

The girl in the mirror in front of me is tied in a straitjacket and sitting on a wheelchair, not because her legs are numb, but because she is paralyzed.

"It happened after your accident," Waltraud says. She looks happy I am finally realizing my dilemma and facing my fears. "You're the only one who survived, but like this." She points her prod at my feet. "See, that's what the doctor meant. Facing your fears. You made up this silly story about a rabbit appearing in the mirror so you wouldn't confront the reality of your paralysis."

My eyes scan the room for my Tiger Lily but it's gone. I feel lonelier, pushed into a dark corner too tight for my size.

"I'd like to be alone," I say, still holding the tears, but not sure for how long.

"I can't object to that. You're a lucky girl. The doctor denied me the satisfaction of your shock therapy for the whole week." She turns to walk away, but then stops and looks at me in the mirror. "But I am sure you will do something stupid and be my slave in the Mush Room again." She laughs and closes the door.

Alone again. I can't stand any of this. Whether it's true or not, I close my eyes and pray to God to get me out of this, even it means to send me back to the insane world I have supposedly imagined. I don't mind to be mad. I don't mind the madness in the world, if only I get up walking again. If this is really my real and sane world, then I am in love with my insane one. Whether I am imagining it or not,

I want to be the girl who saves lives. Please, I want to wake up from this.

Chapter 60

"You're all right, sweetie?" Fabiola's generous smiles lands upon my face and blesses it with safety I have always needed: a rare moment to feel that someone truly cares for you.

I don't reply to her, though. I realize I am in the back of the Pillar's limousine, stretched with my head resting on Fabiola's lap. The first thing I do is stare at my legs. They look all right. But it's not enough. I wiggle my toe. It's all right. But not enough. I bend my knee, and it works. I am not crippled. Then what was all of this? A bad dream? Or am I living in my imagined world right now?

If so, then so be it!

I don't mind.

"Where am I?" I straighten my back on the seat of the Pillar's limousine. The chauffeur is driving. Fabiola, the White Queen, sits so elegantly next to me, and the Pillar is in the front passenger's seat. I guess Fabiola made him sit there, against his wishes.

"We're in—" the Pillar begins, his head turned back to face me.

Fabiola shushes him immediately. "We're in the Pillar's limousine, driving to London. You seem to have entered the mirror back into our world, but a bit later than fourteen minutes." She hands me a glass of water. "Thank God almighty you weren't *that* late. A few seconds after the fourteen-minute range usually causes dizziness, but not great harm. At least this is what Lewis' transcripts say about the Blackboard. You just came back unconscious and the Pillar thought you'd died. He sent for me to help. And I am glad I could."

"Sent for you?" I gulp the water, still not quenching my thirst, neither for water or the questions piling up. "From the Vatican?"

"It took me about four hours, including the drive and wait at the airport," she explains. "Gone are the days of Wonderland, when I was able to travel to some place by the blink of an eye."

I remember entering Einstein's Blackboard a few minutes after midnight. What would the time be now? How long did it take me to wake up? I dig my hand into my pocket to find the watch. It seems I have lost it, along with the letter.

"I took my watch back, if you don't mind." The Pillar shows it dangling from his hands. A weak smile is plastered on his face. He is really annoyed that we're occupying his backseat. As usual, he can't stand up to Fabiola, and I still wonder why.

"It's three o'clock in the afternoon," Fabiola says. Her soothing voice has the power to bring such horrible news with ease. Otherwise, I would have panicked. It's only two hours to the Muffin Man's deadline.

I can't panic. I can't complain. Whatever happens in this mad world, I love it. Because if I am truly crippled in an asylum in real life, I can't go back there, no matter what. I love it here. My arm itches, right where my tattoo is. Right where it says: *I can't go back to yesterday because I was someone else then.* I wonder if "yesterday" only means "reality."

"I was unconscious for *that* long?" I ask.

"What you did wasn't an easy task," Fabiola says. "I mean, none of us can go back in time through that mirror. Lewis' leftover papers say only 'the Girl' can."

"Does that mean I am *the* Alice?"

"I can't say," Fabiola says. "'The Girl' mentioned in his transcript could be anyone. We're only suggesting it should be Alice."

"But I passed."

"It wasn't easy. You were almost going to die. I had to use special potions I rarely use to bring you back," Fabiola says. "I'm truly sorry; I still can't confirm you're the Real Alice."

Although I love Fabiola, I am rather mad at her. Why can't she just tell me I am *the* Alice? I need to hear it so much now, because I am so afraid I will lose consciousness and go back to that scary "reality" of mine again.

"Don't listen to her," the Pillar sneers. "Religious people are always hesitant and old-fashioned. They can hardly cope with anything that's new to their ancient beliefs. As if we're not supposed to evolve and create." Fabiola tries to shush him, but the Pillar doesn't care. Not when the subject comes to me being the Real Alice. "You are the one and only, Alice. You want me to prove it?"

"Pillar!" Fabiola raises her voice elegantly, though.

"Yes, please prove it." I lean forward.

"If you're not the Real Alice, why did she save you?" The Pillar points at Fabiola, who lowers her eyes, escaping mine. "Why are we now sending you on a last new mission? Ask her!"

I stare back at Fabiola, whom I can't believe could be lying. Ever. But why is she shying away from my eyes?

"When Galileo discovered the earth's rotation, the likes of Fabiola killed him for opposing the 'man up in the sky,'" the Pillar says.

"Stop it!" Fabiola's jaw tenses. "We could argue about who you are all afternoon," she says to me. "And let people die." She breathes briefly and closes her eyes, as if meditating. When she opens them up again, serenity has caught her. Is it possible she can show a darker side sometimes? "We do have a new mission, Alice," she says. "It's less than two hours before the Muffin Man mass-poisons millions of people. You're the last hope for millions of people."

"So, he didn't change his mind?" I am disappointed I couldn't change the course of events when I was back in Wonderland. I can't even begin to think what this means. Does it mean Lewis couldn't save Gorgon's kids? Oh my. I feel like I am going to vomit again.

"No," the Pillar says. "We don't have time to tell you what happened, since it didn't work anyway."

"So, that's it?" I am not going to cry. I have seen too much already. I know that crying doesn't solve anything.

"There is one last thing you can do," the Pillar insists as we enter London. "And it's not even an option."

"I'll do it. Time is running out," I tell them both. "What is it?"

"I feel ashamed that our final hope is what I am going to tell you." Fabiola exchanges looks with the Pillar and turns back to me. "The Cheshire called me in the Vatican a few hours ago."

Chapter 61

"Called *you?*" I know it's rather insulting to call Fabiola, but it must be one of his sinister tricks.

"Phone call, Skype, WhatsApp?" the Pillar says, but we dismiss him.

"He came to me in the form a repenting woman in the confession room," Fabiola says. "I don't want to talk about it."

"And he made her an offer she can't refuse," the Pillar mocks.

"The Cheshire said he knows how to stop the Muffin Man," Fabiola says. "And before anyone comments, I know how humiliatingly ironic this is. The man who created an evil murderer to terrorize us is also telling us how to get rid of him."

"He is mocking us. It's an analogy." The Pillar's seriousness returns.

"For what?" I ask.

"In the Muffin Man's mind, the food companies create food that gets us sick, so we end up going to the medicine companies asking them for a cure for the food. Both medicine and food companies are owned by the Black Chess corporation. They sell us the poison and then the cure for it. The same thing the Cheshire does now."

"I don't want to confuse her with all the details about the Black Chess Corporation now." Fabiola waves a hand at the Pillar. "The fact of the matter is the Cheshire demands he only tells *you* the how to get rid of the Muffin Man." She is looking at me. "He will meet you in Mudfog Town—"

"Mudfog, where everyone is dead now. It looks like a smaller version of England's Black Death in the 1600s," the Pillar comments.

"Is that where we're going?" I ask.

Fabiola nods. "You will have to shake hands with the devil to save the innocent. I know this is the noblest thing to do."

"Noble, my tarts and farts," the Pillar mumbles, but I can hear him.

"Are you ready to meet him?" Fabiola asks me.

I nod.

The chauffeur stops his car. I assume we've arrived in Mudfog.

When I pull down the window, the town reeks of the dead. The sight of them sprawled on the ground is really no different from any zombie movie I have watched.

"No one cleaned this town yet?" I can't believe this.

"They said they did in the news." The Pillar winks, but then his face changes. He stops and looks at me from top to bottom. I don't know what he is looking for. "Did you read my paper about Jack yet?" he asks.

"No. I didn't find it." I dig my hand in my pocket and don't find it again.

"Strange, I searched for it in your pockets while you were sleeping and couldn't find too," he says. "Would you like to know who he is before you go to meet the Cheshire?"

The idea of knowing has been paired with the word *horrifying*. When I woke in a physiatrist's office, I ended up with crippled legs. Whether it's the truth or not, I am afraid that knowing who Jack is will have the same effect on me. And I'd had that feeling for the last couple of days.

"I think I'd see the Cheshire first." I pull the handle. "I might return to you briefly when I know what he is asking from me." Gazing outside, I see an overweight kid somersaulting and dancing atop a wall. His moves are impossible for his body figure and shape. I know it's the Cheshire. I step out.

"Tell him the Pillar says 'meow'!" the Pillar chirps from inside before I shut the door behind me. "And if possible, can he tell us how to stuff a head inside a watermelon, because I think it's brilliant!"

Chapter 62

Amidst the corpses, I walk toward the overweight boy dancing upon a wall. His egg-shaped body reminds me of Humpty Dumpty in *Through the Looking-Glass*. When I get closer, I notice his head is cut off. He wears it on and off, and even kicks it like a football and runs after it. His overalls are spattered with blood. I am going to talk to another dead boy.

But the silence in the town of Mudfog isn't quite silence. A corpse stands up and greets me here and there. "Welcome to my frabjous playground of madness," they say, possessed by one of the Cheshire's nine lives.

"What a golden afternoon we have!" the boy greets me with open hands, pointing at the sinking sun in the distance.

"It's almost four o'clock." I stop before him, craning my neck up, just like Alice did in the book when talking to the cat on the tree. "Get to the point."

"Not before you see this." He walks on his hands on top of the wall while dribbling his head like a ball with his legs.

"Good for you," I say. "You belong to a circus."

"Why do you hate me so much, Alice?" He stands straight and jams his thumbs behind his overall straps.

"If you don't talk, I will walk away," I say.

The boy lets himself fall, and pretends his neck is broken. His head rolls right under my feet. He props himself up without a neck. His head underneath me talks to me. "Did I tell you my name is Humpty Dumpty?"

"A pleasure," I say with pursed lips. "I've had it. I am walking."

"Could you please give me my head back, then?" His face snickers at me. "How do you expect me to talk to you without my head on my shoulders?"

I kneel down, pull it up, and throw it in his hands. He catches it with ease and hinges it back on.

"Talk," I demand. "Fast. No games."

"Look at you," the boy says with both resentment and admiration. "You're not scared of me anymore."

"That's not fast enough." I am terrified. Somehow, I've learned not to show it.

"Oh, and you have learned good comebacks." He rubs his fatty chin.

"The only comeback you will get is my fist in your ugly chin." I think my fear to awaken crippled again is what moves me now.

"I am beginning to like you," he says. "Here is the deal. I will help you kill the Muffin Man and stop him from mass-poisoning everyone."

I want to ask why he would do that, but I have a much more important question. "Killing him isn't going to solve it. He must have already poisoned food across the country. I need to know what kind of food and where to find it."

"You believed that?" He pulls out a yo-yo and plays with it.

"He was bluffing?"

"Not exactly," the boy says. "At the moment, nothing has been poisoned yet. But he, and a few acquaintances, will start poisoning a lot of candies and junk food across the country."

"I'm not quite following."

"Poisoning the food as he promised wasn't going to work. At best a few people would die, and then a pattern of which foods are poisoned and which aren't will present itself. We had a greater plan. To shock you and do nothing, and then right when everyone on the news calls the Muffin Man's bluff, the poisoning starts without warning."

"Because the food he poisons now will take about week to get into the market, and then when it starts there will be no going back." I am thinking their sinister plan out loud.

"Touché! I'm a brilliant cat." He grins. "Although it all could have been stopped if the Queen and Parliament confessed their wrongdoing, which we knew they would never do."

"This means I have to stop him now."

"Right on, tough girl." He fists a hand, mocking some comic superhero. "If you kill the Muffin Man, all his acquaintances will stop immediately, and you will truly have saved Britain."

"How can I kill him?" I try to be blunt and precise, like the Pillar.

"That's the easy part." He pulls my umbrella from behind his back and opens it with a joker's smile on his face.

"How did you get that?"

"I had to snatch it from your cell when I visited you last time," he says. "I've always been curious about those gadgets Lewis Carroll invented. Fabiola knows a lot about those, but she wouldn't tell me." He meows like a sad cat waiting to be fed. "But that's all right. I always get what I want eventually. I'm a cat, after all."

"So you know I'm not mad," I say. "You have my umbrella and know I used it to escape the tower at Ypres."

"I don't know that," he says. "You know why? Because we're all mad here." He throws the umbrella my way.

I catch it, and without hesitation, I aim it back at him. I pull the trigger and shoot him. I don't get chances like these often, and I should have killed him in the morgue.

A bullet that looks like a sharp tooth slithers through his stomach and doesn't come out. I think I managed to finally kill the Cheshire Cat.

Chapter 63

"Ouch," he says. "That tickled." He grins that awful grin again. "That's why I met you in a dead boy's form, because you can't kill what's already dead. Nice reflexes, though. The bullets inside this weapon are very scarce, so don't shoot me again, please."

"What kind of bullets?"

"Bandersnatch teeth, another Carrollian invention. You know what a Bandersnatch is, right?"

"A monster lurking in the Wonderland forest, according to the books, like mentioned by Carroll in the poem."

"You had three bullets inside. Now two." He furrows his brow. "No other bullet can kill the Muffin Man, unless you're planning to get close to him and fist-fight a big man like him."

"Where is he, so I can stop him?"

"He is in Uxbridge in London, inside the Cadbury factory, stirring some hot chocolate and pouring pepper into it."

"Wait a minute. Something isn't right." Uxbridge shouldn't be far from here. I just don't understand why the Cheshire wants me to kill the monster he created himself. "Why are you doing all of this? You're tricking me."

"It's simple, really." He pulls out the Bandersnatch tooth and hurls it away. "I planned this mess from the beginning only to send you a message. By *you*, I mean the Pillar, Fabiola, and the whole world."

"Which is?"

"I showed you an example of a man crushed so hard by society he flipped back with anger against it." He is proud of it. "It's a textbook on how to create a terrorist or criminal. Crush him with society's cruelness, take his poor soul to a madman like me, and infest his brain with revengeful thoughts so powerful that he only sees humans as bridges to his cause. Then you've got yourself a first-class *nuthead* killing for reasons that make no sense."

I stare at him speechlessly.

"What?"

"I just haven't seen anyone sicker than you," I admit. "What are you? What drives your hate to humanity so much?"

"Humans, of course." He spreads his hands wide. "They made me what I am. The same way I made the Muffin Man. I am a reflex to human cruelty and madness; only you weren't prepared for such a powerful reflex like me. And guess what? I am just showing the Pillar and Fabiola how weak human souls are, how I can use most of them against them in the coming Wonderland War. You know how many mistreated men and women walk the streets every that I could take advantage of?"

"Somehow, I don't think this enough reason to want me to kill the Muffin Man," I argue.

"I want to see if *you* can do it." He steps forward, his dead eyes gleaming with life. "I'm still am curious about you." He throws the yo-yo away. "Either you won't be able to do it and go permanently insane so I'll stop thinking about you, or you'll kill him, and prove you're the one and only Alice that Lewis trusted so much."

"Then what happens?"

"If you are her?" he asks. "Oh, baby. That's a new ballgame on its own."

I am not sure I want to risk being pushed to further madness. I'd risk waking up crippled in my cell again.

"But I don't think you could shoot the Muffin Man," the Cheshire dares. "You're too weakened by what you've seen in Wonderland. Deep inside, you think he had been a good man mistreated by the grumpy Queen of Hearts, who killed his children."

"We're not sure about that," I object. "Lewis went to save them. He might have—"

"No, he didn't." He grins. "Doesn't it show already? If Lewis had saved Gorgon's kids, he wouldn't be still doing this now. What? You thought you could change the past? The Pillar used you as an experiment to see if the Einstein Blackboard works. Gorgon Ramstein's kids were found dead, their hands scraping at the locked door of their mushroom house, trying to reach for a handle that wasn't going to budge anyway."

I am holding on to the umbrella as strongly as I can. If that really happened, I can't picture it in my mind. Is the Muffin Man supposed to pay for the cruelty of the world, or is he supposed to be killed to save those who, some of them, had been cruel to him?

"I can't believe such a thing happened to the Muffin Man." My jaw aches when I speak. I'm fighting both vomit and tears. But like the Pillar said, I can't keep on whining about the insane world. I have to be stronger, although I don't know the recipe for that. "What happened to Lewis when he saw them?" I am angered I have to get my information from the Cheshire, but I can't imagine how Lewis reacted to this. I know how much he loves children.

"Well for one, he st-t-tuttered f-for a-a while." The Cheshire mocks Lewis's shortcomings with a meaty smile from his fatty lips. I barely keep myself from shooting him again. "But then, after he gathered himself, the mathematician priest had an epiphany of a lifetime."

"What do you mean?"

"Lewis Carroll finally knew what could save the poor children of Victorian times," the Cheshire says, mockery underlining every word. "He decided if children could not get clothes, friends, and goods in real life, he was going to give it to them lavishly in a book. A book full of oversized mushrooms, cakes that make you taller, marshmallows, tarts, and more. All free, but only in the figments of imagination of the poor children."

"You mean..."

"I mean the Muffin Man's story is actually the inception of the *Alice Underground* books. He actually believed that if Gorgon's kids had such a book they might have not starved so quickly. A 'food for the soul' thing, if you know what I mean." He rolls his eyes, obviously envious of everything Lewis did.

"My God."

"Yes? How can I help you?" The Cheshire tilts his head and raises his eyebrows. "Just kidding. Come on, let's see if you can pull the trigger, so-called Alice." The Cheshire shows me his latest grin. He disappears, evacuating boy's head and torso so they fall down to the ground.

Chapter 64

Cadbury factory, Uxbridge, London

The Pillar takes care of getting me into the factory. It isn't that hard, now that it's abandoned. Who wants to make chocolate for a world withering away half an hour from now?

In the elevator to the factory's manufacturing floor, the Pillar pushes the stop button.

"You can do it," he says.

"I know I have to," I reply with my umbrella in my hand. "But I am afraid to hesitate, knowing what I know about what happened to the Muffin Man's children."

"If we consider every Bin Laden-like terrorist's miserable childhood and make excuses for him, the world will end up perished in a few days," he says. "Everyone is responsible for themselves. You can't blame the world for what happened to you." He stops for a breath and asks me, "Now, do you want to know who Jack really is before you do this?"

"I am not sure."

"It's all up to you. I am only reminding you in case you don't come back alive," he says. "Who knows what might happen up there?"

"I think I know who Jack is." I finally falter under the pressure. Why should I deny it? I woke up crippled in a world that seemed to be the real world, while all of this, although it feels real, simply can't be real, because it doesn't make any sense. "Jack is just a figment of my imagination."

"Go on..."

"I made him up to compensate for his absence after I killed him in the school bus for reasons I can't remember..."

"And?"

"He just pops up whenever I am in great danger because it feels better thinking he came to save me." I am crying already. "I made him up so I don't feel guilty about him. Sometimes I think people see him, but I could have made that up as well."

"Is that all?"

I crane my head up at the Pillar. "I am ready to admit that, but I want him to stay near. Please, don't make him disappear," I say to the Pillar, throwing myself in his arms. It has been so long since I needed to let these words out.

"I can't make him disappear, Alice." The Pillar doesn't put his arms around me. He just lets me do whatever I want, but doesn't show his sympathy.

I pull back and ask what he means.

"All you've said is wrong," the Pillar says.

"Does that mean Jack is real?" I wipe my tears with the back of my hand.

"Not really."

"What is that supposed to mean?"

"Are you ready for the truth?"

I nod eagerly.

"Jack isn't a figment of your imagination, Alice," the Pillar answers. "He is a figment of his own imagination."

"What?" I can't even comprehend the sentence he just said. "A figment of his own imagination?"

"When people die in this world, sometimes they aren't ready to cross over to the other side," he explains. "Usually it's someone they have left behind that keeps them attached to the living world. It's not something that happens often. Maybe one in a million." I'm beginning to see where this is going. "There is no doubt you killed Adam—I mean Jack. He just wasn't ready to leave you alone in this world. He believes there is something you haven't learned yet, and he can't leave without helping you with it. Don't ask me what it is, because I don't know."

"You mean he is a dead man walking in my life?"

"He doesn't know that. If you ask him where he slept last night, he usually can't answer it, right?" the Pillar asks.

"He is in a haze himself, driven by only one force in this temporary figment of existence."

"One force?"

"His love for you."

My tears burst out again.

"He will appear when your heart needs him the most. He will be seen by others and he will be effective," he says. "If he kills someone, they will die. He is rather true when he is present. Think of him as a living soul borrowed from the other side."

"This so confusing." I hiccup. "But it means he will always be there for me."

"Like a guardian angel." The Pillar chews on the words. "I pretended I didn't see him because of the emotional pressure he will put on you. The world is in danger, Alice, and emotions make us weaker. You can't be like that. You have to learn the art of bluntness in order to face the enemy."

I pull the umbrella up and wipe my tears. "You have it all wrong, Pillar," I tell him. "I don't know what you know about love, or what happened to you in the past that made you so blunt and without feelings, but love strengthens, not weakens. Why didn't you just tell me he was a figment of his own imagination long ago?"

The Pillar stays silent. I sense there is more he isn't telling me.

"If there is anything else I should know, please tell me now."

"There isn't," he says. I believe he is lying. "Do me a favor and don't call for Jack with your heart when you confront the Muffin Man. I want you to know your powers and what you are capable of doing. Jack and I can't be there for you forever."

"How can I do this?"

"Just don't think about Jack up there when you meet up with the enemy," the Pillar says. "Be yourself. Everyone else is taken."

"I will." I like the idea. I can't keep using Jack or the Pillar's help to get me out of every problem. "But still, you have no idea what it's like to be in love." I push the elevator button up, ready for a kill.

The Pillar seems slightly insulted by my words. For the first time, I realize that this ruthless killer was definitely in love one day. The kind of love that maybe left him the way he is now.

Chapter 65

Cadbury factory, chocolate stirring floor

I ask the Pillar to leave me alone with the Muffin Man.

"If you say so," he mumbles as the elevator door closes. "I would have liked to see a chocolate factory just like in *Charlie and the Chocolate Factory*," he teases.

The sound of working machines and drills surrounds me as I walk in between. The factory is huge; I am worried it will take me too long to find the Muffin Man.

Surprisingly, it's easier than I thought. Gorgon Ramstein is humming his own nursery rhyme as he is working.

"Muffin Man, Muffin Man. Do you know the Muffin Man, who lives in Drury Lane?"

I take off my shoes so I can surprise him and he can't hear me coming, my umbrella held up high like a loaded gun.

"Muffin Man, Muffin Man. Do you know the Muffin Man, who somehow lost his brain?"

A few rows of stacked-up material later, I see him standing behind a huge, round machine. It looks like a bathtub, with chocolate stirring inside. It has huge mixing fans that are so long and sharp they could cut through a person. The Muffin Man has tons of pepper sacks next to him. He begins opening one to pour the pepper into the mix.

"Muffin Man, Muffin Man. Do you know the Muffin Man, who's gone utterly insane?"

"Stop!" I stand firm and point my umbrella at him. It's surprising how I got a straight window for a shot so easily. It occurs to me that I must have been taught to use this umbrella before—or was my clash with the Cheshire in Ypres just about enough? "Or I will shoot!" I say.

"How did you know I was here?" He is utterly surprised, one of the sacks open in his hands.

"That doesn't matter." I manage to control my voice. I have to be loud enough so he knows I will shoot. "I need you to put that sack down, sir." I don't know how it works, but the Cheshire said if Gorgon is stopped, his acquaintances will stop.

"How did you find me?" He is perplexed. "You should be out there with all the panicked people, trying to find the poisoned food or stay away from it."

"Please, sir," I repeat. "Put down the sack of pepper."

The sound of stirring machines demands I raise my voice even more.

"The only one who knows I'm here is the Cheshire." His jaw tenses. "Did he tell you I was here? Why would he do that?"

"Because he is the Cheshire. You shouldn't have trusted him." I'm trying to use this conflict. "I promise you won't be hurt if you stop, sir. We will consider you an ally who helped prevent millions from dying." I am lying. I talk as if I am the police or something. Anything to stop this from happening. "I promise I will tell you anything you want to know once you put the sack down." I readjust the position of my feet. Holding a gun up for a long time turns out to be a hell of a task.

"I will not put the sack down," he says. "I don't care if you caught the Cheshire and made him confess. The world has to pay, or the Queen of England apologies publicly."

I want so badly to ask him if this means the Queen of England is the Queen of Hearts, but I won't. I have to strike with iron hands. The killer has to be stopped or killed.

"Sir, for the last time." I can't quite breathe steadily. "Put the sack down, or I will shoot."

"Shoot as you want," he says. "Bullets can't kill me."

"I have Bandersnatch bullets, sir." Why do I keep saying "sir"?

The Muffin Man suddenly panics. He realizes the power in my hands.

"Then it's really the Cheshire? Did he sell me out?"

"For the last time, sir." I grit my teeth. "I mean it. The last time. Put the sack down, or I will shoot."

"You know what she has done to my children in Wonderland?" His sadness begins to surface. It's sincere, I can tell. "Can you imagine your children scraping the doors and windows for three days without food?" This isn't helping me. The image haunts me. "Do you know how many times I asked the Queen of Hearts to kill me and just send someone to open the door for them? I mean, they were just children." An image of Lewis crying *I couldn't save them* blocks my vision and my reason. I don't want to soften from the Muffin Man's words. I am not sure I can hold on any longer. "Then in this new world, I told myself I would start all over again. I told myself the cruelty of Wonderland couldn't be in the human world. But once I warned the government of my scientific discoveries about the crimes committed by food companies, they killed my lawyer and killed my children. AGAIN!" he screams. His veins are about to spurt out of his neck.

His screams are absorbed by the stirring machines of the factory. Another injustice done to him. Every part of me translates his words to "Pain."

A tear trickles down my cheek. I don't think I can take the shot. "I understand your hardships, sir." My voice is fragile. The voice of a liar. How in the world can I understand such cruelty? "Once you put the sack down, we can talk about it."

"No we won't." He cuts the sack open, some of it already pouring in. "You look like a good girl. You don't know much about the world. And you don't have the guts to—"

I take a spontaneous step back. I don't know why. Then I close my eyes and shoot him. I can't let him play with my emotions.

The shot echoes briefly before it's sucked by the noisy machinery again. It's followed by Gorgon's mocking laugh. I open my eyes, and he is already pouring the pepper. His laugh of evil, as hollow as his voice, resonates and reminds me of my failure to stop him. The Pillar is right. Gorgon has been mistreated, but it doesn't give him the right to kill children and people. I'm beginning to adjust to some kind of moral compass I can follow. Saving lives always comes first.

A hand pulls the umbrella from me and pushes me away.

It's the Pillar. He has come back, and he will take the shot.

Seeing him do it, I feel like burning from inside out. I am not a failure. If I am meant to save the world, then I will freakin' save it. I pace ahead, pull my umbrella back from the Pillar, and watch the astonishment in his eyes. I push him out of my way and aim at the Muffin Man, who has emptied one sack inside already and has pulled his falling hair back so I can see his empty eye socket. He sneers at me, knowing I can't shoot him.

"Take the shot, Alice!" the Pillar shouts behind me.

The Muffin Man reaches for another sack and opens it, staring blatantly at me. I have one last Bandersnatch tooth left.

Afraid I will miss the shot, I run toward the Muffin Man, aiming at him. Closer is better.

On my way, he has emptied another sack. Damn it. He is reaching for a third.

I am running so fast I wonder if I'll end up flying. I circle around the huge stirring tub. Its sharp fans are glinting and scarily sharp. I am afraid I'll trip and fall inside.

"You can't kill me!" he yells, inches away from me.

I don't hesitate. I aim at his heart. It's the heart that kills, right?

The Bandersnatch tooth hits him in the heart, but sticks in his double-breasted jacket as if it's made of steal. The one-eyed Muffin Man grins at me and pours the third sack.

I go crazy, filled with such anger I think I am going to explode. Without thinking, I run toward him, pull one of the sacks, and hit him with it on his back. It seems impossible that I could hurt such a big guy.

The look on the Muffin Man's face is priceless. He didn't expect it, bending over on the edge of the stirring tub, gripping at the edge with his hands. Still, it's not enough to hurt him.

I hit him again.

He bends closer with his head, staring right at the stirring fans. His tall body helps him to hold on. I prepare to hit him once more, but he steadies and pulls the sack from me. The look in his one eye says he is going to push me into the tub.

The Pillar interferes and whips Gorgon with his hookah hose, as if he were Indiana Jones. The hose is like a snake, tightening around his neck on its own. Gorgon chokes, and the Pillar pulls. But the Muffin Man is stronger. I run around and add my strength to the Pillar's.

"Don't pull," the Pillar complains. "Kick him into the stirring machine!"

Provoked, Gorgon somehow twists his arms and manages to start choking the Pillar with his one huge hand. The two of them end up almost tangled together.

"The Queen should've made you sneeze harder," the Pillar slurps with a squeaky voice, his neck reddening under the pressure of Gorgon's hand. "So your other eyes would have popped out too!" His face is about to explode like a pumped balloon. He still has his grip tightened on the hose.

I turn back and keep kicking as the Pillar pulls, but it's all in vain. I kneel down to grab another sack, but stop when I glimpse Gorgon's glinting kitchen knife.

I pick it up. It's so heavy. And I keep staring at it.

"Nice-looking knife, eh?" The Pillar can barely talk as Gorgon still chokes him. "Stab him!"

I don't know how I feel about stabbing him. The gun is easier. You pull the trigger from afar, feeling almost no responsibility for the deceased's pain—no wonder most of the killing in the world happens that way. A knife seems too personal. Too close. There is no escaping the responsibility.

"Better stab him, or just stab me!" the Pillar says. "Because if I can't hold any longer, he will surely chop me and serve me as a caterpillar soup."

I raise my hands and stab the Muffin Man in the back. He arches and stares at me with utter disbelief. The look in his eyes scares me. I stab him again, his blood on my hands.

Then again, and again.

Doing this reminds me of Edith telling the girl I came back from Wonderland with a kitchen knife in my hand. What the heck happened to me in Wonderland?

The Pillar takes advantage of Gorgon's brief weakness and pulls him closer to the edge. I catch on and put my final signature and kick the Muffin Man into it. He falls, bending over the edge of the stirring tub. The Pillar seizes the opportunity and kicks him in too a couple of times.

Finally, the Muffin Man falls down. The slicing blades of the stirring machine finish him off.

I shy away from the spattering blood all over the chocolate, a bit dazed. Killing someone, even if it's for the good of millions, shatters something inside you.

"Huh." The Pillar mops his forehead. "That was some stubborn beast."

"I could have just kicked him myself," I tell him.

"I know, brave girl, although it took you like forever to stab him. I just couldn't resist a kick in the butt. It's such a relief. We should do this more often." He adjusts his tie.

"Glad that you know I could have done this without you." I throw the knife away.

"Are we fighting over credits now?" He pulls his hookah back. "You know no one will know you saved the world tomorrow, right?"

"I know." I clap my hands clean of the pepper. "I'm an insane girl in an asylum. The world isn't supposed to know about me."

"Think of yourself as Superman," the Pillar suggests. "All the world's greatest heroes stay anonymous."

"You've got a point." I let my shoulders fall under the weight of exhaustion and follow the Pillar to the elevator. "I'm starving. Do I get to eat a nice meal, maybe?"

"Full of delicious carbs, saturated fats, and unhealthy sweets?" He looks irritated.

"Yes?" I tilt my head.

"Marshmallows, greasy pizza, and lots of ketchup?"

"Yes?"

"Ice cream, fudge, marmalade, and lots of cream?"

"Yes?"

"But of course." He rolls his cane with all the mirth in world. "As long as you promise to lick your finger and make a mess while you eat."

"I promise I will make a mess, just like we did before at the Westminster Palace."

"That's my girl," he chirps. "I know a boy who's been dying to get you to eat with him at Fat Duck, the best restaurant known for mock turtle soup in the world." He pushes the elevator button.

"Jack?" The smile on my face is so wide it hurts.

He nods. "But first, I need you to go to court with me," he says. "It's just a small favor."

"Court?" I am suspicious.

"It'll be fun, I promise." He snickers as the elevator door opens.

Inside, I glimpse the stirring tub for one last time. "Aren't we supposed to warn the health administration of the few sacks that fell in?"

"You forgot about the man who fell in too." He presses the button to the ground floor. "But hell no. A few body fats and blood of a dead guy in a few chocolates won't hurt. We eat gross stuff all day and no one complains."

The elevator door closes. The Pillar tries to hold a sneeze.

"Pardon me," he says. "Achoo!"

I stare at him, terrified again.

"Gotcha!" He points at me and smiles.

"I wasn't afraid." I shake my shoulders.

"Oh, you were." He nudges me as I stare at the elevator's numbers.

"Not at all," I insist. "I was wondering if it was 'achoo' or 'atishoo.'"

I bite my lips. He buries a smile.

Chapter 66

The Royal Courts of Justice, London

I am sitting among the crowd, wearing a brand-new dress we bought with Margaret Kent's credit card. It's a fantabulous dress I chose with care in Harrods. And I am not planning on spattering it with blood. I will wear it on a date with Jack once the Pillar finishes his absurd joke in the court.

He stands in front of the judges, wearing a lawyer's coat and speaking with impeccable seriousness. The crowd sitting next to me loves him for filing a case against the Queen of England.

"Ladies and gentlemen of the jury," he says. I don't think this is the way you address the court in the British system. But that's the Pillar. And this is my insane world. I am beginning to love it. "I demand you look into the following case: the People versus the Queen of England."

The judges are about to laugh at him, but they act accordingly.

"We, the people of England, demand to know who pays for her nuts?" He raises his hands theatrically and talks with grace, like a nobleman. "We demand to know if she gets her nuts from the taxes we pay."

People in the crowd nod and are about to clap.

"Because I don't remember paying for the Queen's nuts." He winks at the crowd. "To be or *nut* to be, that is our sincere question. And we demand an answer."

The judge waits until the crowd hisses into a fading quietness and then asks the Pillar to approach the bench.

"I may only approach the bench with my assistant." The Pillar points at me. I blush in my soiree dress.

"Why would you need her to approach the bench with you?" the judge asks.

"I have a hearing problem, and she would be kind in reciting words I mishear," the Pillar says. "You know how words like 'tart' and 'fart' are almost the same."

The judge looks like he is going to sentence the Pillar with a death penalty for insulting his court. But he and his assistant judges cope with him, knowing they will eventually jail him for week or so. To them, the Pillar is a big joke they'd laugh at it with cigars and cognacs in their hand by the end of the week.

I don't want to be in it, though. I want to have my first date with Jack.

"From the way we are having this conversation, I believe you can hear me well," the judge says.

"I can only hear when you're afar. The closer I get to you, I can't hear you," the Pillar says. "It's a new disease. Only discovered a few hours ago."

"All right," the judge puffs, about to scream and pull his wig. "Maybe you two approach the bench."

We do.

"Are you aware of ridiculing the court with your atrocious case?" The judge leans closer with gritting teeth.

"I stand by the people," the Pillar says. "People need to know about their taxes."

"I don't care about you or your people," the judge says. "I will give you a chance to apologize to the court or I will let you proceed with the case and jail you for disrespecting the court by saying the word 'fart.'"

"I said 'tart.'"

"You said 'tart and fart,'" the judge insists.

"I said 'tart and tart.'" The Pillar is pushing the limits. "It would be disrespectful of me to say 'fart' in court."

"You said..." The judge's anger peaks, but he remembers to cool down. "Never mind." He breathes slower. "Have you made up your mind on whether to drop your nonsensical charges?"

"No," the Pillar says. "I insist. And you know what? You will approve of them, and have the Queen of England come to this court and explain herself. And you will not jail me."

"Is that so?" The judge smirks.

The Pillar pulls a few photos out of his pocket and throws them at the bench. I can't see them, but the judge blushes with anger and helplessness.

"This is a picture of your wife running away with an eighteen-year-old Nigerian." The Pillar sorts the photos for him. "This is your son killing a woman with his new car in a hit and run. A case has never been filed. And this is you in your tiger-striped underwear in—"

"Stop," the judge hisses.

"Sorry I couldn't number the negatives." The Pillar flashes his fake smile. "I was in a hurry."

"All right. All right." The judge tucks the photos under the desk, afraid anyone will see them. "You may do as you please. Go back and say whatever you want. I will accept the charges and file a case."

"I love it when the authorities are cooperative," the Pillar says. "One more thing, though."

"What now?" The man is about to have a heart attack.

"We need you to help us book the Fat Duck restaurant tonight," the Pillar says. "Table for two, romantic dinner, extra-nice waiters, and pay it with your own credit card—I mean, my taxes."

"Will be done." The man really wants the Pillar to disappear from the face of the earth.

"And if it's not too much to ask, can we have Sir Elton John play the piano tonight?"

Chapter 67

Fat Duck restaurant, London
The best mock turtle soup in the world

Later that night, I am having the date of my life. Jack looks very handsome with his super dimples and extra care for me. The service is amazing and the waiters are super nice to us. And to my surprise, Sir Elton John is playing the piano. He is singing a song called Mona Lisa's and Mad Hatters. A man with a peculiar hat on a table nearby raises a cup of tea and greets Sir Elton John for the choosing the song, which turns out to be a real song, not a figment of my imagination. I can't see the man's features from here but his table is filled with giggling young girls — I don't want to even think about who this man is.

We try the fabulous mock turtle soup and love it. Jack says it's going to be our "love soup." Every couple should have a love song, so why not be creative and have a love soup?

Jack wears a nice black suit and looks really handsome in it. He isn't one to really eat with a fork and spoon. Neither am I. But we both play aristocrats for one night.

"I have brought you a gift," Jack says.

"I love gifts." I blush.

"It's an unbirthday gift," he says.

"Unbirthday gift? Like in..."

"Like in the *Alice in Wonderland* books." He nods. "Everybody gets birthday gifts one day a year, but you can give an *unbirthday* gift any day. And I want to gift you every day, Alice."

"What is it?" I am excited.

Jack pulls out a small book and places it in the table. "*The Nonsensical Art of None Fu*," he says. "It's a rare copy. Presumably the only one available in the world."

It's not the kind of gift I was expecting, but I take it. I am sure I need to learn this None Fu for future missions.

"I have made up my mind, Alice," he says. "I know what I want to be."

"What?" I am excited to know.

"An actor," he declares. "I feel I have it in me. Those moments in Drury Lane were eye-opening."

"Speaking of then, how did you escape?" I feel the need to ask.

Jack stops his fork midway to his mouth. First, I think he doesn't want to tell me. But then it's apparent he doesn't remember. The Pillar told me that he wouldn't have answers for certain things like that.

"It's okay," I say, and change the subject. He talks about his love for cards for a while. Although not that romantic, I do listen with care. All that I need is knowing he will be there for me for a long time. It's a good feeling, and a good start.

Then he brings something up.

"I just feel so lost sometimes, Alice," he says. "When I am not with you, sometimes people don't notice me. It's like I am invisible or something. Sometimes I don't remember where I live. Sometimes I don't want to do anything at all. If it weren't for you, I don't know what I'd be living for."

It aches me to death when he says "living."

"What else, Jack?" I hold his hands across the table. He has no idea how good this feels to me. I wonder if we're going to kiss tonight. "Is there something you feel you want to tell me, maybe?"

The Pillar said Jack hasn't left to the other side because he needs to tell me something, that there is one last mission he can't leave without accomplishing.

"There is this one thing I wanted to tell you about..." He hesitates.

"I am listening, Jack. We shouldn't keep things from each other."

"Well." He pulls his hand away, and this time I feel lost. "It's nothing." He waves his hand and cleans his lips with the napkin. "I need to go to the bathroom." He stands up and leaves before his spills the reason for his stay. I don't push him. Whatever he needs to tell me before he leaves forever can wait, so he stays as long as he can with me.

I watch him enter the bathroom.

But I am still curious. What did he want to tell me? Is it fair that he isn't crossing to the other side for me? As much as I want him here, how long should he suffer from feeling lost and sometimes invisible?

I wake up from my thoughts to the Pillar sitting next to me.

"Look at all those people enjoying their food." He points at other customers. "If they only know how precious it is. If they only know that there are people who killed to get them that food."

"Why are you here?" I wipe my mouth with the napkin. "Jack will be back any minute, and I don't want to upset him."

"Hey, Rocket Man!" The Pillar waves at Sir Elton John, playing the piano and hiding behind his sunglasses. Sir Elton John greats him back with his chin up. It's as if they have been friends since long ago.

"Why are you here, Pillar?" I insist.

"I just remembered a small detail I left out about Jack, and thought you'd better know it."

"Not now," I say. "I am emotionally confused, and Jack will be back any moment."

"That's why you need to know."

"Is it about what he wanted to tell me?"

"I have no idea what Jack wants to tell you or why he refuses to die," the Pillar says. "I only know this: in spite of your utter need to have him around, something no one can blame you for, since we all need love, it's not good for him as much as it's not good for you."

"How so?"

"Every moment Jack spends here, he is opposing the balance of the universe. People are destined to die, and others are destined to be born every day. We have no idea why, and frankly I don't want to know," he says. "So, every day Jack spends with you, he is upsetting the guys on the *other* side."

Should this explain Jack's confusion and unhappiness when he is alone? "Define 'upset.'"

"The books, and Fabiola, say that in his case he is decreasing his chances for entering heaven," the Pillar says. "Each day for Jack here, he is living in sin, and could end up in hell—literally—for you."

"You don't strike me as believing in God, Professor Pillar."

"I don't," the Pillar says. "But Jack does."

I look at him, puzzled.

"Everyone has their own belief, Alice," the Pillar says. "You believe you're mad, you're mad. If you believe you can walk on the moon, trust me, one day you will. If you believe you're going to hell in favor of helping the one you love, you'll help the one you love...and you will go to hell."

"I don't believe I can be the reason for Jack's hell."

"The one thing that stands up to the insanity of the world is belief." The Pillar is lecturing, as always. "Scientists will say belief is hocus-pocus, but guess what? The insane world is hocus-pocus too. You only fight hocus with pocus."

"But—" No words will express how I feel. I need Jack, but I can't be selfish and do this to him. I am confused and heartbroken, without someone breaking my heart. I don't know what to do. "But what can I do?"

"The only way for Jack to die, against his stubborn wish to stay and be your guardian angel, is if you tell him to his face."

"Tell him that he is dead?"

The Pillar nods and takes a sip of the mock turtle soup. "Delicious turtle," he remarks, enjoying the taste, although

I know there are no turtles in this soup. "Very delicious for a creature *that* slow." He wipes his mouth with my napkin and then checks his watch. Finally, he whispers in my ears, "Let Jack go, Alice." He whispers. "Tell him he is dead and let him go. You killed him once. Killing him again shouldn't be a problem."

The Pillar stands up and leaves. I don't see him do that, but I feel his weight lift off the bank I am sitting on. My eyes are fixed on the bathroom's entrance.

Jack hasn't returned, so I occupy myself with checking his None Fu book. I notice it's a used copy, borrowed from the Radcliffe Science Library, which is in Oxford University. I open the book and am startled by what I see on the first page. Someone wrote a dedication to me. It says:

Alice,

I found the book you were looking for.

The handwriting is bad and the ink is thin and fading. I don't fully comprehend this, but then I look at the stamp from the library. It indicates the book was borrowed about two years ago, some time before I was admitted to the Radcliffe Lunatic Asylum. I wonder if Jack knew this about the book he gave me.

I turn the page, only to find more writing on the margins. This part is written in pencil.

Something tells me I shouldn't read it, or at least wait a while.

I raise my head, and I see Jack coming out of the bathroom. He looks like a shining star. The smile on his face could revive me if I were dead. The grace of his walk could save me if I am crippled. His name on my lips could be my prayer against the madness of the world. He just looks so suitable for me, as if we were star crossed. I can't believe I am asked to let him go.

Jack is approaching me as I sit looking at him with starry eyes filled with moisture. I have no idea what I will do. Will I tell him the truth and lose him, or selfishly lie to him and have him nearby.

I can't let him go, and I can't let him stay. Either way I am cursed.

Afraid that he would read my thoughts through my dilated eyes, I lower my head and peek back into the book to read the note. It says:

P.S. *Don't forget to water my Tiger Lily? Btw, I gave it a thought, and I agree we should take that bus trip you wanted to.*
Love, Adam.

The End...

Thank You

Thank you for purchasing and downloading this insane book. I'm so happy to share this story with you and I hope you enjoyed reading it as much as I enjoyed writing it!

I know there aren't many travels and riddles in book 2 like in book 1. I needed to develop the characters more. The next books will have tons of locations, riddles, and mad facts about Lewis Carroll and the world as the story unfolds. *I've created a special Pinterest page for you, though, where you can see for yourself all the places and riddles Alice and Pillar visited. You can access it through my Facebook page which you can find online.*

Insanity 3 will be released in February 2015, so stay tuned for more madness.

Thank you, for everything.

Author's Notes:

Like I said, I don't want to give away all historical and mad facts mentioned in the series, as I plan to use them as plot devices in future books. However, here are a few facts I was asked to mention by readers who received advance copies:

1) Addresses and locations used in the series are all real, including the Fat Duck restaurant and its famous mock turtle soup—even the Kattenstoet festival is real; check the Pinterest page.

2) Fat Duck restaurant is owned by Gordon Ramsay, famously known for Hell's Kitchen TV series. Not our Gorgon Ramstein/Muffin Man/Cook in the book.

3) Einstein's room in Oxford University is real, and it was Lewis Carroll's studio two centuries ago. As for Einstein's Blackboard, it can only be found in the Museum of the History of Science in Oxford. I have no idea if it can time travel, but wouldn't be cool if it does?

4) Lewis obsession with poor Victorian children, especially girls, is true. It shows in his photography, which will play a crucial role in future plots. They are maddeningly interesting, dark, and very mysterious if you take a look at them.

5) According to my research, particularly a few BBC documentaries, legal controversy about the double bar chocolates is true. I am sure the food companies didn't kill the Muffin Man's family, though. Lol. But the debate is there, and not a figment of my imagination.

6) The Iain West Forensic Suite, an extension to the Westminster Public Mortuary in London is also true. It's high tech and was developed by the government for intricate investigations.

7) Lewis wrote the Queen of Hearts alluding to Queen Victoria. There is a lot of research that supports the fact. Alice in Wonderland isn't just a children's book filled with amusing mathematical facts, play on words, and nonsensical arguments. It's also a political satire concerning the Victorian era.

8) Last but not least, the Queen of England's case about her nuts did happen in real life. You can Google it and get the details. However, there isn't the slightest intention to offend anyone with the possibility of her being the Queen of Hearts. (so far, we can't really tell if she is. Further explanations will take place in book 3.) The way most of this series is written I try to stay true to Lewis Carroll's work in its context. If the Queen of Hearts was alluding to Queen Victoria, then in a modern fictional adaptation it could be the Queen of England (which again, we aren't really sure about yet.)

Thanks again for being mad.

Cameron.

About the Author

Cameron Jace is bestselling author of the Grimm Diaries series and Insanity. A graduate of the college of Architecture, collector of out-of-print books, and is obsessed with the origins of folk tales and the mysterious storytellers who spread them. Three of his books made Amazon's Top 100 Customer Favorites in Kindle 2013 & Amazon's Top 100 kindle list. Cameron lives in California with his girlfriend. When he isn't writing or collecting books, he is playing music.

41856749R00146

Made in the USA
San Bernardino, CA
21 November 2016